THE CEO'S REVENGE

GEORGIA LE CARRE

For Elizabeth Burns

A good friend and a beautiful soul.

ACKNOWLEDGMENTS

Much love and many thanks to:

Elizabeth Burns
Nichola Rhead
Brittany Urbaniak

PROLOGUE

SAVANNAH

https://www.youtube.com/watch?v=2g5Hz17C4is

-It wasn't me-

The French doors leading to the pier beyond the bar were open, and I could detect the lights from yachts bobbing on the dark water. The smell of the salty night air mixed with the food aromas floating off the dishes of the other diners. My stomach rumbled with hunger, but I kept my gaze fixed on the multi-colored lanterns hanging outside, and took a sip of the soda water I'd requested from the bartender.

I'd been sipping at it for the past forty-five minutes. I refrained from looking at my watch again. Where on earth was Max?

The feeling of crushing disappointment slithered over me like a snake, but this was not the first time he'd stood me up. Of course, he always arrived later with an armful of gorgeous flowers, and an impeccable and totally believable excuse.

They could be distilled down to one word: work. He was on the verge of something big, something so big that, once he was done with it, our lives would change forever. He was always so charming, so sincere, so sorry, I could not even bring myself to be angry. After all, he was doing it for us. Our future.

So... I would allow him to take me into his arms and let him make it up to me, but after he was only a faint manly fragrance on my pillows, I could not help worry if work was always going to be a very big part of his life, and me a secondary afterthought.

It had not always been like this .

The first six months after we started dating had been sheer bliss. I actually felt as if I'd died and gone to heaven. Then out of the blue he got sucked into work, into a big opportunity, a thing that was supposed to change both our lives forever. Since then, I lost count of the number of times Max had missed our dates. I exhaled slowly. There was just no denying the sting of feeling ignored and unimportant. I don't know why I'd allowed myself to think tonight would be different.

Maybe because it was my freaking *birthday*!

I had programmed the date into his phone calendar. Heck, I even reminded him a couple of days ago. All of that had to count for something, but clearly, it did not.

I smoothed the bodice of my sexy new dress, picked specially for this occasion, and a sigh came up from deep within me. The anticipation with which I had dressed earlier as I eagerly looked forward to spending my twenty-first birthday in the restaurant he had taken me to on our first date now made me cringe. There was no denying it now. I was head over heels in love with a man who couldn't even be bothered to turn up for my birthday dinner.

Sadly, I looked around the fine room at all the other happy couples.

My eyes dropped to the small rectangular dark blue box on the pristine white tablecloth. I fingered it pensively. Though it was my birthday, I had a gift for him. God, what a fool I was. With another heavy sigh I slipped it into my purse.

Damn you, Max.

All I wanted to do was sob my heart out, but no. Maybe later, alone in the shower. Taking a deep breath, and schooling my features, I prepared myself mentally to walk out of the restaurant with my head held high. I anticipated the subtle looks the other diners would throw my way. It sure felt like I was wearing a billboard that screamed 'STOOD UP AGAIN'.

Just as I lifted my head and prepared to stand, I saw a tall figure approaching me. My heart leaped joyfully only to crumble once more as my eyes moved upwards and detected his perfectly coiffed wavy blond head rather than Max's dark brown carelessly sexy straight hair. It was Robert. Physically, he was built very similar to Max. He was also his best friend and business partner.

I leaned back into my seat and waited for him to approach. The corners of his mouth tilted up in an easy smile. I smiled back and he leaned down to lightly brush my cheek with his lips. I detected the scent of the expensive cologne he always wore.

"Happy birthday, Savannah! Did you get the flowers I sent you today?"

My smile widened at the memory of the absolutely massive bouquet of roses I found on my desk at the end of recess. It sure made all the other staff curious.

"I did. Thank you so much, Robert. They were absolutely beautiful."

He shrugged casually. "Beautiful roses for a beautiful woman, but I'm sure Max topped my little bouquet, though. Max is a ladies man. Knew exactly what they wanted and gave it to them."

My smile slipped slightly and I looked away from him. Max had not sent anything for my birthday. Breathlessly, I'd waited all day. Twenty-first was a landmark birthday, after all. Nothing. Not even a card. I hid my disappointment by anticipating how he would make up for it tonight. Obviously, that was not going to happen either. I cleared my throat and looked up at Robert. I found him watching me with a strange expression that confused me and made me frown.

Instantly, he hid his thoughts behind a suave smile. "I should amend that statement. He *used* to be a ladies man. Not since he met you though."

My fingers tightened on my purse, but I managed to keep my voice casual. "Speaking of Max, did you see him at the office by any chance? He was supposed to meet me here, but I guess he's caught up with work as usual."

"Caught up with work?" He scratched his chin. "I don't think so. I was the last to leave the office just now, and he was not there."

"Oh," I exclaimed, surprised.

"Ummm... I don't want to bore you with work details, but we've been having some issues lately. I had to call an emergency meeting, which Max stormed out of halfway through. That was hours ago, though."

"What?" A feeling of confusion crept over me. Hours ago? "But if he left that early, why isn't he here?"

"He's a fool who doesn't realize what he has." Robert's

voice was soft, but he was watching me blankly, his real thoughts masked.

I swallowed, feeling suddenly nervous under his intense, unfathomable stare. *Keep your focus, Savannah. Find out what's really going on.* "What's the problem that called for the emergency meeting? Is it the software again?"

"Ummm. Not quite."

"Well? What is it then? It has to be something important to make Max forget even my damn birthday." I felt the heat in my words. Angry tears were stinging my eyes.

He looked away, but before his gaze swung away, I detected pity. "It may be best to hear it from Max himself."

"I would gladly do that if I could only get a hold of him. I've texted and called. No response. And now to hear that he left the office hours ago... and he still hasn't shown up. For—" I stop suddenly. My anger collapsing instantly and horror replacing it. "Oh, Robert! What if something's wrong with him? What if he's had an accident? Or he's been mugged? What if he's lying hurt in an alleyway some-where, and here I am bitching at him for being late?" I could feel my voice rising hysterically, but I couldn't help myself.

The thought of losing Max filled me with terrible, terrible fear. I loved him with all my heart. He was my first love and I was convinced he would be my last. I placed my hand on Robert's arm. "Robert, please help me find him. I feel so silly and childish for behaving like this when he needs my help. Yes, he's stood me up before, but he has always called and explained. Always. He hasn't called tonight and worse I haven't been able to reach him either so something must be very wrong. Please, Robert!"

"Savannah, calm down." Robert patted my hand sooth-ingly. Even in my agitated state, some distant part of me realized his fingers were lingering on the bare skin of my forearm.

"Max is a big boy. I'm sure he is fine."

I leaned back, dislodging his fingers. "But what if he isn't? You have to help me find him. Please, Robert. I have this terrible feeling in the pit of my stomach. Something is wrong. I know it."

And that was no lie either. When I woke up this morning I felt as if something was not right, but I dismissed it as nothing, and when all the e-cards and birthday wishes started coming into my phone from my circle of friends the sensation dissipated slightly. Later, I put the unease down to Max not calling. Now I know it was my intuition, a premonition, warning me of some impending doom.

I stared deep into Robert's eyes, not hiding the tears and fear in mine. I saw him soften a bit.

"Okay. Let me see what I can do. Let me call Lillian. She might have some idea where he might be." He pulled his phone out of his pocket, dialed, and placed the call on speaker.

I waited impatiently for Max's secretary to answer the phone.

"Hello?" Her voice was clear, but cold.

"Lillian, I've got Savannah with me. We're trying to find Max. Have you seen him, or know where he might be?"

"I haven't seen him since he left the meeting, Mr. Channing. Maybe he went back to the office after I left."

"Well, he wasn't there when I left fifteen minutes ago. But you may be onto something there. Thanks, Lillian."

"Sure." His secretary ended the call abruptly, which was weird because she was always very warm and chatty with everyone.

Robert looked at me and smiled apologetically. "Everyone's a bit on edge with this latest issue we're having, but she made a good point. What do you say we swing by the office to see if he's gone back? And even if he didn't, we can check his desk to see if there are any clues as to what's going on with him. He has been acting weird for weeks. Have you... er... noticed anything?"

I frowned, puzzled. "No, nothing out of the ordinary. What do you mean by 'weird'?"

"Oh. Just not his usual self, you know. At first I thought it was the new software he was working on. You know how intense he gets with his projects. But when he finished that job, he was still on edge all the time..."

He allowed his words to fade away and I felt raw panic take hold of me. Whatever was going on with Max was more serious than I thought. How had I not noticed any signs? I thought back to when I'd seen him two days ago. We had hung out in my apartment, and he'd seemed his normal self. We finished a big tub of ice cream whilst watching four episodes of *Billions* back-to-back, then we played a video game until something I did triggered him, and he carried me off to bed like some marauding caveman. The things he did with my body showed him to be very normal. He left after breakfast, smiling at my reminder of my birthday dinner.

I stood abruptly. "Let's go."

Robert left a few bills on the table and led me out. A million thoughts raced through my head as we headed to the Stein-Bart Innovative Software office. The dashboard read a little past nine, and though I was doubtful that Max would have gone back to the office at this time, it did not hurt to start by ruling that option out. If he was not there, I would go to his apartment next. I would not stop until I found him. It cut me to the core to think that he was in some kind of trouble and had kept it from me. Ever since we'd been seeing each other, one of the things I had been truly happy about was how open we were with each other. And now to find that he had been hiding something from me just did not sit right with me.

I was out of the car before Robert could attempt to assist me. I rushed to the entrance and waited impatiently for him to punch in the security code to let us into the building. He nodded to the night watchman and we went into the elevator. I stared at the panel as we rose up the floors. At the fourth floor the doors swished open and Robert walked ahead of me down the corridor to the room where Max had his office. There was no light within. Robert switched on the light and the room illuminated. I must have been hoping to find him here, because my stomach flipped to find his chair empty.

"Damn. He's not here. Let's check his desk to see if there's anything there that could give us a clue. A name. A number. Something."

As I stood over him, anxious and full of dread, Robert began to open the drawers and look through the papers. Nothing seemed out of place as everything was neatly arranged, as was Max's style. Everything except –

Robert reached for a blue folder that seemed to have been hastily shoved underneath a pile of papers in the bottom drawer. As he opened it, I felt my knees grow weak. I groped for the chair as spots swam before my eyes. I blinked several times. I had to be dreaming. Robert snapped the file shut and tried to put the file back into the drawer, but I snatched it off him.

"Don't, Savannah," Robert implored.

I completely ignored him. With shaking hands I went through the pictures inside the file.

I looked up at him, tears blurring my vision. "Max is cheating on me."

"Max loves you."

I tossed the pictures onto the desk bitterly. "Sure, he loves me."

Robert stared at the pictures speechlessly. He looked just as shocked as me. The images of Max naked in bed with another woman were seared on my brain. They had looked as though they had just finished making love as his hair had that tousled look which I was all too familiar with.

"Damn! Max! What have you gotten yourself into, my friend? But now it all makes sense."

I looked at Robert sharply. My voice was raspy with hurt and anger. "What makes sense?"

He looked at me with that strange expression from the bar once more, before he dropped his gaze. "It would be better to hear it from Max himself, Savannah. It's not my place-"

In a flash I leaned forward across the desk. I saw the surprise in Robert's eyes as I grabbed his tie and yanked him towards me.

"Max is not here to tell me what the hell is going on," I snarled looking into his eyes, "so you had better start talking. Now, which part of this shitshow makes sense to you?" I bit out the last bit through gritted teeth.

He swallowed. "I suppose she must have been blackmailing him. That's why he needed so much money."

I scowled. "Money?"

"The meeting today, the one that Max stormed out of. I called it to tell him we were going to press charges for embezzlement if he didn't return the money."

My heart dropped to the pit of my stomach. "Embezzlement?"

"It's been going on for months and he has been very clever at covering his tracks, but this week, finally, our accountants were able to trace the payments back to him."

I let go of Robert's tie, and stood back, shattered. I stared at him, my head shaking with disbelief. No way. It couldn't be. This was not the Max I knew. Max was the most honest person I'd ever known. He would never cheat Robert. Or... would he? Was it all a lie? "But he's your friend. Your business partner," I babbled. "He would never do that to you."

Robert adjusted his tie. "Well, clearly he has. I wanted to make it easy on him by asking him to return the money and I would forget it, but I guess he doesn't have that kind of money so he pretended to be offended and stormed out. I have to be honest and tell you that it doesn't look good for him, Savannah. I'm afraid he could be going to prison for a very long time."

"Prison?" I whispered as I struggled to process what Robert was telling me.

"Embezzlement is a serious crime." He picked up one of the pictures, shook his head in disgust and flicked it away from him.

How strange. Even after seeing the repulsive pictures and knowing that Max was nothing more than a common thief, I wanted to wipe away that look of disgust from Robert's face. Even after what he had done to me, I couldn't bear for anyone to insult him.

My hand rushed forward, not to punch Robert's face, but to cover my mouth. I closed my eyes. I needed a moment to try and make sense out of everything. But nothing seemed to be computing. It was all too much for me to take in at once. I had been so sure he was the one. From the moment I had seen him at that bar two years ago, I had felt an instant connection to him. I had felt him to my core as my inner soul told me I had found my soulmate. The more my friends tried to tell me I was too young to settle down to one man, the more sure I was that I had found that one man I wanted to be with forever.

I saw us growing old together. I saw him, with gray hair. I saw our children, our grandchildren. And now to find that my mate had betrayed me broke my heart into pieces.

I felt a dark cloud sweep over me as my heart came to grips with the decision I would have to make.

I opened my eyes. My hands were steady as I picked up the photos from the desk and placed them back into the file, slipping only one out and into my purse. I looked up at Robert. My cheeks burned with the pity I saw in his eyes.

I lifted my chin. "Could you take me back to get my car, please?"

"Savannah, I'm really sorry. This is so fucked up. I never wanted you to find out this way."

"It's okay. None of this is your fault. Thank you for being a good friend, Robert."

"I feel like a heel, though. God, I wish I'd never suggested you come here."

"I needed to know. And I'm glad I know." Then I walked out of the office and went straight to the elevator. He followed me out and stood next to me. He said nothing. There was nothing to say. It felt like hours passed before the elevator doors opened.

The ride back to the restaurant was in total silence. Images and memories of Max and me floated in and out of my mind. The last few weeks especially, showed me the signs had been there but I had not paid attention to his distance and preoccupation, writing it off as the usual work stress. But now it all made sense.

I thanked Robert once again as he walked me to my car.

"Will you be okay, Savannah? Are you sure you can drive? Do you want me to follow you home or anything?"

I shook my head. "No. I'll be okay."

I reached up and brushed my lips against his cheek. "Thanks again for everything, Robert. You've been a great friend to us both. Shame Max didn't appreciate you."

"Promise to call me if you need me?"

"Of course. Take care."

I got into my car and pulled away. I watched in the rear-view mirror as Robert grew smaller, feeling as though Max was growing smaller and smaller in my heart. By the time I reached my apartment, I was sobbing my heart out. I knew that I would have to find a way to heal my shattered heart from Max's betrayal, but not now. Now I would just mourn the loss of him. For it was a big loss. A very, very, very big loss.

I went through the rest of the week in a daze. There was no word from Max.

I did not try calling him.

I did go to the seafront and fling into the ocean the pearl necklace he gave me, though. As soon as the milky beads touched the water, I was full of unbelievable regret. I dived in, fully clothed, after it, but it was gone forever.

The way Max was gone forever from me.

1

SAVANNAH

(Four years later)
https://www.youtube.com/watch?v=G7KNmW9a75Y
-flowers-

Twenty-three pairs of eyes were fixed on my face as the bell rang. I could hear a pin drop. I could feel them squirming at the silence that ensued. Finally, I opened my mouth, and the class seemed to draw a collective breath in anticipation.

"You may go to lunch."

"Thank you, Miss Maitland!" they chorused happily as they dashed out of their seats.

I began to count to ten. Even before I got to seven, the door was already closing behind the last child. Smiling to myself at their incredible zest for life, I turned towards my desk. I loved my job as a middle-school teacher, but there were days when I needed a break and today was one such day.

I could feel a headache starting behind my eyes.

Quickly, I packed my things and headed towards the teacher's lounge, making sure to lock the door behind me as I did. Mid-semesters were coming up in a few weeks and I did not want to run the risk of any mischief with tampered tests. I knew my eleven-year-olds well enough to know how sneaky they could be.

I entered the lounge, sank into the closest chair, and slipped my shoes off. I pulled out the pins that had tightly held my thick hair in a bun all morning and allowed it to fall down my back. Some of the pressure behind my eyes eased. I leaned back and closed my eyes.

"Rough morning?"

My eyes opened and my gaze found Stacey standing over me, a cup of coffee in her outstretched hand. I smiled thankfully and took the hot beverage from her. Cupping it in my palms I took a sip.

"I've had worse, but it could have been better. I just don't know what's gotten into them this morning. I had to reprimand them at least five times, and only when I threatened to call their parents, did they settle down a bit."

She waved her hand in front of her face. "I swear, it's that time of year. I don't know what it is about March, but it just drives them all so giddy and feral. My crew is the same."

I laughed. "You sound like you're talking about a field of wild ponies."

"It's the spring thaw that's doing it. All winter they've been frozen and now that it's warming up, they're getting feeling in their little bodies again."

I considered Stacey's theory as I took another sip of coffee.

"You might be onto something there, Stacey."

"What else could it be?" Dayton, another teacher, looked

at her over my head as he plopped himself on the arm of the chair I was sitting in. Automatically I leaned forward out of his reach while pretending to reach down and massage my feet. Dayton had this annoying habit of encroaching on other people's personal space. At first, I took it personally, but then I realized that was just the way he was with everyone.

"I just hope they will settle down soon before I lose it completely," I said as I stood and stretched. I could feel the kinks in my back straighten out a bit and the relief was heavenly.

"Want a back massage? I'm really good," Stacey offered.

"Thanks, but that would put me to sleep for a week. I need to wake up," I said, as I slipped my shoes back on and made a beeline for the pantry to find myself a snack. I came back with a bag of chips and went to stand by the window overlooking the parking lot.

I thought about when I started teaching at Dunrobin Middle School. I'd been fresh out of college and getting this job had been the only bright spark in my life. In fact, that summer had been the worst one of my life and one I wished I could wipe away forever from my memories. But now and then old images, three dimensional, moving, complete with color, sounds, and smells, encroached into the peace of my mind.

Almost as if I had conjured them, I felt them begin to come up before me. That terrible birthday... me standing by the ocean, the feel of the wind in my hair as I flung my beautiful pearl necklace into the relentless waves. The glint of the milky beads as they disappeared from view. He gave that necklace to me. I remembered again, how divinely sublime and vast the sky had seemed, and how small, fragile, and broken I'd felt then.

I pushed the painful recollection away forcefully. I was no longer that girl. She was long dead.

As a matter of fact, my twenty-fifth birthday was only a month away. The past four years had been good to me and I supposed I could say I had accomplished quite a lot in that time.

A year after getting the job, I started an online course to complete my Masters in education. I enjoy learning and got that under my belt in two years.

I glanced at my watch. Lunch would end in ten minutes, but I always liked to be there before my class returned. I went to the coffee machine and got myself a coffee before heading back to the classroom. I straightened a couple of desks that had been moved out of place in their owners' hurry to escape.

As I pushed Simon's desk back into place, I wondered what it would be like to have a child. As soon as the thought came, I pushed it aside impatiently. To have a child there would need to be a partner. And a partner was definitely not in the books. Of that I was one hundred percent sure. My heart would not be open to being hurt in that fashion ever again. Going to the sperm bank was too clinical for me. Maybe later, much later in life, I would consider adoption. For now, the subject was closed.

I sat at my desk and looked around the room at the teaching aids which had seen better days.

It was no secret that Dunrobin was no elite school. As a school in the poorest part of the state we suffered from a lack of funding and provision. How wonderful it would be if the fundraiser I was working on was a success and we were able to replace all the ancient computers in our classrooms.

I pulled out the notepad I used to keep track of my thoughts. The fundraiser was actually my idea. It popped into my head last autumn. I approached the principal and he had agreed to allow me to plan and execute my idea. I pulled my team together quickly and we worked hard for many months to solicit assistance from the business community.

In just a few weeks Dunrobin would be having its first ever 'Spring Fair' in its history. It had been an amazing experience and I was very proud of our progress. Our next committee meeting was next Monday and hopefully we would all be able to report success on all our various tasks to date.

The bell rang for the end of lunch and I put the notepad away and went to stand by the door. As my students poured into the room, my heart swelled with great affection for each little child.

I prayed and hoped our school got the funds we needed.

SAVANNAH

My weekend was satisfying. I spent almost all of it painting my apartment.

By Sunday evening I stood back proudly to survey my handiwork. I had gone with a mostly monochromatic theme throughout. Various shades of peach and cream were present in all the rooms, with a pop of color on an accent wall. My living quarters were small; one bedroom with en-suite bathroom, a square kitchen, and a living area that also served as a dining space. It was what I had called home since my college days and it still suited my needs just fine.

My mother didn't think so. In her words, 'it was cozy... for now'.

With a dreamy gleam in her eye, she would refer to a time in the near future when God would send her a son-in-law and grandchildren, and I would need to house them for her in suitable lodgings. Whenever that discussion came up, I did not burst her bubble by telling her I had no intention of being in any sort of relationship ever again.

Four years ago, when the pain was so fresh it felt like a

knife in my heart, I would vehemently and bitterly insist that I was through with men and relationships forever. She was very gentle but firm and stated that was only the pain talking. I was young and would soon be out and about on the dating scene once more. She believed since I was an attractive and sensible woman the suitors would soon be pounding down my door.

I didn't argue, but I knew my mind was made up against anything of the sort.

As a child, I'd watched my parents, the love they had for each other, and had dreamed of having a love like theirs. Even as my father lay dying from terminal cancer, their love for each other shone out of their eyes. And afterwards even though she was only forty-one my mother declared my father was the only man for her and she would never again remarry.

I wanted a love like that. And for a brief moment, I thought I had it. But in a blink of an eye it had all fallen apart.

I looked around the apartment. Once he had walked these rooms barefoot and shirtless. An image flashed into my head. Him, leaning against the kitchen doorway, biting into an apple as he watched me make a cup of bitter tea for him. I shook my head to dislodge the bright image of him and frowned. It had taken me a long time to wipe away every trace of him in my space and this paint job was to be the final task. There was to be not even a reminder of the soft blues he had helped me put on the walls so long ago. Or the things our paint-splattered bodies did on the canvass covered floors afterwards.

My eyes darkened. Why was I having all these flash-backs and memories suddenly? It was not any special season. My birthday was weeks away. His was in the fall. We had met in winter. So why all these memories in the middle of March? Why all the thoughts of that devil Max Blackstone who not only shattered my soul, but also ruined me for any other man?

I wiped my hands on a piece of rag, put the brushes to soak, and jumped into the shower. I was exhausted, so after a quick meal of grilled chicken, mashed potatoes and a can of green beans, I slipped into bed.

Tomorrow is Monday and I could lose myself at work again. Max was gone. He was rotting in some prison and never coming back. The last memory I had before sleep claimed me was Max whispering, "You're the only woman for me, Savannah."

He lied.

Then I fell asleep.

MONDAYS ALWAYS MOVED FAST. There was so much to do. Finally, the day was over and my fundraising team and I gathered in the old computer lab for our weekly meeting.

"How is the donation sheet from the PTA coming, Monica?" I asked.

"Mrs. Gibbs is to get back to me tomorrow when she has heard from all the parents. Not much has changed, she said. We still only have the offer of a projector and a couple thousand dollars in pledges."

My heart fell at the news. "What about the bake sales we've been having so far, Lisa?"

She tried to look bright, but didn't succeed. "The profit isn't much, but it is a profit nevertheless."

"Can I get a report on income and expenditure to date on that, please?"

She nodded. "Sure. I'll let you have it before the end of the week."

I turned to another colleague. "Any improvement with the cookie drive, Lance?"

"Slow. You can't blame anyone. Times are hard and people are holding on to their pennies."

I looked around the room. "It's going to take more than a few pennies to reach our goals. The 'Spring Fair' seems to be our only hope. And much as I hate to put all my eggs into one basket, we have to pull out all the stops there. How many commitments do we have, Stacey?"

"We're still getting rides from 'Wild Rides'. They've agreed to loan us the equipment for free. All they ask is for us to feed their staff."

"Awesome! What about food?"

"Captain's Bakery will provide a thousand buns and rolls for burgers and hot dogs. Sammy's is also on board to donate the meat we need for those. We've also got a promise of condiments and napkins from SuperMart."

Already I could feel the positivity snake around the room. I grinned at my team. "Sounds good."

"And you know the parents are all on board with helping to supervise for the day. I'm working on a roster of the various stations and the help we will need in each area."

"If only all this volunteering could be converted to cash. We would have our computers in no time. But it does take cash to care," I smiled ruefully. "But for what it's worth, we will be grateful for whatever we're able to get done."

"We will be. Savannah, I wanted to run an idea by you. It's not something we've discussed before, but, what about alumni?" Stacey looked at me with raised eyebrows.

"Alumni?" I tilted my head inquiringly.

"Yes. We have been so busy focusing on who we have

presently – parents and students. What about those who were here before? You know, those people who are not parents with children in this school, but have made it in life and can write off a big donation as a tax deduction."

I nodded thoughtfully. "You're on to something there, Stacey. I don't think we ever thought about them. Especially being a middle school. People are usually more loyal to their high schools or colleges, but we could give it a shot."

Stacey smiled triumphantly. "I thought you would agree so I went ahead and got a list of names and contacts for every graduate in the last ten to twenty years. We have quite a few heavy hitters on this list too. I'm sure just one check can cover any shortfall we have."

Dramatically, she flourished a few sheets of paper.

I laughed. "Trust you to be ahead of the game."

Her eyes shone with pride. "I know you can't contact them all so I've taken the liberty of assigning each of us a contact list. I have even drafted a template email that we could use." She pulled another stack of papers out of her bag. "And here is the information sheet to summarize the event and its objectives that we can send."

She passed the sheets around.

There was silence as we all read her paper. I looked up, impressed. "Sounds like a plan. Thanks, Stacey."

"I'll put some work into the draft email tonight as well"

She sat back, pleased. "Awesome!"

The meeting wrapped up shortly after and I traveled back home.

Twenty minutes later I pulled into my apartment complex. In my freshly painted apartment, I popped the freezer meal I'd taken out that morning into the oven and headed to the shower. While it baked, I worked on the draft email for the fundraiser. The television droned in the background as the evening news was read. I was barely listening, the news was all bad or depressing, and I was half ready to switch to a music channel when my ears perked up. My eyes widened and my head spun around towards the television screen. I was greeted with a pair of piercing blue eyes I could never forget.

I felt my heart speed up and my hands grow clammy.

"Max Blackstone, the Tech software genius and one half of Stein-Bart Innovative Software, was today released after serving four years for embezzlement. More in this report."

I sat with my mouth wide open as they showed four-year-old clippings of Max entering and leaving court during his trial. The memories I had been staving off all weekend now came crashing in on me and I felt like a shipwrecked sailor being tossed on a stormy sea.

The last time I had seen Max in person had been just before that fateful missed dinner date on my birthday. The next time I saw him was on the screen of my television. I couldn't help it. I was like an animal that had been starved of food for weeks. I stared at his image hungrily, devouring every little detail. Noting that his eyes were still the same brilliant blue and his gorgeous black hair was just as thick and sexy as it always was, but there were tiny lines around his eyes that had not been there before. His mouth, which used to break into a ready smile at the least provocation, was pressed into a thin, hard line. I watched entranced as the cameras followed him from the gates of the penitentiary to a waiting car. The film cut back to the reporter.

"Blackstone has always professed innocence even in the midst of his trial and has served only four years of a ten-year sentence. And in other news—"

I rushed to turn off the television. There were goose

pimples on the back of my arms. I stared at a blank wall in shock. My whole world felt as if it had turned upside down.

Max was out of prison!

Fuck!

Max was out of prison!

I blinked. What was the matter with me? What did it matter if he was out or not? It had nothing to do with me. He was nothing to me. Nothing. I forced myself to think of the photo I kept in my bureau. The one of him and that other woman. That was my reminder that I needed to have nothing to do with Max... nor any man for that matter. That was my reminder that men were cheats and liars who couldn't be trusted. Ever. I allowed the anger to come. It was the perfect foil and diffused any other emotion that threatened to overtake me. It had kept me focused all these years and I would not let it go now.

Max was out of prison. Good for him.

I went to the kitchen and pulled out my meal. I sat it in front of me and forked it into my mouth. The delicious macaroni and cheese that I had been looking forward to now tasted like cardboard and sat in the pit of my stomach like a solid brick. I washed the taste out of my mouth with a glass of wine. The wine tasted foul.

I drank another glass and started to feel better.

Work. Work was always the answer.

It was nearly nine o'clock. I worked like a demon on the email. Tomorrow I'd take another look before printing it for submission. Before going to bed I checked my emails. Stacey had sent the full list. The list I had only glanced at.

I scanned the thirty-odd names curiously. Then, for the second time that night, I felt as though I had been dealt a blow. There, staring up at me, just above Robert Steinberg, was the email and contact number for Max Blackstone. I stifled a scream. What were the odds that he would end up on my list?

What kind of sick game was the universe playing with me?

I moved my eyes up and back to Robert Steinberg. Robert and I had sort of kept in touch over the years and spoke sometimes.

I sensed he was interested in much more than a casual friendship, but I had never felt that way about him. He was always meant to be in the friend zone. In fact, I met Robert first, but it was Max who stole my heart. Robert, being the gentleman he was, had been gracious enough to step aside.

But I always knew he wanted more.

So both Robert and Max were on the list. I swallowed hard at the prospect of interacting with Max in any way, but I pushed the nervousness aside and remembered the anger.

I had to stay angry.

Ignoring the slight tremble to my finger, I typed Max's email address on my draft email. Taking a deep breath, I then, copy pasted all the other names on the list into the sender's box.

As the cursor hovered over the 'send' button, I half considered deleting Max's address, but then I stopped myself. He was nothing to me. If the children could benefit from him, why not. Anyway, he would probably be in no position to fund anything but himself, so there was almost no reason to believe he would respond.

Before I could give it any more thought, I clicked 'send'.

I pursed my lips. Of course, he won't respond. That would be the best thing for him to do – not respond.

3

MAX

https://www.youtube.com/watch?v=PpsUOOfb-vE
-Jailhouse Rock-

I took a deep gulp of air, opened my front door, and walked into my apartment. It was a surreal feeling.

I was – fucking free.

I could go into any damn room I pleased. I could open the refrigerator and eat anything I wanted. I could shower whenever I felt like it.

I was finally free after more than forty-eight months behind bars.

A smile curved my lips. This was no dream. I'd left my prison days behind me forever.

I looked around.

Everything looked the same as it had that morning the police turned up on my doorstep with a warrant for my arrest. I had left instructions for my weekly cleaning service that there was not to be one speck of dust to be found on my arrival and last week I had asked for my refrigerator to be deep cleaned and fully stocked with all my favorite foods.

I opened the refrigerator and pulled out a bottle of Dom Perignon. I popped the cork and drank straight from the bottle. I unscrewed a jar of beluga caviar, dipped my finger into it, scooped some of the shiny beads, and placed them on my tongue.

Yes... oh, yes.

I took another gulp of cold bubbles, closed my eyes and savored the taste. It was hard to believe that four years had gone by. I thought it would never end, but here I was. Finally, finally free to pick up the reins of my life and continue... but it would not be business as usual.

Oh no.

For one, there was no more Stein-Bart. I would never have believed it four years ago, but it was the best thing that ever happened to me. I didn't need Robert. I thrived without him. From behind bars, I had set up my own operation – BB Tech Solutions.

Nobody knew that the CEO of BB Tech's office was in a ten-by-ten cell he shared with another man. Nobody cared enough to ask what BB stood for, or I would have had to tell them it was short for Behind Bars.

If Robert thought he had destroyed me, he thought wrong. I went into prison accused of stealing a few hundred thousand dollars. Now I was worth millions. All I needed was a computer and internet access and I had both in the prison library where I spent every moment I could. Rick, who had married my sister, Michelle, had proven trustworthy and a good man. He had taken care of all the legwork outside of prison, and I had made sure he was more than handsomely rewarded.

He was now a very, very rich man and about to get even richer.

I walked towards the gigantic windows that overlooked the park across the street. The scene was beautiful, but thinking of what Robert did to me, made the familiar rage course through my veins.

The old adage about being stabbed in the back by those closest to you had proved to be true. He had set me up beautifully. And I knew why. In all the years since we had been partners, I knew I was the brains behind our operation while he just wrote the checks in the beginning.

I was so involved in work I had not sensed his underlying resentment of me and I was too loyal to break out on my own. Hell, I would have carried him for the rest of my life if he had not shown his true colors.

What a shame for him that he completely misunderstood me. I was about to secure us both the deal of our lifetimes, but he thought I was going to betray him and set up my own establishment. To stop me he set me up on a made-up embezzlement charge.

As I sat in front of my lawyer, I understood how much I had misjudged Robert. I knew the only way was to play along and get a reduced sentence. This way I would have a brand new start with no messy battles over intellectual property rights. Of course, Robert took the bait of dissolving our partnership... and I was free of him.

My jaw clenched to match my fists at the thought of my once best friend now being my sworn enemy. All through school I had covered his ass. Yet for reasons only he knew, he had turned on me. They say the past was the past, but those that said that have not been screwed over by someone they trusted.

There were old scores to settle before I could close the chapter on the last four long years.

As was my wont, inevitably, after thinking about Robert's betrayal, my thoughts would always turn to Savannah.

Savannah, the woman I once loved. Deeply.

She made me believe she would be there forever, but she deserted me when I needed her most. She did not call me. Not once. I looked for her, but she never came to court. She pretty much dropped off the face of the earth in the middle of my worst nightmare. Not once did she ask me: What happened, Max? Give me your version because I'm your woman and I'll stand by you, no matter what.

Bitch!

I thought of her with Robert. The image burned my chest. I took another swig of the most expensive champagne money could buy, but it tasted foul.

I would move on from Savannah as well... after exacting my revenge.

I would have the last laugh.

I was not yet sure how, but it was a necessity. Robert's betrayal enraged me, hers tore me to pieces. I had already more than recovered my financial stability while still in prison, but now I needed to heal my heart and soul. I couldn't do that until Robert and Savannah got their just desserts.

Until then, fuck them both. I wasn't about to let them spoil my first day of freedom.

I turned away from the window and looked around. The place was as quiet as a fucking graveyard. Putting some music on, I ordered dinner. The food was exactly what I needed. I'd almost forgotten the taste of good Chinese food.

Afterwards, I got into bed and watched two seasons of *Succession* late into the night, content to be in my own bed with a luxuriously thick mattress and lavender scented sheets. As my eyes drifted closed to the hum of the voices on the television in the background, I prayed for my future. For my future without her.

It seemed so bleak...

As my eyes opened, I lay still, and stared at the duck egg blue ceiling. Memories of the previous day flashed before me and I sat up. I looked around, allowing a tiny smile to cross my lips. It had not been a dream. It was real. I was free.

I rolled out of bed and placed my feet on the floor. My toes were lost in the plush mat by the bedside, but when I lifted them clear and I looked down they made me shake my head ruefully. These feet seriously needed some attention. And while I was at it, so did my hands, face, and hair.

I was no longer a convict, but a man with a plan. I could do with a day at a spa.

My secretary made the necessary booking and within an hour, I had given myself over to the skillful hands of a masseuse. I felt the first shoots of new energy grow in my body. I moved from station to station. By that afternoon, my muscles felt supple, my hands and feet felt like they hadn't felt in years, and they had done something to my hair which made it look pretty good. I looked every inch the successful young executive. Sometimes I did not believe I was just twenty-seven going on twenty-eight. Prison makes you feel like you are a thousand years old. But now I was on to the next phase.

A glance at my watch told me I had twenty minutes to get downtown to my office. I had a meeting with Rick who had been holding the fort. Obviously, I had met most of my staff electronically, but now I would see them face-to-face. All twenty-six of them.

I got into the blacked-out Koenigsegg Jesko. As the beast

of an engine roared into life, I smiled. Life was amazing. Even without her. Yes, even without her.

It was a short trip to my office building.

I gave my name to the parking garage attendant who stared at my car in an awed daze, and entered the underground parking space. I easily found the section assigned to BB Tech and could not help but chuckle at the banner marking the CEO's spot.

Welcome back Max!!!

I watched as the numbers on the elevator panel climbed to the twenty-second floor. The doors opened and I stepped into a plush reception area. To my surprise I was greeted with loud cheers.

Every member of staff was waiting in the lobby. Rick came forward and pushed a glass of champagne into my hand. He raised his glass as did everyone else.

"Welcome back. Hip hip!"

"Hoorayyyyyyyyyyy!!!" my staff yelled.

My face split into a grin as I raised my glass and clinked it with Rick's. I looked around at the staff who were all beaming at me. With Rick's help in recruitment, I had interviewed each of them via video call and felt as though I knew them all. Even staff meetings had been conducted with me on video.

"It's nice to finally meet you all in the flesh," I said.

"You're much taller!" someone shouted from the back.

"And more handsome too!" a woman from the accounts team joined in cheekily.

That had everyone rolling for a few moments. There was some hand-shaking and I made a little speech to express my appreciation for all they had done for the company. Afterwards, they disappeared to their own places of work and Rick showed me to my office. Once he left, I sat for a few minutes silently enjoying the view of the city skyline.

Life was good. Even without her.

There was a faint knock on my door, and I called, "come in." The door opened as I swiveled around to face it. In walked Rick and his assistant.

"I wanted to introduce you to Paul," he said.

Paul grinned. "Settling in okay, boss?"

I got the distinct impression of a brown-noser, like the Tom Wambsgans character in *Succession*. Well, I was no Kendall Roy. "Just Max will do. I'm fine. Take a seat, gentlemen."

When I'd been brought up to date with the different projects they were working on, they rose to leave, but I beckoned for Rick to remain. Paul shot us a brief look, a frown creasing his brow, before he masked it and left. I waited a few moments until he had closed the door before I turned to Rick and spoke again.

So, how's the asshole doing?"

"His ass is in a bit of a bind right now with losing the Chase account last week."

"Does he know who won it?"

"I made sure of it."

I nodded. "Good. I guess he knows BB Tech is my company."

"Max, it's not something I have to plaster on a billboard or hire a skywriter for him to know. He knows exactly who the brains are behind BB Tech."

"Good. He needs to know he fucked with the wrong guy, friend or not. Do you think he knows I'm out?"

"Again, no need for a billboard or skywriter. It's been all

over the news. If he's living in this city, which he is, he knows."

"Good." I went silent.

Rick continued, "I'm sure she does too." He stared at me.

I shifted uncomfortably. "Don't mention her to me."

He hid his amusement. "I didn't mention anyone in particular. There are many 'shes' in this city."

"You know damn well you're talking about Savannah."

"Now that you mention it, I'm sure she knows you're out as well."

"It is of no importance to me whether she knows or doesn't."

"Liar. Michelle always said your right eyebrow twitches when you lie. It's a pity the jury didn't know your little tell. You know you damn well care if Savannah knows."

I felt suddenly bitter. "Only enough to exact my revenge the same way I'm taking my revenge on Robert."

"To be fair she didn't actually do anything bad to you."

"She did not even give me the benefit of the doubt. Simply judged me and deserted me when I needed her most." I didn't tell him my suspicion that she then took up with Robert, which was the real sin I held against her.

"Michelle thinks, and I agree with her that it was not like Savannah to do that. There must be an explanation."

"You're welcome to it when you find it. As far as I'm concerned, she's history," I said coldly.

"Come on, Max. Give her a chance."

"No."

"But-"

"End of discussion, Rick." My voice was harsh.

He held his hands up defensively and stepped back.

"Okay. There will be nothing else said about Savannah Maitland from me."

"And tell Michelle I don't want to hear her theories about Savannah either."

"She's your sister. You should know better than me that she is going to speak her piece whether you want to hear it or not. We agree with you about Robert. But Savannah-"

"Rick. Let it rest, will you?"

"Okay."

I shook my head. "My sister had to choose a man as pig-headed as she is. You're both like damn bulldogs when you're holding on to a point."

"Now who's going back to it. I'm done!"

"You know damn well you're not."

He grinned. "Yeah, I'm not. But I will let it rest for today. It's good having you out, Max."

The tension flowed out of me. "It's good to be out."

"Now let's get on with the business of really putting this company on the map. If Robert thought he was in trouble before, he's going to think hell has been let loose by the time we're done with him."

I nodded in agreement. Revenge had kept me warm in my cold prison cell. "I'm taking him for every penny he's got, and that still won't be enough."

"By the way, Michelle wants you to come to dinner tonight. Seven good?"

"Perhaps tomorrow?"

"Tomorrow it is," he said with a smile.

I looked at the door as it closed behind him, then I swiveled back to face the window. The afternoon had slipped away and the evening sun bathed the sky with a golden light. Memories of sunsets on beaches, her naked skin bathed in pinkish light, her swollen mouth whispering, "I love you, Max... forever and ever," rose up before me. With a frown, I pushed them away hurriedly. I could not afford to wallow in childish memories any longer, not when I had my revenge to exact.

They had to pay for their betrayal. Both of them.

I thought about the conversation with Rick and instantly dismissed his defense of Savannah. My family had loved her to pieces and clearly still did, if Rick and Michelle defending her was any indication. But I would not entertain such foolish ideas. No, I knew better.

I took one last look out of the window before getting up and walking towards the filing cabinet. Outside my room I could hear my staff begin to leave. I was just beginning my first official day as CEO. And sometime after I had everything exactly how I wanted it, I would pay a visit to Robert.

Then to Savannah.

By the time I got back to my apartment, it was close to midnight.

I showered quickly and got into bed. As I allowed my brain to wind down, I scrolled through my phone. My heart skipped a beat when I saw the email address connected to the school where Savanah taught. I stared at it in amazement. The world felt as if it had come to a grinding halt.

"Calm down. It's not actually from her. Anyway, remember you're angry with her. She left you for Robert. Actually, you're fucking furious," I muttered to myself.

Still, I could not help but burn with curiosity at what was in the message. I opened it and felt a bit disappointed to see that there were over thirty addresses the email had been sent to. I skimmed through and realized instantly these were familiar names of old classmates. Robert's name was there as well. The mystery was solved when I read the body. So, they were having a fundraiser and wanted the alum to participate.

Did they now?

I leaned back in bed and stared at the ceiling. I had not planned to hunt down Robert and Savannah just yet, but this invitation to an event at which they would both be present, just seemed like a gift from the heavens telling me to strike the iron while it was hot. I did not have to be told twice.

With a few taps, I sent a brief message.

I'll be there.

4

SAVANNAH

We could not have asked for a more beautiful day for our Spring Fair. The chilly winds of early spring were gone and after a week of rain that had seen vendors and rides calling in to query if the fair would still take place, had given way to one of the warmest April days yet.

Birds were singing and flowers were blooming everywhere. Spirits were high as were the expectations for what the day would bring.

We had debated long and hard whether or not to sell tickets for entry and had voted not to as we would anticipate that the activities and food would be supported and an entry fee might be a turn-off.

By our count with the treasury, we were a little over twenty-five percent towards our target. Projections for sales for the rides and food put that figure closer to the fifty percent mark. So, we needed every cent we could collect in sales and pledges today.

Stacey's idea about contacting alumni had borne fruit and we'd collected pledges via bank transfers from all over the world. There were others who promised to be there in person with their checkbook and to support in any way they could. I pushed away the thoughts about one particular response as I drove to the school field where the fair was being held.

I'll be there.

Even now my heart skipped a beat as I remembered how nervous I'd been all day after sending the email. Robert had been the first to respond and we spoke briefly. He seemed pleased to come and help, but there was no response from Max. I had already given up on him by the time I heard the ping of my phone at well past midnight. I had half a mind to ignore it until morning, but given the nature of the messages I'd been getting, it could have been someone in Japan who was just waking up to my message. So I reached for my phone to check, but the last thing I expected was to see a response from him.

I'll be there.

The three words burned into my subconscious. And I had been nervous ever since.

"He's just another alumnus, Sav. No big deal."

"Ha! But I gave this 'just another alumnus' my freaking virginity, planned to have a bunch of babies, and be with him for the rest of my life."

Forcefully, I killed all thoughts of Max and concentrated on what needed to be done.

By the time I pulled into the staff parking lot, I was all business again. The morning sun lit the Ferris wheel and here and there tents dotted the field in between other rides which had been set up last night. Even now, I saw more trailers drive into the site as last-minute rides and tents were being positioned and secured.

I stepped out and was glad I had chosen to wear low

boots rather than sneakers. The ground was still soft from the days of rain and my sneakers would have sunk right into it. I tucked my black t-shirt into my jeans and smoothed my hands over my hips. My hair was not in the usual bun but hung behind me like a thick rope. The end twitched against my ass as I walked over to the staff tent where some of the other members of the committee were already gathered.

We had agreed that as the committee we needed to be there at least an hour before the volunteers and vendors. Stacey was busy sorting through t-shirts for the volunteers. We had come up with the idea of color-coding the shirts depending on the area in which persons would be working. The committee wore black with the word 'STAFF' printed on the back, while the other groups would wear their colors with words like 'VOLUNTEER' or 'VENDOR'.

"Good morning, boss. Looking good!" Dayton greeted me with a bump on my shoulder. I smiled, pulled my cap out of my back pocket, and fished my braid through before pulling the visor down over my forehead.

"Good morning everyone. Are we ready to kick ass today?"

I was greeted with loud affirmative cheers as my team came up to high-five me.

"Come on, let's make use of these few minutes of quiet before the chaos of the day starts with donuts and a cup of coffee."

I'd only just brushed the crumbs of my donut off my jacket when the cotton candy merchant rolled in to take up her booth. After that it was a never-ending stream of vendors and volunteers. Even before the gates opened at nine, children, parents and other patrons started lining up.

It was non-stop activity all morning. The rides were packed and the food vendors did not have enough hands to sell their wares. It felt as though the whole city had turned out. I was constantly being introduced as the committee chair for the computer lab renovation project and had to explain to several potential donors where the proceeds would go. I'd anticipated this and had a fanny pack into which I placed checks, business cards and other pieces of paper with various bits of information.

At midday, I managed to sneak away with a hot dog and soda and wolfed it down in the privacy of my car. By my mental calculations with just the checks and promises in my fanny pack, we were almost sixty-five percent there. Then when we saw what we took in from our cut of the sales from the rides and food I was sure we would surpass our target. The committee had already decided that any surplus would go into renovating the playing fields.

I grabbed my bottle of water and ventured out into the fray once more. I could see the committee, vendors and volunteers constantly on the go. We were running at top speed and I knew we were tired, but it was worth it. I was already observing the proceedings today, noting gaps in the flow of the activities, and planning for next year to be even more organized with a bigger group of volunteers and a roster for relieving workers throughout the day.

I did not take another break until nearly four o'clock which was close to closing time. I wandered over to the Ferris wheel and tapped Monica on the shoulder.

"Have you had a break yet?"

"Bless you, Sav. I could use a breather."

I took the bag of ticket stubs from her and stepped in to supervise the ticket collection while the ride operator continued.

"Okay ladies and gents. We're wrapping up. Who wants

one last ride on the Ferris wheel today? I've got space for twenty."

With a big, friendly grin, I began to collect tickets from eager patrons. I was about to turn back to the Ferris wheel when I looked up and did a double-take. Suddenly, I felt as if I was spinning out of control.

There, standing a few feet away from me, was Max!

Oh God!

All day I had forced myself not to think about him. Throughout the day I'd met a few people I had emailed, and each time I'd forced myself not to hope that Max would keep his word to be there. At any point that I found myself wondering if he was there yet, I reminded myself that he was not the most reliable person at showing up. His promises were all built on sand.

I was happy that my visor and sunglasses hid any expression on my face. If he only knew how desperately I was drinking in the sight of him as he stood there, looking at me, his own eyes shielded. I did not know if his blue gaze scanned me as I did him.

My God, the man was beautiful.

He wore a soft yellow button-down shirt. Without moving my head, I allowed my eyes to travel downward to the dark blue jeans that hugged his lean hips, and was shocked to find my body was growing warm just looking at him. What the hell was I doing?

Suddenly, the hurt, rage, anguish, and hate that had become second nature to me dissipated like hot breath on a freezing night. I struggled to even remember how furious I was with him. I just wanted to wrap myself around him again. Feel his hard body against mine, his skin like raw silk...

NO! The word was like a scream reverberating in my head.

I forced myself to remember the familiar anger, the hurt, the pain, the anguish, the grieving, everything he had put me through with his revolting betrayal. I rammed the intolerable image of him with the other woman forcefully to my mind. I must never forget that, yes, he was very easy on the eye, but he was actually a disgusting human being who had also tried to steal from his best friend. A kind man who had taken a chance on him and his business ideas. Robert was almost a brother to him, and someone who had taken the risk of backing him financially when no one else would. Max's repayment had been to steal from poor Robert.

Ugh!

I felt the desire evaporate and I set my jaw defiantly.

Taking a deep breath I watched him taking long strides towards me. He was wearing sunglasses, so I couldn't see his eyes, but the evening sun slanted onto his cheekbones, and made him look so darn beautiful, my stomach clenched. *Once this man was mine. I dreamed he would be forever.* Now he was a stranger. I would never feel his lips on mine again. I felt tears burn the backs of my eyes, and suddenly, I knew I couldn't meet him. Not yet, anyway. I just needed a bit more time.

To prepare myself.

I turned on my heel and all but ran away towards another part of the field. I dared not look over my shoulder until I felt I was far enough away from him to be safe. Thankfully, though the grounds were becoming scanty, there were still enough patrons around and things to be done where I could be busy.

I made my rounds, discreetly looking for his black head. He always was the tallest man in a crowd. I spotted him a few times as he walked around, laughing and chatting with a few sponsors who he seemed to know. Why the hell hadn't he come earlier when it was busier and it was easier for me to get lost in the crowd? I could not help but feel as though he had deliberately waited until there would be very few distractions. But then again, I was only assuming he had just arrived. He did not have the look of someone who had been at a fair all day.

I stood with my back against a tent as I scanned the field once more. All I had to do was avoid him for the next ten minutes after which the fair would close and all patrons would have to leave. I could already see the school's security team beginning to round up stragglers who were trying to get into any last-minute rides and food. The clean-up crew were already moving in and some of the ride operators had already started dismantling their equipment.

Ten minutes. That was all.

How hard could it be to stay out of his way for the next six hundred seconds?

5

MAX

https://www.youtube.com/watch?v=GtUVQei3nX4
Drop it like it's hot

A s though I had conjured her up by merely thinking about her, I saw her familiar figure at the other end of the field. I narrowed my eyes as I zoned in on her. My eyes traveled down her curvy figure. Jesus, how beautiful she was. In an instant the noise faded away to a hum and all the people around me dropped away. There was only her and me.

She stood and stared at me, her body as tense as a deer about to bolt.

I wanted her. How I wanted her. I felt as if every pore in my body had opened up and all I could feel was a raging heat. My cock twitched and I was half-erect before I could catch myself.

Then, without warning, she suddenly turned, her thick braid swinging from beneath her cap, and sprinted away. I stopped in my tracks. It actually felt as if all the air had been sucked out of my body.

"What the fuck?"

I gave myself a mental shake and looked down to the ground. I forced myself to remember how fucking angry I was. Damn her, she had deserted me in my hour of need. Of course, she ran away. She was too ashamed to look me in the eye. I might fucking remind her of the pact we made to love each other till after we breathed our last. Sounded so silly to me now, but I was young and in love. She had hurt me the way no one had ever done before and no one will ever do again, and she definitely did not deserve to feel anything but my rage.

I unclenched my fists slowly, and allowed myself to calm down. Then I looked up slowly and at the spot where I had seen her last, not fifty feet from me stood Robert, his blond hair gleaming and not a hair out of place despite the brisk breeze. I did not doubt that a great deal of hairspray had been applied before he set foot out of the house this afternoon. In fact, his obsession with looking perfect used to be a source of much mockery amongst our classmates.

I had not seen him since my release, but I knew that today would be the day since he had confirmed his attendance on the email thread. He had also added a personal message for 'Savvie'. Whether or not that was for my benefit, I did not know, but it sure made me even more determined to get my revenge.

I stared at him from behind the shield of my sunglasses, watching as he mixed and mingled with a group of people at one of the hot dog stands. His smile, even from this distance, irked me. Seeing him behave as if the world was his oyster only strengthened my resolve to destroy him. And he would not have a clue what hit him, the same way he had taken me by surprise. And it would only be a matter of time.

As I watched, he turned away from the people around him to watch Savannah fleeing across the field. Even from a distance I could feel the intensity of his gaze. I felt my throat close up as fury overtook me. Taking a deep breath I expelled my breath slowly. I needed to get my temper under control. I needed to be calm. The past full of my trusting naivety and stupidity could not be changed.

Robert had met her first... wanted her first.

Then I turned up at the bar and she made it clear she wanted me. Though I had briefly harbored a feeling he resented the fact she had chosen me over him, I slapped it away as unworthy of either him or me. He was my best friend, and he himself had assured me nothing could, or would come between us, especially not a mere woman.

In those days Robert went through women so fast I could hardly keep up.

Naturally, I believed him when he told me she would have been just another fling for him. He asked me if I was really serious about her. I told him I was not really serious, I was totally and utterly smitten. Head over heels. She was my life. She was everything to me. He hugged me tightly, wished me well, and told me he was happy for me. One day, he said, he too would find the woman he wanted to marry, and keep forever.

Fool that I was, I made the classic mistake of judging him by my standards. Because that is what I would have done for him.

I took stock as calmly as I could. The past was the past, and unchangeable, but that was okay. I was no longer interested like the love-struck boy I was. Now, I was only interested in the future. As far as I was concerned, Robert and

Savannah could go to hell together. And I would happily pay for their ticket there.

I thought about the two accounts BB Tech had already snatched away from Robert this week. That was just the beginning.

I turned away and walked in the opposite direction as fast as I could. I grabbed a snow cone to cool off. As the ice slid down my parched throat, I felt my eyes once again begin to search the crowd for Savannah.

I found her easily.

She was conversing with a group of children. She had always loved children, and I couldn't help remembering the times we had talked about having kids. She wanted six, but said she would settle for three if I didn't want that many. I laughed and told her she could have thirty-six if she wanted. She made a face I will never forget.

I circled a few more times, always keeping her within sight. She seemed to be on the move, throwing glances over her shoulder every once in a while.

She was avoiding me.

The fairgrounds started to empty. It was now or never. I saw her stop to talk with another staff member at the Ferris wheel. She stayed and the other woman left. My feet moved of their own volition.

I heard her clear voice ring out as she loaded the ride and I stood still, placing myself somewhat in her line of vision. She was laughing at something someone said and her face swung upwards and met my gaze. Her laughter died on her lips and her body stiffened. Time seemed to stand still in that instant. The feeling from when I had first seen her across the field started to sweep over me once more. My feet took a mind of their own and started to move towards her. Just as I was closing in on her she suddenly took flight. I stopped and stared at her retreating form. Well, well, so that was how it was going to be? She was going to keep running away after inviting me here?

I realized I enjoyed having her run. She should run.

For another half hour or so, I played her little game of 'chase Savannah', knowing I was unnerving her each time I popped up in her line of vision. I watched her watching me watching her. She managed to keep away by virtue of the crowd, which was to her disadvantage thinning pretty fast. But when it would be only her and the staff left then what?

Would she have security escort me off the field?

Closing time was approaching fast. I had to make my move. And the opportunity came when she became so engrossed with some staff members, she failed to see me slip away from where she was keeping an eye on me. I circled around behind tents, catching glimpses of her as she looked around frantically. I came up behind her stealthily and stood a few feet away. One of her staff members, facing me, noticed me first. Her eyes widened, which told me Savannah had discussed me. She looked at Savannah and winced. I saw Savannah's shoulders stiffen before she turned slowly. I stepped within arm's reach.

"Hello, Savannah."

She swallowed and licked her lips nervously. "Uh... hello."

"I came."

"I see "

I deliberately let an awkward silence between us grow as the other staff wandered off. From the corner of my eyes, I could see them throwing curious glances our way. Savannah kept her gaze fixed on me. I was close enough to see the gold flecks in her hazel eyes. Her eyes were the things I first noticed about her. They were incomparably beautiful. I'd never seen eyes like hers before.

My mind went back to the last time I had seen her that weekend before her birthday. I felt a rush of warmth wash over me as I remembered that last time we made love and had an instant erection. Thank the fuck I had not tucked my shirt into my jeans. My physical reaction spoke volumes about the hold she still had over me and it was intolerable.

This was Savannah, the bitch, who turned her back on me, and betrayed me with the man I thought was my best friend. My sweetheart, who had not called me after my arrest, thought to visit me even once while I was awaiting trial, or even show enough curiosity to turn up at the court-room. This was Savannah who, instead of reaching out to me as the man she loved, had hooked up with the man who had framed me and put me behind bars.

Running through her sins killed off my erection and I reminded myself that this was no lovers' reunion. This was a face-off and confrontation. I watched as she bit her bottom lip and reached around to fish her braid over her shoulder, all telltale signs she was nervous.

I smiled tauntingly. "A little nervous?"

"M-Me? N-Nervous? No, I'm not."

I took another step closer and was extremely pleased to see her immediately take a corresponding step backwards. I chuckled almost maniacally. It was nice to know I made her as uneasy as she did me. I saw her lick her lips and I licked mine in turn. If the circumstances had been different, I would have drawn her curvy body tightly to mine and devoured those juicy lips greedily.

"You *are* nervous, Sav. I'd say you're as nervous as a mouse in a room full of hungry cats. I wonder why, though. Have you done something to make you jumpy around me, the love of your life? The man of your dreams who you left to suffer alone for four fucking years. Hmmm, Sav? Is that why you're nervous? Perhaps you were hoping I wouldn't show up?"

I saw her chin stick out defiantly. "It wouldn't be the first time you stood me up, would it? I'm more surprised that you did show up, actually. Or perhaps because it's daytime and you prefer to have your sordid little escapades after dark."

I narrowed my eyes. "Whatever that means. If you didn't want me here, you shouldn't have arranged to have that email sent to me."

"Don't flatter yourself. I sent it to all the alumni. You had the choice to pass. So don't blame me for your presence here."

I shrugged. "I'm here to support my old school."

"Good. Support duly noted."

"Savvie! Sweetheart! There you are! I've been looking all over for you. Monica told me I could find you here!"

I looked up to see Robert had come around the corner of the tent. I felt as if he had punched me in the stomach when he put his arms around Savannah from behind, and embraced her tightly. He looked at me, a carefully practiced half-smile on his lips.

"Hey there, Max. I heard you were out. Long time no see."

I looked at him expressionlessly for a few seconds. All the hatred I felt was like red-hot lava in my guts, and my hands itched to curl into a fist and slam that irritating smile off his ridiculous face. But not now. My time will come. Without a word, I turned on my heels and walked away, feeling both their eyes boring into my back.

SAVANNAH

I watched as Max walked away. His long legs carried him halfway across the field before I could even react to his departure.

Damn him.

When I first saw Lisa's expression, she knew all about my relationship with Max, my heart felt like it had dropped to the pit of my stomach. The hairs on the back of my neck stood up as I turned around to face him.

Dizziness threatened to overtake me and my knees felt weak, but thankfully, my moment of weakness went as the venom spewed between us. He was furious, but so was I. Good. That would mean there was no hope of any sort of lovey-dovey reunion. The battle lines were drawn and I would keep them that way. How dare he expect me to play the dutiful girlfriend while he was having affairs behind my back.

Since he had so emphatically stated the only reason for his presence was in support of his school, I would collect whatever he was willing to donate and call it a day, but damn it all... if he didn't make my stomach tight with desire.

And I could not stop thinking about what he would think if I were to lunge at him and taste his lips. He was obviously not thinking the same thing because his face was hard and stony.

Thank God, Robert's voice rang out. I was so disturbed I barely felt his arms come around me. My usual response to his closeness was always to step away, but not this time. This time I welcomed it.

I felt strangely empty and suddenly annoyed by Robert's presence.

"What was that all about?" Robert murmured close to my ear.

I stepped out of his embrace and turned to him with a forced smile. "We were discussing his donation."

One blond eyebrow rose. "Oh? I guess he didn't give back all the money he stole after all if he is able to donate to charity." His lips tightened. "Or maybe it's what he's scammed from me since he got out. I lost two more accounts to him this last week, you know. It's like he's out to ruin me still. Ripping me off the first time wasn't enough for him." Robert's face twisted into a spiteful glare as he watched Max walk away.

"Let bygones be bygones, Robert," I said, even though I didn't know why I said it.

Robert swung his eyes back to me, his expression hurt. "So a sixty-second conversation after four years of suffering merits forgiveness? Remember, I'm not the only one he wronged, Savvie. Or have you forgotten what he did to you and how I had to pick up the pieces?"

I rolled my eyes. "Don't be ridiculous, Robert. You're exaggerating, don't you think?"

"I prefer to err on the side of caution. He was my friend

and turned on me. I'm not going to allow that to happen again to you or me."

I turned to look across the field once more and frowned to see Max coming back. My heart plummeted once more as he walked up to us.

"I like to be a man of my word. I promised I would make a contribution to my old school so here it is. I'm prepared to meet any shortfall in the budget for the refurbishment of the lab."

"Keep your dirty, stolen money. We don't need it. I wonder where you're skimming it from now. Maybe you'll be behind bars before the ink on the check even dries."

Max turned his stony face to Robert. "You worry about your money and I'll worry about mine. And, for your information, my money is clean and untouchable. I can't say the same for yours."

I looked from one to the other as they engaged in a dangerous silent war. Out of the corner of my eye, I saw the security team approaching and knew I needed to diffuse the situation immediately.

"Gentlemen, now is not the time or place for this. Please. People are looking."

"Let them look, Savvie. Why shouldn't I defend myself from the slurs this bastard has been throwing around since he got out?" He faced Max again. "Do you think I don't see the side-eyes as people wonder if there's any truth in the allegations that I framed you? Do you think I don't know that you're still saying I framed you or that you're trying to ruin me on top of everything?"

I watched as Max ignored Robert and stepped up to me. He pressed a card into my unresisting hand. "Let me have the figures as soon as possible so we can talk about my legitimate donation."

Then he turned and walked away once more. My eyes followed his determined stride and rigid back. Each step resonated with anger and I could not help but feel as though I was caught between a rock and a hard place. Behind me, I could feel Robert fuming.

"He's got some nerve even showing his face to us."

It was on the tip of my tongue to remind him that there was no 'us' but I could not be bothered to entertain Robert any longer.

"Be careful, Savvie. I know you need the money but I wouldn't take a cent from him. If you'd like, I can have my accountant look at your books and see how much more you need and if you can find another source for funding."

"The school's accountant is taking care of that, Robert, but thanks for the offer."

I looked at my watch and saw it was past closing time. It had been a long day with an unpredictable end. "I've got to go, Robert. Thanks for coming. I really appreciate it."

"Anything for you, Savvie."

He reached out to hug me once more, but I stepped back with a frown. We didn't have that kind of relationship and I didn't want to give him the wrong impression. I saw his face grow hard and anger flare in his eyes, but just as suddenly as it had come it was gone. A benign smile was in its place. He inclined his head slightly before walking away in the same direction Max had gone.

I stood looking at his retreating figure, wondering if I was going to have to send security to the parking lot to break up a fight if Max still lingered. I knew who my money would be on in such a fight. Robert would be too conscious of messing up his hair or sweating off his cologne to throw a proper punch.

"That was awkward."

I turned to find Stacey at my elbow. What was it with all these people sneaking up on me today? I smiled grimly. "You started it, you know."

She placed her hand on her chest and raised her eyebrows in shock. "Me? How did I get dragged into this triangle?"

"You generated that damn alumni list. And gave ME their names. So. Yes. I. Do. Blame You." I punctuated each word with a stab of my pointer finger at her chest.

"Well? Would you have reached out to him otherwise?"

I tilted my head and looked at her curiously.

She stared back innocently. Too innocently. I knew Stacey well enough to know she was up to something. My mind raced back through the series of events over the last few weeks.

I frowned. "You had the list out before he was even released."

She shrugged. "The timing just worked out perfectly, I swear. I just thought it was worth a shot seeing that he was an alum and all. Did it work?"

"You *did* see World War III barely averted just now? Right?"

"It wasn't that bad. Besides, I'd pay money to see someone mess Robert's hair up."

"Stacey!" I burst out laughing. "You're impossible!"

"But you know it's true. Listen, Savannah, from one friend to another, I don't know what went down between you and Max. Yes, we all know that Robert said he stole some money and he got sent to prison for it. But as far as I can tell there is still a lot of chemistry and unfinished business between the two of you. Maybe now that he's out, you can fix things or at least work him out of your system. As your friend I want you to be happy. I'm tired of seeing a beautiful woman like you turn guys down because you're protecting your heart. You need to heal. And maybe you need to be healed by the one who broke your heart in the first place."

"Maybe I don't want to be healed... or the damage is irreparable?"

"Nope. I'm the perennial dreamer and happily-ever-after believer. You can be healed. Both of you. Now let's see if we can help to lighten some vendors' loads by assisting with their disposal of any leftovers. Heaven knows I'm not going to sit in a drive thru, nor am I going home to cook after a day like today."

I laughed and threw my arm around her waist. "Well, that makes two of us."

BY THE TIME I got home, I was exhausted so I popped the bag with all kinds of leftovers into the freezer, and stuck a few slices of pizza into the microwave. Then I had a hot shower and shampooed my hair thoroughly. Leaving it wrapped up in a towel as I hungrily wolfed down the pizza and washed it down with a can of diet soda I found somewhere in the refrigerator.

With my hunger assuaged, I combed out the knots in my hair and while it air-dried, I sat at the dining table with all the bits and pieces of paper and checks I'd collected throughout the day. I began to add up all the checks and made a list of all the promissory notes we'd received. A quick calculation showed that with our cut of the vendors sales we would achieve about seventy-five percent of our target.

That still left twenty-five percent to be funded. Though it

sounded like a small percentage, I had to remember that getting to the seventy-fifth percent in the first place was as a result of hundreds of donations, countless emails and phone calls, and much begging and pleading. And quite frankly, we were all begged out. I felt as if we could go no further and were all tapped out with raising funds. I did not believe I could ask anything else of the committee of me either.

I went back through the figures again, and realized that if I removed the promises made, our gap widened closer to a forty percent shortfall. That was alarming. What if these promises were not fulfilled? We were hoping to start renovation works in the summer.

My thoughts turned to Max. Could I trust him to honor his pledge of picking up the shortfall? Where could he have gotten so much money in the short space of time he had been free? Was there any truth in what Robert had said about being sure of where Max's money was coming from before taking it?

I fished his card out of my purse and stared at the simple bold lettering.

I turned the card over in my hand. BB Tech. Wondering what BB stood for, I walked over to my laptop on the kitchen counter and booted it up. A quick internet search showed a company which was barely four years old, but was already making waves in the technology industry.

From all indications, they were doing good business, but my jaw dropped when I dived deeper and found out that the company had netted no less than eight figures in the last two years alone. Max had become a wealthy man even behind bars. Come to think of it, he had not been lacking in funds when he had been arrested either.

Not for the first time, I wondered why he would need to

embezzle. But then I remembered the blackmail bit. Which made me remember the photos. And the memory made me cringe. I was the clueless idiot in that scenario, but as I looked at the company's site now, my gut instinct told me that any money from Max would be above-board. Perhaps he had turned over a new leaf, at least financially.

It would seem I could trust his money, but I would never dare trust his heart again.

I would get the final figures from contractors and suppliers for the total cost of the renovation and find out exactly how much the shortfall was. Then I would approach Max armed with figures and keep my fingers crossed as he wrote the check. Once it cleared, I would be finally done with the likes of Max Blackstone.

7

MAX

https://www.youtube.com/watch?v=aGCdLKXNF3w
-there's a room where the light won't find you-

I sat in my car for a few minutes after leaving the fairground.

It took every ounce of willpower not to go back and rip Robert's arms off for daring to touch Savannah. The very thought of what I wanted to do made me angry as I felt conflicted between remembering that Savannah and I were no longer together. She had abandoned me. And slam her against a wall and fuck the living hell out of her.

"That's what happens when you start thinking with your dick, you fucking dick."

My jaw clenched as I saw Robert walking through the parking lot. Again, I found myself having to restrain myself from getting out of the car and taking my anger out with my fists. Violence was not my nature, but four years behind bars messes up even the most peaceful of people. I had to use my fists a couple of times until I found my feet and fixed a very complex software issue for the penitentiary.

It was all special perks and privileges thereafter.

I took a deep breath and watched Robert head in the opposite direction. He disappeared behind some cars and I was relieved I had not allowed my anger to get the better of me. I much preferred the current revenge route I was on anyway. Punches and a black eye would fade, but running his business into the ground would be forever.

I started the engine and pulled out of the parking lot. I felt too on edge to end the day and head home. I turned in the direction of downtown and before I knew it, I was pulling into a parking garage and heading down the side-walk towards *Chewsdays*. As expected, the bar and grill was still scantily populated. A few hours later and I would have been lucky to find a wall to lean on while I sipped a drink.

I slid onto a stool near the end of the bar with a good view of the room.

The bartender made his way to me. "What will it be?"

I put my credit card on the bar counter and pushed it towards him. "Two double whiskeys, no ice."

He gave me a look before moving off to make my drink. I guess not many people ordered two stiff drinks in one go at this time of the evening. The way I felt right now, two of those were going to do nothing to get me out of my current mood. I'd have to crawl out of here on my hands and knees before I could get the sight of his filthy hands on her out of my system. The drinks arrived and I downed both and ordered another two. This time the barman's eyebrows shot upwards.

I stared into the depths of the amber liquid, my head was alive with the past.

I remember feeling as if a horse had kicked me in the

stomach when I first saw her. Robert and I were at a bar to celebrate our newest account and the night was going well. Then I went to the toilet and by the time I came back Robert had managed to buy a girl in a red dress a drink. He was leaning close to her and whispering something in her ear. All I could see as I made my way to them was that she had long thick hair that fell in waves all the way down to her great ass. When Robert caught my eye, I winked at him, and mouthed, "great catch." But then I drew alongside her and she turned those incredible hazel eyes on me and I froze. I actually froze. I couldn't move. My heart felt as if it had stopped beating. My jaw went slack.

Robert was staring at me strangely, and I knew I was making a fool of myself, but I couldn't stop staring. I think it was lust at first sight because I wanted her like I'd never wanted anybody else ever. I could feel the desire for her vibrating in my guts. I was like a caveman who was claiming his mate. I swear, the way I felt, I would have killed any man that stood in my way that night.

"Have I got spinach on my teeth or something?" she asked self-consciously.

I shook my head and felt Robert give a hearty thump on my back. "This here is Maximus, but everybody calls him Max. He works for me. Does all the complicated software stuff only real nerds understand."

I understood what he had done. That was the classic needle in a banana. The insult inside the compliment. He had made himself the Alpha and me the beta. I hated him for it, I understood. She was a prize he didn't want to lose to me.

She smiled brightly and extended her hand. "Well, Max. It's a pleasure to meet you."

Finally, I found my tongue. "The pleasure is all mine." I

reached out and enclosed her hand in mine. Electricity flowed through our skin. She must have felt it too, because her beautiful eyes widened.

For the rest of the evening, I had to catch myself several times because I was staring so hard at her. Admittedly, there were a few times when I caught her staring back. I could tell Robert was irritated and wanted me to make myself scarce, but there was no power on earth that could have made me drag myself away from that delightful creature. As the night began to wind down, she looked directly at me and said she needed a software upgrade for her laptop.

Robert fumed, but I snapped up the dangled bait.

The following morning, being a weekend, I showed up on her doorstep. The problem with her device was something I solved in less than five minutes. After that there was nothing left to do, but invite her out to lunch. The rest, as they say, is history.

Robert gave me the cold shoulder for a couple days before getting over it, and we went back to business as usual, or at least, I thought we did.

As for Savannah and I, we moved on to the next level. I had been in awe to know I was her first. For the first time in my life sex was sacred. I held her as if she was a delicate piece of china, and made sure she suffered as little pain as possible. I knew exactly how to please her and taught her how to please me. We were perfect for each other. If I had not been framed, I had no doubt we would be married with at least one child already. Maybe child number two or even three would already be on the way.

Considering how much she loved a big brood of kids, I found it surprising she was not married and fretting over a few already. Maybe Robert had changed her mind. He was not the paternal type. Or maybe she had only pretended to want what I did.

No. She was a woman who was driven by her passions and knew exactly what she wanted. There was no way Robert would have been able to impose his childless, fancy-free mentality on her.

I ordered another drink and let my mind drift back to that summer. It seemed like a blissful dream now. Then I had decided to venture out on my own and started working harder, twice as hard actually. I still had to keep my end of the bargain to Robert and could only develop material for my own business afterwards. I knew Savannah was unhappy with the state of things, but I kept most of my plans to myself as I wanted it to be a surprise.

Lo and behold, the surprise was on me when Robert managed to concoct the whole embezzlement scam. My lawyer told me that all the evidence Robert's side had was circumstantial, but at that point I also found out that the gentleman's agreement contract with Robert trapped me intellectually to his company for a lifetime. If Savannah had been there for me, intellectual property be damned, I knew I would have fought harder to stay out of prison. But she wasn't and I knew I had to break his hold over me. Through my lawyer I made an offer to Robert. I would plead guilty if he would release me from our contract.

His answer came back lightning fast. Yes. My lawyer drew up the papers and we both signed it. Even though I was going to prison, I had actually bought back my freedom.

I ordered a burger and fries to go with it.

The first week of my incarceration was not the night-mare I thought it would be. Well, maybe the nights were. I kept waiting to wake up in Savannah's arms. For her to tell me I was just dreaming, but I was now back in the land of the living. But morning brought the same hard mattress, the metal toilet, and the stained gray walls.

Still, the day was preferable to the night. There was a pecking order in prison and I quickly learned my place. I was not there to remain indefinitely like some other inmates, and therefore did not need to prove anything or attain any ranks. What I did need to do, though, was not become a target or punching bag for others.

As soon as I gave out my fair share of black eyes and busted lips, they learned the computer guy could pound more than just laptop keys. They stayed out of my way and I stayed out of theirs.

While my lawyer worked on the dissolution of my partnership with Robert, I had the unexpected fortune of gaining favor with the prison administrator. Not only by retrieving some lost crypto due to a hack of his system, but making him some substantial crypto gains in the process. To do this, I needed my laptop from home. The special privilege was granted and afterwards I'd been allowed to keep it.

It had been a game changer.

Working with Rick, I quickly got BB Tech up and running Within the first year, the company was already turning a healthy profit. Old clients of Robert's found me and word spread that the brain behind his company was back on the scene. My reputation preceded me and soon other potential clients found their way to me. No one seemed to give a shit that our meetings were being held from a laptop in a prison library.

BB Tech became a great success.

The burger and fries felt solid in my stomach as I paid for my meal and drinks. I wisely ordered a cup of black coffee to go. I was neither drunk nor tipsy, but liquor in my system before getting behind a wheel was asking for trouble.

Hopefully the caffeine would counteract the creeping effects of the alcohol long enough for me to make the short drive home.

I sat in my car and sipped half of the hot brew before I started the engine and pulled out of the parking garage. Night had fallen and with it had come a slight chill. The air smelled as though there was a storm brewing and I felt my spirits lift somewhat. There was something about rainy nights that just invigorated me.

At the thought of night rain, a memory surfaced unbidden.

That night I booked a cabin in the hills for the weekend: but it never stopped raining and we had to stay indoors the whole time. On our second night there, a storm came through. We stood at the window of the cabin looking out at the sheets of driving rain and the streaks of fierce lightning. I still remember the citrusy smell of her shampoo. My arms had been around her, pretty much the same way Robert's had been today.

Maybe that was why it had irritated me so much.

She had taken my hand and slipped it down her body. I found her pussy hot and wet. A few strokes of my fingers brought her swollen clit out of hiding. My cock started to pulse in anticipation of what was to come. My jeans melted to the ground and soon we were skin to skin. Suddenly her naked body darted away from me. She grabbed a blanket from the couch. The next thing I knew, she wrapped it around her shoulders and flung me a teasing smile.

Then she threw the door open and danced out into the crazy storm.

I watched with my mouth open as she threw open the blanket on the lawn and laid down on her back, her legs spread wide. The rain pounded on her naked body, bounced off her pink pussy lips. I stood frozen, mesmerized, but the second her fingers reached down to her pussy, I shuddered and came alive. I needed no further invitation to join her. We made love in the pouring rain. I drove into her over and over again. The intensity of the storm was no match for the intensity of our passion as we cried out in ecstasy. It was not until she started to tremble from the cold that I scooped her up in my arms and carried her inside.

My cock was tight with need as I pulled into my parking space.

I switched off the engine and sprinted up to my apartment. I stripped immediately and stepped into the shower. This was one of the things I had taken for granted in my life, but showering with ten other men has a way of making you appreciate privacy.

I grasped my hard dick and began to jerk off.

In my mind Savannah was sucking me. She didn't want to, of course, but she had to. She had no choice, because now, I had the upper hand. She was my bitch. I could do anything with her. Fuck her anyway I wanted. First, that swollen mouth. I was going to fuck it hard and fill it with my cum. She always loved the taste of my cum. She was going to swallow a whole load of it.

I came in a rush. The hot water washed away my release. I leaned against the tiles, panting. Fuck her. Fuck her. What had caused her to turn on me the way she had, and with Robert of all people? I had dismissed the notion that she had been a part of the conspiracy to frame me. On that point, I believed Robert had acted alone. But why Robert? There were so many other guys she could have chosen to be with.

There was no doubt she was going to have to pay for abandoning me when I needed her most, though. And I knew just how to dangle her like a puppet on a string. I had something she needed. I knew her well enough to know that if it was a personal need, I would not have a bargaining chip. But anything to do with her kids was a different matter altogether. She needed money for the computer lab, and I was going to see to it that I made her work for every goddamn last penny.

I slung a towel around my hips while my laptop booted up. I smiled with satisfaction at the prospect of what I would do to make Savannah grovel.

SAVANNAH

"I legit thought we were going to have to send for the fire brigade! Like seriously, he looked as if smoke was going to come out of his ears any moment." Stacey scarfed down a sandwich after the Monday debriefing committee session was over and there was only Monica, Stacey and me left in the room.

"Were they fighting over you?" Monica asked wide-eyed, as she reached for a soda.

"Don't be so silly," I muttered. "They are enemies from a long time ago."

"I don't know about you, but I think he's still carrying a torch for you. I saw it in his eyes."

I shrugged as I reached for another sandwich. "That torch is called hostility. He was incredibly angry with me. He thought I should have stood by him."

Stacey opened her mouth and I raised a hand. "Look, I really don't want to talk about Max right now."

"Got it." Stacey grinned. "You have to admit that it was a great day, though. I see this fair as just the beginning of bigger and better projects we can take on for the school. I mean, this time around we're renovating the computer lab. Next year we can take on something else and so on for the years to come."

"Speaking of alum, Savannah, how did we do with the profits and pledges? Did we reach our target?"

I sighed. I hated to be the bearer of bad news. After Saturday night, I had spent a good portion of Sunday calling the pledges I'd been given. Sad to say, many of them were not donating as much as I had anticipated. "We are twenty-seven percent away from our target."

"What about Max's promise?"

I looked at Stacey sharply. I'd told her what Max had pledged, but I was hoping that we could work with what we had and do a partial renovation and raise the rest of the funds another time to finish the project. I did not relish the idea of taking Max up on his offer.

"What promise?" Monica raised her eyebrows curiously.

I felt as though I could throttle Stacey, but I was being childish. Of course, my feelings must take second place. "Max offered to pick up whatever shortfall we have."

Monica's eyes became as round as saucers with excitement. "Whoa! That's amazing. So, what're we waiting for? We just need to tell him how much to make his check for? Right?"

I hesitated and she repeated herself. "Right?"

"I... um. I don't think we should get all our hopes up just yet. Suppose his offer was not genuine? The shortfall is close to a hundred thousand dollars, you know."

"A hundred thousand?" Monica scoffed. "If we're talking about Max Blackstone, the software genius, believe me, he won't feel that."

"True. But—"

"There's no 'but', Savannah. He offered. We need it."

I turned to look at Stacey. Her eyes were focused on me and it gutted me to see the hope shining in them. I took a deep breath.

"Fine, but we'll need Arthur to do the official figures and give us a detailed breakdown of what the renovation will cost in terms of equipment, material and labor, and how much of it we already have. I don't want to approach him with incomplete figures. This way he will see that we are legitimate and we are not asking for more than we need."

"How soon can Arthur do that report?" Monica shot back.

"As soon as I give him our final figures. Some pledges have asked for a few days to honor their commitment. So, hopefully the latest should be by Friday and I will have the final figures for Arthur. I should be able to approach Max by next week. If he's good for his word, I project we will have a brand-new lab ready for the new school year." I smiled tremulously at the thought of the feat we had undertaken coming to fruition.

Monica stood and opened her arms to both of us. There were tears in her eyes. "We did it. We really and truly did it!"

It was as though the reality finally hit us and we all hugged tightly in a group hug. Then Monica had to run and Stacey and I were left alone.

"That was a sneaky move, you know," I said quietly.

She shrugged "I love you, Sav, but whatever you and Max have going on has no place in our renovation objective."

"Max and I have nothing going on," I huffed.

"Of course not. Let me correct myself. Whatever you and Max will have going on—"

"You're still using the wrong tense, Stacey," I rolled my

eyes at her cheeky grin. "There is nothing going on between Max and me, nor will there be."

She gave me a funny look. "We'll see what time has to say about that, won't we."

I narrowed my eyes on her. "Do you know something I don't?"

"I know something is not right. I don't believe he stole that money."

"Er... news flash. He pleaded guilty."

"Sometimes people make deals for a lesser sentence, you know?"

I shook my head with exasperation. I couldn't discuss this with Stacey. She was just too naïve. "Look. I know you mean well and think the best of everyone, but in this case you're wrong, okay?"

"No, you're wrong," she shot back passionately. "You should be Mrs. Blackstone with a couple of little Blackstone's running around. I don't take you to walk away from a man in trouble or to be the snobbish type to hold a guy's prison record over his head. I saw how you looked at him. Hell, you were vibrating with need."

"Stop being so dramatic. I wasn't 'vibrating with need'."

"Well, whatever it was, fix it and get the hell on with being happy and in love again. I could eat some wedding cake."

"So, go get married then."

"No thanks. I'm far too picky. I'll wait for yours."

I crossed my arms over my chest. "You don't stop, do you?"

"Nope. And I'm usually right on the money too. You and Max were made for each other. You'll get back together. You'll see."

"You finally got the tense right – were. There is no more Max and me. All I want is to get the check, and call it a day."

My tone brooked no further conversation on the matter and though she made a face, she said nothing else. We finished cleaning up in a matter of minutes.

THE REST of the week was taken up between classes and working on the final report to present to Max. I half-hoped that he would be one of the cop-out pledges who called to say he could not honor his word after all. It would give me some more ammunition to fuel my anger at him as well as make it clear that he was no good. I had nothing to regret. But all week, no call nor email came from him. I turned the figures over to Arthur on Friday afternoon and he promised to have the official report ready by Monday.

I spent the weekend grading final assignments as we were heading into two weeks of end of year tests. I started working on my report cards as well.

We had another committee meeting on Monday for me to present the final report. As I had predicted, the shortfall came to approximately ninety-seven thousand dollars and some change. Everything was neatly put together and accompanied by the necessary pro forma invoices and other related documents. I promised, with a pounding heart, to call Max the next day.

Tuesday afternoon after the last student left, I sat staring at the business card on my desk. The letters swam before my eyes as raw panic took hold of me. I felt like a giddy school-girl about to talk to her crush. No. Wrong analogy. I felt like a prisoner about to have an interview with her jailor about the possibility of early parole. I tapped the card a few times before picking up the phone and dialing. It started to ring.

"Hello?"

"Max Blackstone?" I kicked myself mentally. It was his personal number and there was no need to ask if it was him. Stupid!

"Speaking."

I could hear the amusement in his voice. I cleared my throat and rushed on. "This is Savannah Maitland from Dunrobin Middle School."

"I know it's you, Savannah. To what do I owe this call?"

"I would like to discuss the donation you promised for the lab."

"What about it?"

"I did as you asked and have a figure for the shortfall."

"Okay. You can come by my office so we can discuss it further."

I almost swallowed my tongue. "I beg your pardon?"

"I said, come by my office so we can discuss the matter further."

"But, why? You said you would fill the gap. I don't think there's anything further to be discussed that we can't do over the phone."

"But I would prefer to discuss it face to face."

"So that's it then. This is your way of backing out on your promise. Typical. You build up our hopes and when the time comes to back your word you come up with excuses." I knew I sounded irrational, but the anxiety I was experiencing just thinking about having to interact with Max again was flooding through my veins.

"I'm not making excuses," he said, his voice deliberately patient, "nor am I being unreasonable to prefer to discuss financial matters in person. I don't see what the big deal is."

I continued to lash out. To be honest I was now almost hysterical and had no idea how to regain control of my emotions. "The big deal is how hard the committee has worked and how hard all our parents and children worked to make this a reality. And now you're being a scrooge!"

"I'm being a scrooge because I want a face-to-face meeting? Or maybe you're being selfish thinking of how you don't want to face me and just want a check in the mail. You're the one who's not thinking about all those parents and students."

I felt as though he had struck a nerve with how on point he was. "Go to hell, Max!" I swore, seething with anger.

"I've been there. I didn't really like it so I came back. I bet you didn't expect me ever to be free again, huh?"

"I don't give a damn what you do."

"Clearly you didn't and still don't. But then again, this isn't about us. This is simply about you getting off your high horse and out of your selfish desires to come to my office and discuss the terms of the donation."

"It's not a loan. What terms could there be to discuss?"

"I'm sure it's not a few pennies we're talking about. There will be documents you need to show me."

"I can email them."

"And they will need to be examined and discussed on the spot."

"The accountant can do that. I can give you his number and you can both arrange a meeting at a mutually convenient time." I knew I was grabbing for straws desperately, but I couldn't help it.

"Stop being so cowardly, Savannah. It doesn't become you. Now are we meeting at my office or will you find another source of funding? I don't have all day."

I took a few deep breaths as I struggled to calm myself. I

felt as though I was caught between a rock and a hard place. But I felt myself relenting when I thought about going back to the committee with a negative report. How could I explain to them that the donation fell through because I did not want to face my ex-boyfriend?

I took a deep breath, feeling as though I was about to walk the plank, step up to the gallows, face the firing squad, and every other life and death scenario that there could be. I swallowed hard.

"When?"

"Are you free now?"

"Now?" I squawked.

"I'm sure school is over for the day. I'm still at the office if you come by right now."

At first I was going to negotiate to see him tomorrow, but I realized the quicker I got over this meeting the less anxiety I would have to put myself through by waiting another twenty-four hours. The thought comforted me. "I'll come now," I mumbled.

"Good. The address is on the card. I'll see you in a few."

Without another word, he disconnected the call.

I stared at my phone. Bastard. I allowed myself the luxury of sitting and taking deep relaxing breaths for a full five minutes. Then I got up, packed up my belongings and left. I headed to the parking lot and was soon on my way downtown. It was just before peak hours so traffic was still light enough for me to get there in twenty minutes. I groaned when I realized that this evening I would be going with the rush hour traffic. I saw myself sitting in the parking lot marking papers while waiting for traffic to ease. There no way I was going to be sitting in bumper-to-bumper traffic for two plus hours. All these inconsequential thoughts passed my brain when what I was really afraid of was seeing him again in an enclosed space.

Would I be able to control those old feelings?

I parked in the visitor's section in the parking garage, surprised to find that the security guard was expecting me. I followed his directions and quickly found the lobby. As I watched the elevator climb to the twenty-second floor, my heart began to race.

Get in, collect the check, get out.

That was all I needed to do.

Get in, collect the check, get out.

And then never see Max Blackstone again.

I kept my fingers crossed, praying that it would be that easy, but somehow I could not shake the dreadful feeling in the pit of my stomach that I was about to face the challenge of a lifetime.

9

MAX

https://www.youtube.com/watch?v=6vwNcNOTVzY
-Gold Digger-

core one for me. I could barely conceal the feeling of triumph that raced through my body as Savannah disconnected the call. As I had hoped they had fallen short, and substantially too, for I knew if she had another choice or could have done it differently, she would not have called me. All last week I had waited, knowing it must not be me who reached out to ask whether she needed the donation. She had to call me first. And it had come to transpire that they did not need my money then I would have found another way to deal with Savannah. One way or another she was going to be beholden to me.

I pressed the intercom and it crackled to life.

"Yes, Max?"

"I have a Savannah Maitland coming by the office in a

few minutes, Sheila. Could you please clear her with security?"

"Sure thing, Max."

Impulsively I added, "could you also have Derila deliver some refreshments?"

"Anything in particular?"

"Iced coffee, heavy on the cream in one of them." Impulsively, I added, "And one of their donut assortments."

"Got it."

"While you're at it, get me a couple of bottles of water too."

"Your fridge is stacked, Max."

"Is it?"

"You've never checked or you would see that it is."

I could hear the amusement in my secretary's voice. I got up to check the mini fridge in the corner of the office and was surprised to see that she was right. I laughed.

"What kind of robot are you?"

"The kind that knows what you need before you need it. It's my job to make you happy."

"Thank you, Sheila."

"No problem, Max."

I ended the connection and turned around to look out at the skyline. Sheila's cues of being interested in a much more meaningful relationship than that of boss and secretary were becoming more obvious. She was a genuinely nice, curvy woman with long, thick hair, blue eyes, and well-toned legs that were almost always on display in the short skirts and dresses she wore. Apart from the color of her eyes and mouth, she was Savannah to a T.

Even putting my own personal office romance taboo issue aside and the simple fact that I would only be losing a very efficient secretary eventually, to date Sheila would make me feel like I was trying to replace Savannah by finding a near duplicate. But the thing that bothered me most was the weird, but unshakeable feeling that I would somehow be cheating on Savannah. It shouldn't be an issue as not only were we no longer an item, but we both hated each other.

Still, the strong feeling remained.

I glanced at my watch. While Savannah and I were dating, I'd never invited her to my office. I think it was some perverted sense of loyalty to Robert. Didn't want to rub it in his face. So this would be the first time she was going to see me in my work space. I shook off the feeling of anticipation and reminded myself that her visit was business, not pleasure, and the whole purpose was to exact my revenge.

I got busy rearranging the papers on my desk. I had to remind myself this meeting was strictly business. I was not waiting for my lover. I was waiting for the bitch who so ruthlessly betrayed me.

Even after all the pep talk, I almost jumped out of my skin at the knock on the door.

"It's only me," Sheila said, as she walked in wheeling a cart filled with the stuff I had requested. She looked at me as though she could see my thoughts and found it amusing.

"Thanks, Sheila."

"No problem. Should I send Miss Maitland straight in when she arrives, or do you want to keep her... waiting for a bit?" she raised one perfectly arched eyebrow.

I frowned. Was I really that transparent? "No, you can send her straight in. Just buzz me on the intercom first."

She smiled. "Sure."

Sheila swung her ass as she turned to leave. I watched her figure retreating and felt nothing. Not even a twitch of interest. Then I got up, went to the cart, and lifted the lid on the tray. The donuts smelled warm and looked soft. I wondered why I got them? I wanted to punish Savannah, not treat her to her favorite sweet. I picked up the platter, walked to the bin, and watched the donuts tumble into it. It was a strangely satisfying feeling.

Maybe, I was getting over her after all.

I went back to my seat and pulled out a notepad and jotted down my thoughts for a new project I was about to embark on. When the intercom crackled to life, I pressed the button.

"Yes, Sheila?"

"Miss Maitland is here to see you."

"Good. Show her in." I leaned back in my chair and waited for the door to open. First Sheila, then the woman behind her came into the room.

To see them standing side by side made the physical resemblance even more striking. But sexy Sheila with her tight blouse stretched across her bosom with hints of her full cleavage, coupled with her long legs, was no match for the sensible button-down shirt that Savannah wore which hung loosely and only hinted at the ample breasts I knew were there. Her slacks were loose and only cinched in at the waist with her belt to give any indication of her shape.

Sheila's hair flowed from a high ponytail atop her head while Savannah's was in a bun at her nape. Sheila wore a full face of make-up while Savannah looked like she had barely swiped some lip gloss onto her lips.

But still, it was the woman on the left who made my cock jump to life and thicken, and my body ache. Damn you, Savannah. Four years of longing welled up inside me in an instant, and I wished for nothing more than to wipe away the last four years and pick up where we had left off with our relationship.

I tore my eyes away from Savannah and looked at Sheila, who had been watching me as I stared at Savannah. I detected a slight hardness to her mouth and tone.

"Thank you, Sheila. That will be all."

She nodded and gave Savannah one more look before she left the office. As the door closed behind her I turned my attention to Savannah once more. I stretched out a hand, indicating one of the empty chairs in front of my desk.

Without a word she sat.

I regarded her for a few moments before standing and walking over to the cart. I took up the iced coffees and handed her one. She looked up at me and I felt as though I was being sucked into the depths of those hypnotizing hazel eyes. My mind went back to the many times I had stared into those eyes and dreamed of the future...

Her face was deliberately expressionless and she was careful not to let our skin touch, but her eyes widened as she took a sip of the coffee. I could see it in her eyes that she was caught off-guard by the fact that I remembered how she liked it.

Part of me wished I had not binned the donuts and the other part of me sneered at my own weakness and desire to please her.

"I haven't had iced coffee in a while. Thank you." She smiled at me softly.

I could feel myself falling all over again for her and that irritated me. I inclined my head politely. "You have some documents for me to look over?"

It was like a shutter came over her face and she dropped her eyes. "Yes. Yes, I do."

She reached into her bag and withdrew a folder which she slid across the desk. I took the folder and opened it. As I perused it for a few minutes, I could feel her eyes on me. My face remained blank throughout. I had to give it to her though: the records were impeccably done. If this were a pitch for a loan, she would have gotten it with very little trouble. But I had to remind myself that this was not supposed to be made easy for her.

"As you can see, we've gone to great pains to secure the most reasonable costs for material, labor and equipment."

I fixed my gaze on her and she shifted uncomfortably in her chair. "You mean cheap."

She frowned. "Affordable."

"Why not just get things done properly so that they will last longer. This is a serious investment."

Her frown deepened. "Investment? It's a donation. An investment makes it seem as though you will have some returns to get."

"I would like to ensure that my money does not go to waste and then you're back at square one in a couple years putting on fairs to renovate the computer lab once more. So, I think it would be wise to make sure the effects of this... investment is long-term." I raised an eyebrow. "Second-hand computers?"

Her shoulders squared defensively. "We don't have the money to buy new, apart from the ones that have been donated. All they require is a software upgrade."

"They require much more than that and I'm perfectly happy to pay for extra costs."

She blinked with surprise, then a look of fear or was it caution came over her face. My little Savannah knew things were getting too good to be true.

"Look," she began, "I didn't come here for you to undo months of legwork and elimination in sifting through the options. Nor do we wish for you to undo the various contracts and agreements that we have made with those who will be doing the work and providing the equipment. All I need is a check for the balance, please."

"And you think I'm just going to write a check for a hundred thousand dollars, almost a third of your budget, and not have a say in how it is spent? Think again, Savannah. I think you're more intelligent than that."

"Why the fuck did you make a pledge you have no intention of honoring, Max?"

That struck a nerve and I clenched my jaw. My word was something I had never reneged on in my life and I was not about to start now. But neither was I going to allow Savannah to know that she had the upper hand in any way. I knew I could write her a check for five times the balance if I chose. But this little game of make Savannah squirm was not going quite the way I planned.

"Why raise the hopes of the children only to have it dashed because of whatever imaginary ax you think you have to grind with me?" she continued glaring at me.

I was sure I saw tears glittering. Instantly I felt gutted, a sour taste filling my mouth. I had wanted her to grovel, but seeing her hurt face didn't feel good at all. It actually turned my stomach. An old image flashed into my head. She was crying because she had seen a dog killed on the side of the road. I had held her tightly. My jaw tightened. This was not turning out the way I thought it would. I turned away from her and pretended to look at the skyline.

"Maybe you don't have the money. Maybe... you were just playing with us," she yelled, her voice cracking with emotion.

I turned back and saw her hands clenched into tight little fists. She had small hands, my Savannah. She needed both to circle my cock. Ah, hell. Suddenly, it occurred to me that there was nothing more I wanted than to take her into my arms and kiss that delicious mouth. I forced myself to remember that mouth didn't come to court to see me. Didn't call. Didn't care. That was a lying mouth. Yet, here I was, lusting for it to be wrapped around my cock.

The crazy effect she had on me infuriated me and made my voice cold and harsh. "Tell you what, Savannah. I'll write that balance off and more with one swipe of my pen, and you can have it all right now, with no future interference from me ever... with only one condition."

Her eyes narrowed. "Condition?"

"Have sex with me."

The moment the words left my mouth her face went white, a knife turned in my gut, but I did not stop, my voice was sarcastic and mocking.

"I'm not into fucking men in the ass and I didn't have the privacy to jack off when the need arose so four years was a long, long time for me to go without. You're altruistic, always helping the next person. Help me. Have sex with me to remind me what a good, wet pussy feels like. If memory serves, that tight pussy of yours never could get enough of my dick. Maybe after you've broken me in I can go out and taste all the other pussies of this world. Four fucking years-worth of them."

She gasped then, but I was relentless. I needed to get my pound of flesh. "And if you're as good as I remember, I'll even add a little extra if you want. We'll call it even then."

She sat deathly silent, staring at me in disbelief.

I tilted my head and looked at her through half-closed lids, watching the strong emotions chasing across her face as her eyes flashed angrily and her throat worked convulsively. Then, she licked her dry lips and I felt my cock thicken. In my head those glossy lips were already wrapped around my length, as she sucked me just the way I'd taught her.

She took a deep breath, making her chest heave. "Go to hell. Actually, why don't you take your filthy money and give it to the slut you were with on my birthday when you left me waiting in that restaurant? I'm sure she can remind you what it feels like to be with a woman enough for you to go out and get four years-worth of pussy. Or maybe just start with the legs and chest you have sitting in your office out there. I'm pretty sure she would oblige."

I scowled. "What the fuck are you talking about? You did it at the fair as well. You keep going on and on about me cheating on you and I never did. Or does it just irk you that I finally saw through your charade and your gold-digger colors showed."

She gasped in shock. "Gold digger? Are you calling *me* a gold-digger?"

"The truth hurts, does it? When I got involved with you, people warned me you were too young."

"We're only two years apart," she bit out furiously.

"Yes, but I was already a millionaire and you barely knew what four figures looked like, much less seven." As I spoke, I remembered it was Robert who first cracked the joke about her being a gold digger. I'd not believed him then. I'd even taken offense and told him off, but what was one to believe when she left me to rot and picked up with the next shiny thing. Robert himself.

Robert and her deserved each other. Raw bile rose into my throat at the thought of them together.

Fuck him.

And her.

My voice was downright evil now. Even I could hear the degradation and sin in it. "We can do dinner first if you like, then go back to yours or mine, I don't mind which. We'll spend one night together where I get to fuck you as many times as I want in any orifice I want. You will not say no to anything I ask. Once I've had enough of your body, I'll write you a check for the amount you want. After that we'll part ways... forever."

Every word felt bitter, but I had to see the charade through.

What was truly shocking was the suffocating feeling in my chest. I didn't want her to accept. I was hoping and praying she would say no! If she said yes, it would confirm once and for all she was indeed what I'd accused her of being: a gold digger, and it mattered greatly to me that she prove me wrong.

This was my last hope in this cruel, dangerous world.

I wanted to be wrong. God, how I wanted to be wrong.

I leaned forward and steepled my fingers underneath my chin. "Well?"

10

SAVANNAH

https://www.youtube.com/watch?v=k4A5XuMz_Tw
-Killing Me Softly-

I stared at Max in disbelief. What kind of monster was I dealing with? His words cut me to the core. How could he sink so low as to think I would trade my body for his money? Our eyes clashed. I held his gaze as I reached for my bag and stood.

He watched me expressionlessly.

I reached across his desk and retrieved the file I had brought. I rammed it into my bag, zipped it, and shouldered it before looking at him. He was watching me through lidded eyes. I took a deep breath to calm myself. I would not sink to his level and engage in a shouting match or filth slinging. I spoke softly and carefully.

"I have never, in my life, taken anything that was not rightfully mine, nor have I ever used feminine wiles to get what I want so I don't intend to start now. That is not how I was raised. You of all people should know that, or have you forgotten? Or maybe you think I went to one of those fancy plastic surgeons who repaired my hymen when I started dating you and I was just spreading my legs for anyone who came my way. You were my first. All my life, I have worked hard for everything I have. I have never accepted charity for myself. I have always thought of others and their needs. But as much as we need this lab and the equipment, I am not going to allow you to belittle and shame me in order to get it. On our own we raised over two hundred thousand dollars. Many people didn't even believe we would even get twenty thousand. But we did."

I paused to take a breath, I couldn't stop my chest from heaving with the painful emotions running through my veins like poison.

He looked at me coldly. "Well, since you're so good at raising money, I suggest you raise the shortfall if you don't want to accept my offer."

"I don't understand why you're doing this, Max. We never asked you for this. *You* offered. And now you're behaving as if we, or better yet, I, owe you something."

"You sought me out and emailed me."

"You could have just attended without spending a cent. As a matter of fact, if it bothers you that much to deal with me, you could have even ignored the email and pretended you didn't see it. I didn't ask you for anything. You chose to attend. You chose to seek me out, or have you forgotten how you pretty much stalked me all afternoon? You chose to open your mouth and make a huge speech about picking up the slack. Or was that for Robert's benefit to make him see how you throw your money around? Was it for bragging rights? And now that it's time to pay up, you want to back out of your commitment? What about your reputation?

What do you think people will say when they hear the great Max Blackstone stiffed a couple of middle schoolers out of a computer lab?"

He threw his head back and laughed. "My reputation is the least of my worries. I'm an ex-con."

"Oh stuff it, Max. You make it sound like you were locked away for forty years or something."

He leaned across his desk. "Four hours, four days, four weeks, four months, four years, four decades, four centuries, I don't give a fuck. I was locked away for a crime I did not commit. So I'm sorry... not sorry... if it offends your delicate sensibilities that I have no qualms about not defending the reputation I couldn't care less I have right now."

Our eyes met and held. I could see the rage boiling inside him. I stared at him, furious at the stand he had taken. I felt my heart plummet and bitter tears burn the backs of my eyes at the prospect of walking out of here without the check, but I refused to allow them to fall.

"So, you prefer to walk out of here empty-handed than take one for the team? That's a bit selfish, isn't it?"

"Selfish?" I looked at him incredulously. "I'm selfish when you're the one who's going back on your word?"

"One night in exchange for a computer lab for so many poor, under-privileged kids."

"How could you?" I gasped.

"Take it or leave it."

I took a step backward, then another. Then I turned and ran to the door, reaching blindly for the handle as the tears had started to fall.

"Savannah—"

Whatever else he had been about to say fell on deaf ears as I fled the office. I did not care who saw me as I ran. I took the stairs, afraid that if I waited for the elevator he would follow. After a few flights, I sat on a landing and allowed the sobs to wrack me for a few minutes. Thankfully, there was no one who felt the need to get their steps in and I had the staircase to myself. When I felt in control once more, I wiped my eyes and continued my journey downward. I changed my initial plan of sitting in the parking garage while traffic ran off. I preferred to sit in traffic bumper to bumper, burning precious gas than to be anywhere near Max at this point.

I drove into the traffic and kept the windows up to keep out exhaust fumes and provide me some amount of privacy as I processed what had just taken place. The tears came once more. The last time I had been this emotional was during that turbulent time when I found out Max was not only an embezzler he was also cheating on me.

My thoughts went back to that night of my twenty-first birthday as I had sat in the restaurant waiting for him, a small box in hand. That small box was still in the back of a drawer in my dresser on top of a picture. I had not thought about it since the night I had put it there when all hell had broken loose in my young life.

After Robert had shown me the pictures, I had naively still held out hope that Max would reach out and we would be able to talk. I was so young I actually believed there might be a different explanation. I had believed in him until the last possible moment. But when the news of his arrest had broken, I had no choice but to believe that if his embezzlement was true, so was the point of his cheating.

I had decided that I wanted to face him one last time and look him in the eye as I confronted him. But fate had other plans. The morning I planned to visit him while he awaited trial, I woke up in pain with cramps. In total panic I saw the blood on the sheets.

And immediately, I knew: I was losing my baby, just like I had lost its father, and there was not a damn thing I could do about it.

At the hospital, I was informed sudden stress levels could affect the fetus, especially in the first trimester and it often led to miscarriages. I remained hospitalized for two days and was told to continue with bed rest for another two weeks when I returned home as my blood pressure was high enough to cause a stroke. Someone my age should not have such an elevated blood pressure.

My mother saw to it that I obeyed the doctor's orders. As a result, Max's trial came and went, and he was behind bars before I was back on my feet.

The memories of my miscarried child came up before me, and for the first time since it happened, I allowed it to come rather than push it back. The tears which pricked my eyes, I gave free rein to the flow.

The stress, elevated blood pressure and eventual miscarriage had only one source: Max. I was fine when I went to the doctor to confirm the result of the pregnancy test kit. I was eight weeks pregnant and doing fine. How silly of me, but I had taken the little plastic strip, wrapped it up in a pink bow with blue dots, and placed it in a gift box. That's how excited I'd been to share my big news with Max. We'd often talked of wanting to be together forever and having a family so I was expecting a night of happiness and celebrations. I would have been better off taking the advice of my friends, who warned me I was too young. It was madness to settle down with the first man who came my way. I thought I knew better. I thought I'd found my soul mate and life partner all in one.

Yeah, after I lost my baby and Max it got bad. There was even a point when I wondered if I was losing my mind.

But time, the quintessential healer, did its job. After a season of unbearable sadness, each day became easier. I could actually wake up and go on with life. Slowly, painfully, I came to grips with the fact that I could not change what had happened. I could not change Max's infidelity or the fact that he was an embezzler. Nor could I bring back my baby. I could only move on alone and with the firm resolve never to put myself in such a position ever again.

I had not expected to have to deal with Max ever again in my life.

Still, perhaps this was for the best. I needed closure. Perhaps I still needed to see Max's expression when I told him he had been a father-to-be for a few short weeks. Then I thought about the scene which had just unfolded in his office, and my stomach...

The Max I had known was gone, replaced by a bitter, cynical stranger. The man I had known thought too much of my integrity to ever make the kind of suggestion he had. Then again, can a leopard ever change its spots? Perhaps the Max I thought I knew had never really existed? Perhaps the Max I walked away from an hour ago was the real Max all along?

Had I dodged a bullet four years ago when we were forced apart?

A new wave of anger washed over me as I remembered the callous thing he said to me before I fled from his office.

One night in exchange for a check. Take it or leave it.

The fucking nerve of him. As if I had some kind of obligation to grovel for his money. Actually, how dare he? Max and his disgusting proposition could go to hell for all I cared. The committee would understand I was not going to sink to those depths for a man who was clearly playing sick mind games.

I was shaking, but for the rest of the drive home I was determined not to give him one more ounce of my energy. Instead I concentrated my thoughts on how we could compensate for the lacking funds. I should take another look at the figures and see where we could trim things down a bit. Perhaps we could revert to the original plan. Scaling down and doing the project in phases. Miserably, I saw indefinite cake sales when school started in the fall. Perhaps we could try for an autumn event or something else on the same large scale as the fair.

I pulled into my apartment complex and still full of adrenaline and excess energy walked briskly to my apartment.

As soon as I got in through the front door, I kicked off my shoes and went straight into the kitchen. I grabbed the freezer meal I'd left thawing and stuck it into the oven, but I shoved it so hard it thumped the back of the oven and bounced forward.

Get a freaking grip of yourself, Savannah.

Taking a deep, calming breath, I positioned the tray in the middle of the grill and gently closed the glass door. There. I could do this.

An hour later, I settled down at my little kitchen island with a steaming casserole on one side and the project file on the other. There was no time like the present to attack the issue at hand. As I ate I worked out a new strategy. By the time the last forkful of food was gone I had formulated my new plan.

Just before bed, I sent a message to the committee stating that we needed to have an emergency meeting tomorrow afternoon. I did not give a reason. Then I went to bed and lay awake until dawn appeared in the sky. The whole time memories of the past washed over me and silent tears poured down the sides of my temples.

THE LOOK on all their faces as they walked through the staffroom door the next day told me they had already figured that the news I brought could only be bad.

How bad the situation was they did not know, though.

When I finished telling them, they stared at me in disbelief. I avoided Stacey's gaze. I knew she was not going to buy the bullshit story I had made up that Max's promise had been retracted because his accountant had advised against a donation of that amount, or any donation for that matter as he had only been released a few weeks before.

I had no idea why I felt the need to protect him, but in a way, I was protecting myself. There was no need for them to know the real reason we were not getting the money.

"So," I paused, linking my fingers together, "though we are not back at square one, we are now in a bit of a bind and we'll need to decide what gets priority now and what will have to wait for later." I looked around the room. There was silence as they looked at each other.

Before any of them, or specifically Lisa, could ask any awkward questions, I rushed in. "I was thinking we could reduce the number of laptops for each classroom. That would take quite a chunk out of that balance, wouldn't it?"

No one answered. They just stared at me with defeated, disappointed expressions.

I looked down at my file, hating Max with a vengeance. "Anyway, I did some quick math. If we make it a good cut, something like one third, that could cover almost half of the shortfall." I turned my gaze hopefully onto my colleagues. "Can you guys think of what else we can cut or delay?"

They must have understood I was feeling terrible, my swollen eyes would have been a dead giveaway, and they responded with all kinds of suggestions. In an hour, we trimmed the deficit down to less than five thousand. Once we wrapped up the meeting I went to my classroom to finish working on my end of year reports. I did not have to look up when there was a knock on the door to know that it was Stacey.

She walked in, took a seat in the front row, and folded her arms across her chest. "Now tell me what really went on, Savannah."

The desire to breakdown and cry on her shoulder was intense, but I tried to keep my voice steady. "It's too awful, Stacey. Just know that he made me an offer I had no choice but to refuse. I'm sorry I let you guys down."

"Max let us down, Savannah. Not you," she said gently.

I swallowed hard. The tears were threatening again, but I blinked hard to keep them at bay.

"You've gone above and beyond anything we could have asked and none of us can think of a better committee chair. You have not let us down at all. I'm so proud of you, and for what it's worth, I was wrong. I'm really disappointed in Max. I thought this would be his chance to redeem himself in your eyes and it would heal whatever wounds between the two of you. I truly believed he needed someone like you in his life, but, I guess, he blew it. It's his loss."

I looked into my friend's eyes and smiled. "Thank you."

"Anytime. Look, is there anything I can do?"

"No, I'll be alright. I just need a bit of time on my own."

"Okay. Just remember, we've got your back on this. And

we *will* have our lab." She stood and tapped the desk as she walked out. "Don't stay too late. You're a teacher not a slave."

"I won't," I smiled softly. The smile remained long after she had left. It was amazing what a few kind words and positive energy could do. Alone in my classroom I mused on Stacey's last words. We would have our lab indeed, and it would not be because of anything Max Blackstone had done.

11

MAX

I had to admit: I felt like a world class asshole after Savannah left. I fought the urge to chase after her. The last thing I needed was for her to think I was begging her for sex. The desire for revenge still beat in my chest but it felt like something alien inside me. I felt confused and conflicted. One meeting with her and she had reduced me to this mess of emotion. Of course, I wanted to make her pay for deserting me. For going with the man who had double-crossed me.

But the image of her face, shocked, hurt, and white as a sheet horrified me.

Part of me began making excuses for her. She had no obligation to remain with me. Just because I was head over heels in love with her didn't mean she had to be too. She didn't deserve to suffer for that.

I ran the fingers of both my hands through my hair.

What point would I feel satisfied that my revenge was complete, or if I would be stuck in a never ending cycle to get back at her? For Robert, it was easy. There was no conflict. It was clear cut. Wipe out his business without an ounce of regret. When he couldn't even afford the hairspray that kept his stupid hair together, I'd walk away satisfied.

But Savannah was a different matter altogether. Even the sight of her crying was hurting my soul. A voice in my head was already telling me to consider the earlier scene as enough of a punishment.

I avoided Sheila's eyes and grunted a dismissive reply when she asked if there was anything wrong with the donuts.

Once she was gone for the day, I worked until long into the night. Every now and again I had to fight the desire to pick up the phone and call Savannah. What could I have said anyway? I had not meant my offer? That would be a lie. I crave Savannah's body.

I've been craving it day and night whilst I was inside and since I've been out.

I told myself Savannah was feisty. She didn't give up easily. Once she started something she held on till the very end. I held on to that one slim thread of hope. The figures I had looked at were proof that the school desperately needed my money. After she had cooled down for a few days, she would be back.

I had played and the ball was now in her court.

THE REST of the week passed in silence. It was already Friday and there was still no word from Savannah.

I decided to give her the weekend. Monday. She would call at the start of the week.

But Monday evening found me staring at my silent phone. Seven days. It had been seven fucking days since she had come to the office. And she was still silent. What kind of game was she playing? Or was it that she had another source of funds? But if that had been the case, why would she have even bothered to come to my office? No. There was no other donor. She would be back.

By Tuesday afternoon I knew Savannah was playing her own game. She must have picked up how desperately I wanted to feel her body again. I knew I should wait it out, but I seemed not to be able to get my mind off her. She had changed in many ways in four years.

Savannah then had been a young woman, just barely out of her teens. There had still been an air of innocence about her and a wonder in her eyes for the world. She took my breath away every time I looked at her. I basked in the wonder that this woman loved me. My love for her had kept me chained to my desk for long hours as I worked twice as hard to branch out on my own and make all her dreams come true. I wanted to give her the big house and the big family she wanted. She thought I was a workaholic. Little did she know that I just wanted to surprise her with the news of my own company at the same time I proposed.

And I had been so close too!

The Savannah of today still bore hints of the woman who stole my heart the moment I laid eyes on her. Her raven hair still made my fingers itch to undo her strict, no-nonsense bun and run my fingers through the silky strands... like old times. Her easy smile lit up any space she stepped into, except that it was no longer mine to expect when they alighted on me. And her eyes! Those stunning eyes of hers will always pull me into their mysterious gold and green galaxy.

I stopped my thoughts.

What the hell was I doing? I was furious with her. It was Robert's lips on hers now, his hands roaming her luscious curves, and his body joined to hers. My hands clenched hard. Did she cream for him the way she did for me? Had he discovered that sensitive spot on her back that a simple stroke of my finger would make her wet with uncontrollable desire even when she was angry and claimed to be not in the mood? Did she whisper in his ear as her body tightened around him while she peaked in ecstasy?

These thoughts and more drove me crazy. But it was a good thing. It kept me from thinking with my dick and becoming weak.

Clearly, Savannah was no longer as accommodating of others and their foibles as she had been then. Now she had a stubborn streak as was evidenced by her silence. I could not help the reluctant admiration of her strength and defiance even though it was not in my favor.

Another day passed.

To my intense irritation a glimpse of Sheila's dark hair brought back a haunting memory of her. Unfortunately, for me, Sheila turned at that very moment and whatever she saw in my face made her blush.

I was developing an obsession, and I didn't like it one bit.

This was not how my great revenge was supposed to play out. Being the gold digger she was, she was supposed to come back groveling for the money and I was supposed to string her along some more. Dangle more and more shiny objects in front of her face, while I tired of her body. I should not be the one waking up in the middle of the night with a rock-hard erection, or giving my secretary the impression I was lusting after her.

After everyone else had gone off to celebrate Friday night, I sat alone staring out of my office window. I remembered a time when I was working on a project that had me sleeping on the couch at the office for three nights in a row.

When I had gotten home that weekend, I found my apartment cleaned from top to bottom and meals for a week stacked in the freezer.

I frowned. She *must have* loved me at that time.

There was yet another time when she told me to come over straight from work. I had been exhausted, but had gone nevertheless, and man, was I ever glad I did.

She had undressed me and led me straight to the bathtub filled with perfumed oils. After a good soak, she laid me out on the bed and gave me a massage. I was rejuvenated enough to be able to thank her repeatedly.

In the short two years we had there had been so many wonderful experiences. It was hard to think about the changed woman who now behaved like a stranger. What had gone wrong? Why had she left me to suffer alone? I had failed to believe Robert's claim of her being a gold digger, but it would seem he had not taken his own warning seriously? Or maybe he was just getting his rocks off while he could.

The longer I sat staring into space the more thoughts of revenge against Savannah seemed ridiculous. I'd been so shocked and angry by their betrayal I had let my emotions get the better of me. I felt as though I had erred in my assessment of her. The anger and rage I had felt had been stoked by her four years of silence. But just seeing her had made me remember the kind of person she was.

There had to be some sort of explanation for her actions. I should at least give her the benefit of the doubt. I should give her a chance to make things right and explain why she deserted me in my hour of need. Even if she was a gold digger, one call would have not hurt. So why not?

My curiosity peaked. I needed to know what had happened.

I left my office and drove to my favorite watering hole. But even a few drinks could not dampen the need to know what had caused Savannah and me to fall apart so suddenly. I thought we had had something strong and unshakeable. But clearly there was a breach somewhere.

I ordered one last drink, followed it with some strong black coffee and prepared for the drive home. The Friday night liveliness of the bar was lost on me. Such a scene could not be enjoyed in my current state of mind.

When I left the bar, it was minutes to eleven and it had started to rain. I was soaked to the skin by the time I got to my car. I drove carefully in the driving rain, my thoughts on Savannah and every possible way I could find to get her to talk to me. Send her flowers? Nah. That had never been her thing. Then a crazy thought crept into my head. I checked the clock on the dashboard. *Don't do it, Max.* But before I could talk myself out of the idea, my hands were already spinning on the steering wheel. The car's wheel skidded on the wet road.

The rain was now coming down in sheets and the wipers were going at top speed.

I parked and dashed into the lobby. Too revved up to wait for the elevator I took the stairs two at a time. A rush of adrenaline sped through my veins as I walked down the familiar corridor and knocked on that old door. What was the worst that could happen? She could call the police and have me arrested? A bitter laugh rose into my throat. Go for it, Savannah. Been there, done that.

I raised my hand to knock once more, but the door swung open. She stared at me in disbelief. I felt my shoes squelch as I stepped past her.

"We need to talk. And we need to do it now."

12

SAVANNAH

I had always loved rainy nights and tonight was no different. I had sat by the kitchen counter looking at the streaks of water running down the window pane, until I heard someone knock on the door. Probably a wrong food delivery again. That would be the second time tonight. But when I had looked through the peephole and seen Max I had almost fainted.

I closed the door and stared at Max. I blinked a few times. Should I pinch myself? Maybe the random thoughts that had been popping into my head all week about him had crept over into my waking moments. But no. This was no daydream. This was reality.

There he was, soaked from head to toe, and dripping all over my carpet.

"Stay there." I turned on my heel and went to the bathroom to find the biggest towel I had. I returned to find that he had actually obeyed and not moved. He was staring at me in a strange way. I was surprised to see he wasn't shivering. What on earth was he thinking to be out in weather like this? I stepped over to him, the towel over my shoulder.

"Strip."

His eyebrows rose with surprise, then a look of amusement filled his eyes.

My mouth tightened. "Don't go there," I warned tightly.

Wordlessly, he pulled off his tie and shirt followed by his shoes and socks and pants. He was about to carry on with his boxers when I lifted a finger to stop him. Though they were soaked and left nothing to the imagination, they had to stay on. I was not going to have him butt naked in my house at this time of the night.

I tossed the towel towards him and he caught it. Then I picked up his wet clothes and went to put them in the dryer. The days of him having clothes at my apartment were long gone. I had donated all his things to Goodwill after he went to prison.

When I returned, he was sitting on the couch using one end of the towel to rub his hair. He looked so alive, so at home, so unconcerned, and so damn delicious, I felt anger stir in my blood. What right did he have to come here and restart my suffering?

"What the hell are you doing here?" I frowned down at him.

He looked up, pinning me with those oh so bright blue eyes of his.

"We need to talk, Savannah. We need to get some things out in the open and cleared up now."

I blinked and my mouth dropped open in shock. "Now? It's almost midnight and raining cats and dogs in case you haven't noticed. Pneumonia is not something to play with and you of all people should know——" I caught myself just in time before I went on to remind him that he was prone to catching colds. There was no need for him to know I remembered that. It might come across as me actually caring about him and that was a message I had no wish to send.

He grinned ruefully. "I guess there's no time like the present. If there was a blizzard raging outside, I would probably still be here right now. It's been gnawing at me all week, Vannah. And now that I have your attention and we don't seem to be spitting venom at each other, I'm going to make good use of the opportunity."

My breath caught as he used his special name for me. I sank into an armchair across from him. "What's there to talk about?"

"For one, I need to get to the bottom of what happened to us four years ago."

I shuddered at the painful memory of those photos and dropped my head to hide my expression.

"Why did you disappear just like that? Not one visit. Not one court hearing. Not even a phone call. Silence. For four years I've been angry with you for abandoning me. Were you with me just because of my financial worth and potential? Was it just my money?"

My head shot up. "Your money? Me after your money? Are you insane, Max? I was under the impression all your money was going to ensure that your sordid secret wasn't leaked."

"What sordid secret? I haven't got a clue what you're talking about."

"I guess we're even then because I haven't got a clue why you keep trying to make me out to be some sort of gold digger."

He leaned forward, his eyes piercing. "You abandoned me when I needed you most. What else was I supposed to think? I thought we had something special. And though no vows were said, I thought we would be together for better or worse. My worst came and you jumped ship."

I sprang to my feet. "You were the one who did the abandoning, Max. You made me look like a fool! Was she worth it?" I crossed my arms and bit my lips as I felt hot tears sting my eyes.

He threw his arms upwards. "I have no idea what you're talking about."

"The hell you don't. I saw the photos, Max. She must have set you up really good for you to steal to pay her off. But I bet you didn't plan to get caught."

"Again, with the damn photos. What the fuck are you talking about?" The pitch of his voice had gone up, a sure sign of his annoyance.

I shook my head in disbelief. He was actually going to deny everything and play the innocent. Well, I would annoy him into confessing. "Are you really going to sit there and pretend that you weren't seeing another woman behind my back?"

"What?" he spat out, his expression incredulous.

I never knew he was such a great actor. I adored him and I thought I knew him inside and out, but how utterly and totally wrong I was. I knew nothing. "So... you weren't seeing anyone else."

His face was like thunder. Hell, if I hadn't seen the photos with my own eyes I would have sworn he was telling the truth.

"Where did this come from?" he demanded angrily. "You're the only woman I was with at that time. There was no one else."

"Liar!" I snarled.

"I've *never* lied to you! There was no other woman. Ever," he raged. "But, since we're slinging shit around, how about explaining why you dropped me quicker than a hot potato and moved on to more lucrative options as soon as you realized I was in trouble."

I pressed my hands to my temples and turned away. "Something is not making sense here. I'm confused."

"Exactly. Now you know why I'm sitting on your couch in my wet underwear in the middle of the night. There is something here that doesn't add up. There is a whole and we each have a half, but until we put them together, we can't make heads or tails of it."

I took a deep breath, fighting for the fragile control that I could feel slipping away. Was he really telling the truth? But I saw the photos. I turned to face him, tears glittering on my lashes.

"How about you start? Start with missing my birthday dinner. Where were you that night?"

"Robert had made an insinuation at a meeting earlier in the afternoon that he believed I was stealing money so I was at home trying to get my affairs in order and prove it wasn't me when the police arrived with their trumped-up charges. I was framed for embezzlement, but I didn't have the time to prove it at the time."

"At no point did it occur to you to call me?"

"Forgive me, but I had bigger issues to deal with," he said sarcastically. "At the very least, I expected you to call at some point. Then I would have been able to explain what was happening. But you never called."

"So why did you plead guilty then?"

"Since you didn't give a damn it seemed to be the smartest thing to do at that time. It freed me from Robert's ability to ever again profit from my work."

I shook my head. "Right, so I'm to believe Robert, your best friend, framed you?"

"Don't be so quick to defend him. Who do you think first put the idea into my head that you were just all about money?"

"I'm sure you misunderstood him. Robert is a gentleman and would never sink to mud-slinging. Anyway, if you loved me, why would you believe the worst of me?"

"I could ask you the same thing, Savannah. If you loved me, why would you be so quick to believe I was seeing someone else?"

"I have evidence of your cheating. You have no evidence of my greed." I bit my trembling lips.

"What evidence?" he pounced, his eyes fixed on me.

"I went looking for you, Max." A hot tear rolled down my cheek and I dashed it away furiously. "I went to your office to look for you. Robert said you had left the office upset. I found the photos of you and that-that woman!"

"What woman?" his shout echoed around me.

"The woman who was blackmailing you and you had to steal the money from the company to pay her off. *That* woman. So, if you want to know why I did not call, I was busy wrapping my mind around the fact that the man I loved and wanted to spend the rest of my life with was not only a cheat, but a thief, so *forgive me* if I didn't come with guns blazing to bust you out of jail!"

"Even if you believed I was cheating, why did you not come to see me and call me a cheat to my face? At least you could have given me the chance to defend myself face to face. Instead, I sat there, day after day, waiting for you to show up, and all I could think was that Robert had been right about you all along. It broke my heart."

"You weren't the only one whose heart was breaking! While you were on trial, I was holed up in my mother's house recovering from the miscarriage caused by the stress of you cheating and stealing!" I screamed wildly at him. The moment the words were uttered I wished I could take them back.

His face was as white as a sheet as he whispered. "What did you say?"

Gut-wrenching sobs such as I had never had since my miscarriage came out of nowhere. I stuffed my fist into my mouth as the tears continued to pour down my face. I squeezed my eyes shut, blotting out his shocked face. All that could be heard in the strange silence were my sobs. When at last I felt as if I had regained some control, I looked at him as he continued to stare at me. He looked shell-shocked. Frozen, unable to move or do anything.

I took a deep breath. "I was eight weeks pregnant, Max. I had found out the day before my birthday and planned to surprise you with the positive test. I had it wrapped in a cute little box and everything."

My voice broke once more and I closed my eyes. I could not bear to look at him anymore. The tears continued to roll down my cheeks, but my voice was now shrill and accusing.

"I waited for hours. You never showed up. God knows how much longer I would have sat there like some lovesick fool if Robert hadn't turned up to wish me a happy birthday. He told me you had left the office hours ago. I was so worried I begged him to help me find you. He offered to take me to the office to check if you might have gone back there. I was so distraught I thought going through your desk would give me a clue what had happened to you. That's when I found those disgusting photos.

"That was when Robert reluctantly told me y-you had been caught stealing and he'd had no choice but to press charges for embezzlement. I was like a zombie that night. I couldn't accept it all. It was too much. I woke up with cramps the next morning and I was bleeding. By the time I drove myself to the hospital and got into the emergency room, it was too late. The doctor's said I was heading for a stroke, my blood pressure was so high! They had to, they had to finish——"

I wrapped my arms around my torso as I started to tremble. "My baby! My poor baby! My baby was gone! And it was all because of you! Damn you, Max! Damn you!"

Refusing to look at him, I collapsed into the armchair, overcome by sobs once more.

But suddenly, I was torn out of my agony by a howl even louder than mine. I swung my head around to find Max's head buried in his hands as he howled in pain. Instinctively, I went to kneel in front of him and took his face between my hands. As he looked at my eyes, tears rolling down his cheeks, I was shocked to see abject pain and misery so deep it must be etched into his very soul.

13

MAX

https://www.youtube.com/watch?v=6dOwHzCHfgA
-I just died in your arms tonight-

"I'm so sorry. I'm so sorry. I didn't know, baby. I didn't know," I whispered as horror, shock, and pain wrenched at my chest. "I didn't know. Please forgive me, please!"

I held the hands that were holding my face and stared into her tear-filled eyes. She used the pads of her thumbs to wipe my cheeks. I pressed my forehead to hers and closed my eyes.

"I'm so sorry, baby. I'm so sorry," I continued to mutter.

"So sorry," I whispered against her lips.

The saltiness of our tears tasted so sweet to me as our lips met. At first the touch was tentative, hesitant, as though she was testing the waters. But when her lips parted slightly beneath mine and I felt her tongue slip out on that old journey to glide along my lips, I couldn't have stopped myself even if I wanted to. I succumbed to the passion that had been bubbling beneath the surface from the second I saw her across the field at the fair.

"I hate you," she whispered.

"That makes two of us," I confessed, my voice harsh with a mixture of sadness and desire.

"No, I really, really hate you, Max," she whispered again, rubbing her cheek against mine like a cat.

"I know," I said as I wrapped my arms around her and pulled her onto my lap. I only wanted to comfort her, but the sensation of her weight on my skin was so achingly familiar, my hands automatically snaked around her back, and pressed her soft curves close to me. I could smell her pussy.

God, how I wanted her.

Suddenly, all I wanted to do was forget. Just for a little while I wanted to forget what a cruel thing fate had done to us and how unfairly I had judged her. I felt her tremble as her arms came up around my neck. "I trusted you," she muttered angrily as her lips found mine.

My cock was rock hard and throbbing as our tongues met and suckled hungrily. I swallowed her soft groan. Her legs were wide open on my lap. I slid my hand down the front of her shorts and under her panties. My finger slid past her engorged clitoris to her swollen and dripping wet pussy.

A soft growl came from deep within my throat.

"Fuck you," she snarled back into my mouth.

There was no turning back now.

With one swift motion I gripped her beneath her thighs and stood. I sucked her tongue hard as I walked us to her bedroom. The rain beat against the window pane, matching the furious beating of our hearts. I laid her on the bed, pulled her shorts and tank top off before yanking my boxers off.

She spread her legs wide and her pussy opened like a pink flower. I bent down to taste it. It was deliciously soft and sweet. Her flavor washed over my tongue like nectar. I dreamed of this taste for four fucking years. I licked and sucked the wet folds. Her hands fisted in my hair, and her clit throbbed wildly with need as I took it between my lips. My tongue circled it while my fingers slid into her, gently twisting and turning to find that familiar ridge.

"Be rough," she ordered, her fingers tightening painfully in my hair.

It was as if she flicked a switch in my head. That was exactly what I wanted too. Four years of need and frustration drummed in my blood as I held her down and jammed my fingers as far as they could go. Her body bowed off the bed in response. She writhed and struggled under the onslaught of my brutal finger-fucking, but I was fucking feral. Merciless. I could tell she was already close, very close to her climax.

Without warning, I sucked hard on her bud and immediately her legs slammed down on the mattress as she thrust up and desperately ground her throbbing pussy against my mouth. It would have been the beginning of an explosive orgasm for her, but I pulled back abruptly, both my mouth and fingers.

Triumphantly, I looked down at her. She was flushed and trembling uncontrollably. Juice was pouring from her pussy. I was almost drooling at the thought of fucking her again.

"Please," she pleaded hoarsely.

Quickly I moved up her body, and positioned my shaft at the tip of her pussy. I felt her heat and wetness coat the head of my cock. I groaned at the exquisite silky feel. I reached down with both hands to cup her full breasts, pinching her nipples as I plunged forward, marveling and reveling in the sensation of her tight pussy sucking in my cock.

Her mouth opened in a gasp of surprise and her eyes widened at the sudden intrusion so deep into her body, but her pussy gripped onto me like a fist. Hell, it actually felt like I was fucking her virgin pussy all over again. Like that first night all those years ago when I had deflowered her.

Completely buried inside her, I paused to allow her body to get used to my size again.

"I need it hard and fast," she said, her voice jerky.

I nodded, but first I bent forward and claimed her mouth in a deep kiss. Her fingers clawed into my skin and her tongue lashed against mine. Then I began to thrust into her. So hard and fast, she jerked like a doll. I felt her legs wrap around my waist as she tore her mouth from mine and her slippery sweat-slicked body moved to meet every thrust.

"Yes! Right there," she cried out while her pussy fluttered wildly around me. The deep pulsing triggered me instantly. She was climaxing. I was barely holding on myself. It had been too long.

"Yes. Yes! Yeeeessss!!!"

I buried my face in her neck, my spine tingling, and my cock growing painfully hard within her as I continued to fuck her like a man possessed. The blood rushed through my veins and pounded in my head when her liquid heat spurted all around my shaft. Her nails bit into my flesh as she muttered the word "yes" mindlessly again and again.

I'd waited four years to hear her capitulation and I felt the rush of my seed like molten lava burst from my cock and fill her. I kept on thrusting into her, unwilling for it to be over. Still, now that the edge was taken off, it was time for me to really get down to business. All it would take were a few more thrusts to keep me rigid.

I pulled out, and in one swift movement flipped her over to her stomach. Then I stuffed three pillows under her belly so her legs were splayed open and her gorgeous ass and pussy were raised and totally accessible to me. I swooped down and stuck my tongue directly into her fragrant, pulsating pussy. Hungrily, I licked the juices running out of her. I could not get enough of this woman. To be honest, I never could.

She moaned and I gave one final lick before I gripped her hips and plunged back into her. I pulled her back to meet me, only to feel her push back on her own. I pushed her legs wider apart and arched my back, knowing that the new angle would drive her crazy.

I saw her head go down and I smiled. Yes, this was *my* Savannah. Only mine.

I kept up the feral pounding until she screamed. Another climax had started. I knew exactly what to do. I slapped her ass hard and instantly, her pussy tightened around my shaft. I reveled on the fluttery sensations as she enjoyed her climax. When it was all gone I gripped her waist and leaned back, pulling her into a sitting position.

I did not have to say anything: she knew the old drill.

Straddling me she pushed herself down on my erect cock.

"All the way," I instructed. "It's all yours. Take it all inside you. Every last inch."

She rotated her hips, taking my cock into a deep area yet untouched. At that moment I thought I heard her sigh. A sigh of pure contentment. It had been so long. Then, I watched my beauty riding me, her gorgeous body swallowing my glistening cock, her hands massaging her breasts.

"Play with my clit, Max. Please. I want to come again!"

I reached around and stroked her clit, pinching it lightly. I was rewarded by a squeal of pure pleasure.

She moved faster and faster, slamming herself down on my cock, while I stroked her clit in the way I had done a million times in another lifetime.

"You like that?" I whispered.

"Yessss! Oh fuck, yes."

She threw her head back and moments later her hot cream bathed my cock. It made me twitch deep within her. She fell forward, her hands gripping my thighs, gasping for air, her body trembling as she came. I flexed my cock within her, waiting for her to recover.

When it was over, I pulled her up to meet my slow deep thrusts. I was no longer in a hurry. I was going to savor every second of my time with her tonight. There had been a time when I had taken things for granted and had believed our lovemaking would always be there. But the events four years ago had proven that life can be turned upside down in a split second, and that tomorrow is promised to no one. So, I would take tonight.

I drew it out as long as I could. My heart raced as I thought about how close I had come to losing this. Where I had believed that she and Robert had been an item before, now I was sure they were not. Savannah was not the kind to sleep around.

Our sweat-slicked skin made the room warm and the sheets damp. As skin slapped against skin the sound echoed and blended with rain which still poured outside. I felt as though every cell in my body was attuned to the sensation and vibration of our souls as our bodies moved with urgency now.

I felt that familiar tingle wash over me once more, and I

quickened the pace. I smiled against her lips and groaned softly as she matched my pace with her own thrusts. We fed off each other. I gave and she took and gave while I took in return.

We raced towards the final destination, climbing higher with every thrust and parry. I felt my groin grow heavy as blood rushed into my cock. She knew my body, and she called out to me.

"Max!"

"I'm here! I'm here! Right here with you!"

"Oh, Max," she sobbed while her body clenched mine, and she came with me.

Our hearts beat against each other, as I lay listening to the rain and the sound of our ragged breathing. The enormity of what we had just done hit me like a freight train. She lost our baby. Poor, poor Savannah. How she must have grieved.

I rolled to the side, taking her with me, not wanting our bodies to become two once more. I leaned down to pull up the blanket over us as I fit her into the curve of my body. I placed my hand possessively over her hip as I kissed her neck softly.

"Go to sleep now, baby."

"Mmm."

I knew her eyes were already closed and that in less than a minute she would be out like a light. I had often teased her by saying that if she ever suffered from insomnia, I knew one sure fire way to get her to sleep. All I had to do was stick my cock in her and administer her brand of sleeping pill, and she would be out like a light.

I could not sleep so I lay listening to her even breathing as she slept. I watched the rain still streaking against the window pane. It felt surreal. Savannah was in my arms once more. balance was restored. It was hours later that sleep finally claimed me.

I woke up to bright sunshine outside. It took me a second to remember I was not in my apartment with my blackout curtains drawn shut. Memories of last night came swimming back and I smiled and tightened my arms around Savannah who was still asleep. I nuzzled her neck as my fingers glided over her hips. I already felt my body coming alive at the thought of waking her up with some lovemaking.

"Mmmmm." She stretched and sighed before rolling over.

I leaned up on one elbow and stroked her cheek. I watched her eyes pop open. At first, they were clouded with sleep. But I knew the moment she remembered last night. Her cheeks went red and she sat up, clutching the blanket to her chest.

"Look," she began, but she was interrupted by a ringing sound.

Startled, she turned her head and looked at her cell-phone, lying on the bedside. With a frown she picked it up and looked at the screen. First, she bit her bottom lip, then she looked up at me, her eyes blank. Not taking her gaze away from mine, she hit the accept button and put the phone to her ear.

"Hello, Robert."

I felt as if I had been punched in the gut. Why was he calling her at this time? Was I wrong about her? Were they still an item?

"Um... yeah, I know. I'll explain later." She paused. "No, not at all. Everything is fine." She chuckled. "Promise. Really. See you later. Yes, okay. I'll wear the red dress." She paused to listen to his response, which made her smile.

"Look, I'm a bit tied up, but I'll call you back in ten minutes, okay? Bye, Robert."

She cut the connection and put the phone back on the bedside table calmly. You could have cut the silence in the room with a knife. Then she looked at me expressionlessly.

"You're in a relationship with Robert?" I asked incredulously.

She shrugged, a careless, infuriating gesture. "A girl gets lonely. Why shouldn't I? He's been good to me."

I felt as if she'd thrown a bucket of cold water over my head. I stared at her. She looked so hard. So distant. This was not the Savannah I knew. "What was last night all about then?"

She pulled the blanket around herself and jumped out of the bed. "Last night was a mistake. Can you please get dressed and leave?"

"A mistake?" I repeated sarcastically.

"Yeah, a mistake," she returned aggressively. "I felt sorry for you. You didn't know about the baby. It took me a very long time to get over it, so I did my part to help you get over the shock."

I got out of the bed, pulled on my boxers, and faced her. "I wouldn't exactly call last night a mistake, my dear. I think last night could be put under the very satisfying fuck category. Well worth the money. The check is in the mail as they say."

"How dare you? I'm not a whore."

"I never said you were. I'll give you some time to consider the idea that perhaps we can come to a mutually beneficial arrangement. Budgets for development projects are inevitably underestimated as you will find yours is. Having looked at your figures it's a given you'll need more money in the near future, and I need a reliable booty call contact for my little black book."

"Fuck you, Max," she yelled.

"Didn't you do just that last night and it sure looked like you enjoyed every minute of it too," I shot back.

"Get out of my apartment," she raged.

"Certainly, but let me remind you of something first." I walked over to where she still stood clutching the blanket to her heaving chest. Deliberately, I stepped into her space causing her instinctively to step back. I backed her up until she was pressed against the wall. Holding her tense gaze, I placed one palm flat on the wall beside her and used my free hand to reach down and cup her pussy hard through the fabric.

She gasped with a mixture of shock and undeniable arousal.

I smiled coldly. "Yeah, that's right. This pussy is mine for the taking, and I'll be around whenever I feel like it... and you won't be saying no, will you, baby?"

I bent my head and licked her throat where I could see a pulse beating madly. There was crushing pain in my chest, but laughing softly, I turned and walked out of the bedroom. I pulled my wrinkled clothing out of the dryer and got into my pants, but wadded up the shirt in my hand. Pushing my socks into my pocket, I shoved my feet into my shoes. My keys were where I'd dropped them by the door last night.

I retrieved them and threw one last look at the bedroom door, but it remained steadfastly shut. I held on to what little pride I had left and walked out of her apartment.

The drive home was a pensive one. I was furious with her and jealousy was burning me up inside, but at least I now knew why she had not come to the trial. I also had some more insight into why she thought I had cheated on her. She had seen some photos in my desk. I tried to rack my brains and think what she could possibly have seen that made her mistake them for an affair. She was always unnecessarily jealous, but ... were there photos from the office party? Had I gotten too close to one of the women at work?

I frowned. Even so, I never kept photos in my desk.

Belatedly, I realized I should have followed up on that line of conversation, but admittedly we had both become distracted. There was so much information I now needed to sift through in order to make some sense of what had happened.

My hand tightened on the wheel. She was still sleeping with Robert.

Well, it won't be long before I destroy him so completely she won't want him. Having tasted her body again, there was no way I was not going to have her, and I did not care what underhanded methods I had to use to accomplish my goal.

14

SAVANNAH

https://www.youtube.com/watch?v=My2FRPA3Gf8
-wrecking ball-

I stood frozen against the wall as I listened to Max walk out of my apartment. My heart felt as though it was going to pound right out of my chest. What had I done?

I pushed my hand through my hair as the memories of everything that had happened came racing back. I felt my cheeks grow hot as I recalled how I had responded to Max's touch. It had been too much like old times for me to resist. All it had taken was one touch. It had always been that way. But everything I knew about him and after four years of convincing myself I was over him, I felt embarrassed to think he still had that power over me.

I rocked back and forth as raw panic rose up within me. This was exactly what I had been afraid of all along. Some instinct deep down had told me the second Max and I ever crossed this bridge, all pretenses at animosity would be gone. My desire for Max still ran deep. And if his response last night had been anything to go by, he wanted me as much as I did him.

I turned to look at my phone. I should call Dayton back and explain. He had just called to update me about something I had asked him to do yesterday and I had gone and confused him by calling him Robert and babbling on about wearing the red dress. Poor guy thought I had been kidnapped and was trying to give him a secret message.

It was the only thing I could think of to push Max away. I had to admit that lashing out at him had been a defense mechanism. But how else could I have responded? If I had not chased him away just now, we would be rolling in my bed right now.

I pressed my palms against my heated cheeks and cringed at how wanton I had been with him last night. I had enjoyed every second of it.

I fled from the sight and smell of my unmade bed into the living room. Sitting cross-legged on the couch, I stared into space, my thoughts racing.

I had had no intention of telling Max about the baby, but in the heat of the emotions last night, all that suppressed pain had come tumbling out. I could not shake the feeling that he was not gone for good. It would only be a bit of a reprieve. So all this time he had held my absence from the trial against me. I wondered, though, had I not been in the hospital if I would have attended, given I was still reeling from his betrayal.

As for that, he had continued to deny any knowledge of any other woman. But photos do not lie. And I still had one of those as proof. I realized I should have confronted him with the photo, but I had been too emotional to think clearly.

Memories of how it had felt to have him inside me once more filled my mind. We had always been dynamic in bed, and last night proved on that point, at least, we were still in sync. Why did it have to feel so good to feel him inside me? I could still feel the ghost of his tongue eating me out last night and my nipples tightened painfully.

"No. No. No. You can't be having these thoughts," I scolded myself, as I felt the wetness grow between my legs.

I jumped up from the couch and walked to the bathroom. Getting into the shower, I turned it on as cold as I could stand and stepped underneath the icy spray. I allowed it to beat me until all traces of desire left me. I was not really into torture so I ran it hot again, before I soaped my body and stepped out.

Somehow, I managed to resist the urge to bring the sheets to my face to see if I could catch the last lingering scent of him as I hastily stuffed them into the washer. I thought, instead, about the insulting offer he put on the table. Money in exchange for sex. How dare he? As if I was some cheap prostitute he picked up off the street, and his parting words were like rubbing salt into an open wound.

True there was no way I could deny I'd not been turned on last night. My body had betrayed me and he knew I wanted him, but there was no way I was going to let him think that. I hated being in the position of feeling as though I was on a rollercoaster. I hated having my emotions toyed with and that was exactly what Max was doing. But I would show him!

There was a way around my problem.

Robert.

Outside of his company, Robert was a wealthy man. His family was one of the wealthiest in the city and he had a hefty trust fund. I frowned when I remembered Max's insinuation that Robert thought I was a gold digger. If I were truly a gold digger as Max imagined, I would have chosen Robert over him. And in the years I'd known Robert, I'd never once asked him for anything. Apart from birthday gifts, I'd never taken anything from him either. Maybe Max was trying to lay the blame for his perceptions of me on someone else.

Robert had always been kind to me and always told me to come to him if ever I needed help. I would give him the chance to help, not just me, but the school, that he had always said he felt great gratitude for, to come up with any small shortfall in the budget.

Taking a deep breath I sent Robert a text. I was deliberately vague, saying only that I needed to talk to him soon. His reply was instantaneous.

Robert: Saw your message, hon. What's up?

Me: I'm in a bit of a bind. Can we meet up sometime? I need to talk to you. I need a favor.

Robert: Sure. What kind of favor? :)

I pondered if I should have this discussion via text message. I typed back.

Me: I'd rather not discuss it via text. This needs a sit-down conversation.

Robert: Sounds like a lunch date to me. lol.

I scrunched up my face. I really would have preferred just going to his office, but beggars could not be choosers. I sighed and bit the bullet.

Me: Sure. No problem.

Robert: Great. I'm out of town right now. Be back sometime on Wednesday. Thursday okay with you?

School would be out for the summer after Wednesday. Thursday was perfect.

Me: That's fine with me.

Robert: Excellent. See you Thursday. Btw, I'm at a vineyard, would you like white or red?

I was taken aback by the question.

Me: Ummm. Neither. I'm good. Thanks.

Robert: Okay. I'm leaving on Wednesday if you change your mind.

Me: Okay. Thanks

Robert: See you Thursday.

Me: Fine.

I stared at the phone. I hoped I was not making a mistake. Robert's interest in me was not lost on me, but unfortunately, I just could not wrap my head around being in a relationship with him. He simply did not elicit those kinds of feelings in me.

The next week ran off and I kept silent about the state of the finances of the project. I hung my hopes on Robert, hoping that he would give me the balance needed. Last night he had sent me the name of the restaurant where we would meet at twelve-thirty. Trust Robert to choose one of the most expensive and exclusive places in the city that went by reservations only. I arrived early and was pleased to find that just using Robert's name saw me being ushered to a table set on a dais in a corner. I had not relished the thought of waiting in my car and having to run the air conditioner unnecessarily. Ten minutes later as I continued to sip my water, Robert arrived.

He looked as he always did. Not a blond hair was out of place, not even when he slid his sunglasses off and the rim caught in his temple. Today he wore dark slacks and a crisp white shirt tucked inside. The neck of the shirt was open and I could see faint tufts of light curls. He smiled as he approached, his even teeth gleaming. I was overcome by a wave of cologne as he leaned down to brush his lips against my cheek before taking his seat across from me.

"Savvie! Sweetheart!" he exclaimed as he slid a bag across to me.

I raised my eyebrows.

"I know you said no, but I did it anyway."

"What's this?" I murmured as I peered inside the bag.

"White *and* red since you could not decide. It's from their rare collection. Maybe one day you'll invite me to dinner and we can share a bottle." He smiled once more and I felt as though the small smile I had pasted on my lips was frozen there.

"We'll see," I murmured as I slid the bag to the seat beside me. I felt as though neon signs were pointing at my mouth, flashing the words 'FAKE!'.

He laughed. "Well, you didn't say no, so that's a step in the right direction."

He raised his hand and a waiter appeared almost immediately. To my surprise he rattled off an order for both of us. I pushed down the annoyance at his presumptuous behavior and waited until the waiter left before saying anything.

"I could have ordered for myself," I said as lightly as I could.

"I know that, but I also know you would have tried to be polite since I'm paying and order something that's not too pricey. I wanted you to have the best today. They make an amazing steak and I promise you, you're going to love it."

He leaned across and took my hand in his. It felt uncomfortable and discreetly I slipped my hand from his under the pretense of reaching for my phone and putting it into my purse before looking up at him.

"I'm in a bit of a bind, Robert, and I really wouldn't be asking you if it wasn't necessary. I can't think of anyone else who can help."

"What is it, hon?"

"We might be a little short on funds to complete the renovation project."

He leaned forward, his eyes glittering. "I thought Max was going to make up the slack?"

"Well, he gave us the bulk, but I have a feeling some of those costs in the budget are underestimated."

"And he won't cover it?"

"Um—"

"He's not going to cover the entire shortfall," he pounced victoriously. "I knew you couldn't trust him. What did I tell you? He's all mouth. I told you, Savannah. He's not a man of his word. To be honest I don't think he even has that kind of money. It's all smoke and mirrors... unless, of course, he's stealing it from hard working folks like me.'

"It's not exactly the case. He will cover the costs, but... er... he has some conditions to which I'd rather not agree."

A strange look crossed his eyes. "Conditions? Such as?"

I shifted uncomfortably. Perhaps this was a bad idea, after all. "He... uh... wants us to be in a relationship again."

"Over my dead body," he exploded suddenly.

I looked around to see if other diners were looking our way at Robert's strange outburst.

"You didn't agree, did you?" he asked harshly.

"I wouldn't be here asking for your help if I did, Robert."

"Good. Good. Yes, you did the right thing coming to me. Of course, I'll help. The nerve of him! After what he did to you, did he really think he could pick up where things had left off?"

Further conversation was interrupted as the waiter came with our first course.

"Bon appetit," he said, opening his napkin and putting it on his lap.

"Same to you," I said, forking a green olive into my mouth.

"So, how much did he stiff you on?"

It grated on my nerves when he falsely accused Max of stiffing us, but I tried to look past it. "Costs may go up one-third more than projected..."

"Hmmm. That's a lot of money. But that's doable for me. It would be a good tax write-off."

I looked at him hopefully. "So, you'll make the donation?"

"Sure. And my word can be trusted unlike some others."

Robert dabbed at his lips, before filling his mouth with a bit of rocket salad. He seemed oddly preoccupied so I didn't say anything either and we ate in silence. I felt awkward as I forced the food past my lips.

"Robert?"

"Yes?"

"You are fine with donating the money in case we need it, aren't you? I mean, we might not even need it."

"Oh, God. Of course. Forgive me, I was thinking about a different problem, but you know what. I am here with a beautiful woman and I'm going to forget my little problems and enjoy her company." He raised his glass. "To relation-ships based on trust."

I raised my glass and echoed his words.

Robert's subsequent effervescence and his attempts to make it seem as if we were more than casual friends having lunch was mildly irritating, but my strong response to his attention puzzled me. I had never let his attention bother me before. It was easy to ignore his overtures. Not today. Today it bothered me. Perhaps because at every turn, I was comparing him to Max. And he was coming up severely lacking. There was something I never really noticed about him before. Beneath a veneer or charm he was shallow.

"Earth to Savvie."

I blinked. "Huh?"

"You were so far away. Did you hear anything I said just now?"

I shook my head and smiled contritely. "Sorry, I was envisioning the renovated lab," I lied.

He smiled. "Ah, yes. A noble endeavor, indeed. Naturally, I want to do my part in helping you to accomplish that goal, but I've just had an interesting idea."

My antennae went up at his use of the word 'but'. Nothing good usually came after that word. I swallowed hard. "What were you thinking?"

"I was thinking that you should take Max up on his offer of a relationship."

That was a quick 180 degree turn from 'over my dead body'. I kept my voice calm. "Why? You just said you'd give us the money."

"And I will. As a matter of fact, I have my checkbook here and I'm ready to write the check. I'm even willing to double the amount you need, but—"

There's that dreaded word again. "But what?"

He flashed a suave smile. "But I need a favor."

My heart sank. So strings attached to his 'donation' too. "I see."

"It's not a big thing, really."

"What's the favor?"

"Before I tell you that I want you to understand something first. Max is angry with me because he thinks I took great delight in his downfall, but that was not at all the case. It suits him to paint me as the heartless bad guy who drop-kicked him to prison, but I was gutted when the auditors proved to me he was the one siphoning money out of the accounts. I had a responsibility to our clients and share-holders so I had no choice but to do what I did. For his part, I get why he keeps saying he is innocent and I framed him for embezzlement. That muddies the water and puts doubt in people's minds about his guilt."

I reached across and placed my hand over Robert's in sympathy.

"You did what was best, Robert. You were a good friend when he needed your help to start the company in the first place. You believed in him when no one else would and he repaid you with betrayal. He repaid us both for our loyalty with betrayal."

He turned his hand over so that our palms came together. "Thank you for that, Savvie. You don't know how much it means to me to know that you believe me."

Slowly, I pulled my hand away. "You stuck by me through those rough patches, Robert."

He smiled sadly and nodded. "And I would do it all again in a heartbeat."

"So, what's the favor?"

"I want you to take Max up on his offer of a relationship."

I jerked back in shock. "What?"

"Don't get me wrong. Nothing sexual, or anything like that. Just to tickle his fancy. Make him feel good again."

I could feel my forehead knit. "How would that help you?"

"As you know Max is now my rival. What you don't know is he seems hell bent on putting me out of business. His company has been snatching up my clients and I'm trying my best to keep up with him. Hands down, he is better at software than I am. That's what made us an unbeatable combination in the first place. I need to stop him from stealing my clients. If you get close to him, maybe you can convince him to end his terrible obsession to ruin me."

I leaned back against the back of the chair and stared at Robert.

"It will be easy for you. You know he's like putty in your hands. Hell, all it might take is a sweet smile or a little flirting. If you won't do this for me then do it for him. This kind of obsession for revenge is unhealthy for any man. It's going to lead him down a dark path from which he might not be able to come back from. He needs healing. We all need to heal."

"Suppose he doesn't allow me to get close?"

Robert gave a sly smile. "Trust me. I'm a man, I know he wants to get close."

Confused, I looked away from Robert.

I had the feeling of being caught between a rock and a hard place. I had come to Robert in order to avoid dealing with Max. But now it seemed as though I would still have to deal with Max, even with Robert's help. I was back at square one. Not exactly at square one, a little voice in my head said. No, not exactly.

"Will you do it, Savvie?" Robert asked hopefully.

I turned my gaze back to Robert. "Yes, I'll do it."

15

MAX

If I had not been able to get Savannah off my mind after seeing her at the fair, it was ten times worse after I'd spent the night with her.

Robert's morning phone call to her sat under my skin like a burr under a cowboy's saddle for days, but I decided I was going to give the little hothead the rest of the week to cool down before I reached out.

While she cooled down at her leisure, I detected a slow rage simmering steadily inside me. The flirtatious way she had spoken to the bastard! The mention of the red dress. My hands clenched on the pen I was holding. It was Friday morning. I only had the weekend to endure.

My thoughts were so twisted, that Sheila had to buzz me twice on the intercom before I noticed.

"Yes, Sheila."

"Miss Maitland's on line one. Should I put her through?"

I could feel my heart kick like a horse. "Sure."

There was the clicking sound of Sheila leaving the line. "Hello."

"Hello, Max. I...er... called to... ah... say thank you for the check."

"The pleasure was all mine," I drawled.

She took a deep breath.

"What else can I do for you?"

"I... actually wanted to come by to discuss something with you in person. I can be there in ten to fifteen minutes if you're not busy."

"I'm not. Come over."

"Thank you."

The line went dead and I sat looking at the phone for a few moments. What the hell was she playing at now? I pressed the intercom.

"Yes, Max?"

"Please let security know I'm expecting Savannah in a few minutes."

"Yes, Max. Will you be needing any refreshments?"

I thought I detected a slight edge to Sheila's tone, but dismissed it as my own tense state.

"I don't think it will be a very long visit, thanks."

"Okay."

I leaned back in my chair. I was going to remain calm. I was going to remain rational. I was going to allow her to say her piece and not preempt her or make any assumptions about the reason for her visit. I would simply listen and see what she had to say.

I sat like that allowing software and programming to take up my thoughts while I waited for Savannah. The intercom buzzed.

"Miss Maitland is here."

"Thank you. Send her in."

I leaned back in my chair and schooled my expression. Sheila's long legs came into view first as the door opened. I looked into her cool eyes and thought I saw a spark of fire there.

"Miss Maitland." She stood at the door and allowed Savannah to pass.

Again, the resemblance between the two women was striking. I almost smiled when I saw that Savannah had clearly come to fight fire with fire this time. She was wearing her hair loose, held back by only a silk scarf. Her t-shirt clung to her torso, outlining the swell of her breasts and emphasizing the narrowness of her waist as it was pushed into her tight black jeans. Her hips swayed seductively with each step. I did not need to look at her feet to know that she was wearing something with heels. Her face was devoid of the excessive make-up Sheila was fond of wearing, but on every other point, Savannah was drawing a line in the dirt and squaring off with Sheila.

I noticed Sheila looked at her with barely concealed dislike.

"Thank you, Sheila."

Her eyes snapped to meet mine and instantly the scowl was replaced by a smile which did not quite reach her eyes.

"Sure thing, Max."

I thought I detected a hint of intimacy in the way she said my name. I saw Savannah's shoulders stiffen and knew that little power-play had been meant for Savannah's ears. The challenge seemed to have been accepted. Not that I cared.

I gestured for Savannah to sit opposite me and watched as she licked her lips, a sure sign of her nervousness. She took a deep breath.

"I'll get straight to the point. I've decided to accept your offer."

I blinked once. "My offer?" I asked quietly.

"Yes. You wanted a relationship in exchange for the rest of the donation. I accept."

"Oh. I see."

"Unless you weren't serious..."

"Oh, I was serious alright. It's just that with all your talk of not being a gold digger, I thought it would have been rejected yet again."

"It's not like that. I have to think of the greater good, and what this renovation will do for the students. I don't consider that gold digging. The money isn't for me."

"So, you're more of a martyr then? A sacrificial lamb?"

She shrugged.

I felt as if a gaping hole had opened up deep inside me. This was the last thing I had expected to hear. And as much as she tried to justify it, the bottom line was that she was willing to give herself and time in exchange for my money. It was a devastating blow to me, coupled with everything else that had come to light less than twenty-four hours ago. I leaned forward. "I have to say, I was not expecting you to have such a change of heart so soon."

"I guess I weighed the greater good and had to make a decision to forget about how I feel personally."

"You make it sound as though being with me is the worst thing in the world," I responded dryly.

"Not the worst thing in the world, but with things the way they are between us, it is a bit... awkward."

"It wasn't awkward when I was eating you out and having you cream all over my tongue last Friday, was it?" I asked sarcastically.

Her breath came out in an annoyed rush. "Do you always have to be so crass?"

"Do you always have to be so pretentious?" I raised my eyebrows. "Come on, Savannah. We both know that the sex between us is always fucking phenomenal. So don't act as though you didn't enjoy every second of what we did."

"That's not the point is it? You're getting what you want. So what is the problem?"

"I didn't say there was a problem. I'm saying don't pretend I'm the only one who wants this."

"But you are," she insisted stubbornly.

"So why are you here then?"

"Because I need the money."

"So, money in exchange for your presence in my bed. It sounds just like what it is if you ask me."

I watched her cheeks burn and I felt not one iota of guilt at her humiliation.

Her chin lifted. "I have a few requests, though."

"Requests?" I arched an eyebrow.

"Yes. For starters, can we keep this between us, please? I don't want any of our family or friends to think we have rekindled our relationship or that we have a future together."

"What else?"

"This is not an indefinite arrangement. It ends when the renovation is complete."

"When will that be?"

"We've just gone on summer break and work has already begun. We're aiming to have it done before the new school year begins."

I smiled. "Basically, a summer fling."

"If you want to call it that."

"Anything else?" My voice was polite. I did not show how absolutely triumphant I felt.

She shook her head.

"Okay. Your conditions are acceptable. I have one of my own..."

She looked at me suspiciously. "What is it?"

"You do not see Robert during our little fling."

"Could we keep Robert out of this?"

Blood rushed into my head and I was on my feet instantly. I stalked around to her side of the desk and hauled her unceremoniously to her feet. Before she could recover from her surprise and react, I crushed my mouth against hers with a fierce and punishing force. I bit her lower lip, until she parted her mouth. Instantly my tongue surged forward, plundering her mouth. I held her to me tightly, even as her hands remained balled fists against my chest. I pressed my hips into her, nudging my erect cock into her belly. I grinded it into her and felt when her resistance broke and she trembled in my embrace.

I kissed her until she melted into me.

Only then did I pull back and put her away from me. She swayed unsteadily and I watched with satisfaction as she sank bonelessly into the chair behind her. Placing shaking fingers against her swollen lips, she kept her gaze down. I leaned against the desk, spreading my legs slightly and placing my hands on the outside of my hips. I wanted her to see the clear outline of my erection that was in her direct line of vision.

"You don't need Robert. I promise I will be inside your body so many times this summer you won't even have time to look at another man. If you're doing exchanges for money, you might as well go the full mile and milk me for all I've got. There's champagne, jewelry, designer wear, and vacations abroad on offer, babe."

She looked up at me, a silent plea and hurt in her eyes.

But I was angry. How could she go with Robert? I looked down at her coldly. "Do we have an agreement?"

I detected a slight nod as she bowed her head.

"Good. I say we start with dinner this evening. Obviously don't make plans to go home afterwards."

I went back to my seat and began to pretend to make jottings on my notepad, clearly dismissing her. From my peripheral vision I saw her stand and turn away from me. I raised my head and watched her walk to the door. As she reached her hand for the door knob I spoke.

"Be ready by eight."

Her shoulders stiffened and for a few seconds she remained frozen, her hand on the knob. Then she pulled the door open and closed it quietly behind her.

I sat looking at the closed door for a few minutes, replaying every nuance of the conversation with Savannah. Disappointment went through me like a knife. All of it was wrong. Her acceptance of her body in exchange for money. Her desire to still see Robert while she was fucking me. So much for the faith I had in her integrity and morals. It seemed she too had her price.

I reached underneath a pile of papers and withdrew the file Byron had dropped off yesterday evening as I was about to leave the office. I slid out the glossy pictures, the images already engraved in my memory.

Savannah and Robert looked too cozy and comfortable to be having just a casual conversation. *Cru* was not a restaurant for anyone with shallow pockets so this had to have been a date. For five days she had been silent. Then suddenly, after this date with Robert she was ready to accept my conditions. It did not take a genius to figure out something was amiss.

I had had Byron following Robert from the day after I got out of prison. But to date, this was the most lucrative report, even more than his meetings with potential clients who I would then target. Yes. This was now more personal. Savannah was involved.

I closed the file and slid it into my desk drawer. I spun around in my chair to look out at the city skyline.

It did not take rocket science to figure out what was going on with Savannah's visit. If she was in cahoots with Robert, it had something to do with me. The question I now pondered was if they had already been scheming four years ago. Had there really been a miscarriage?

I remembered how broken she had seemed on Friday when she defended herself. There was no way she was acting. I paused. I had been wrong about her on so many counts. Was I wrong again? Could it be that she was just a very, very good actress? One call to my sister who had inside links to the nearest hospital could confirm her story. But I was not interested in going down that road.

At least not yet.

Now I needed to figure out what their game was and how to stay two steps ahead of them. I was a fool for Savannah but even blinded by lust for her, the play was obvious. How else could Robert know what my next move was unless he could get information from someone close to me? The moles he had planted in my company had not been doing as good a job as my moles in his company. It had been easy to identify them and feed them faulty information. If it had been anybody but Savannah in the equation, I would enjoy this game of cat and mouse even more. It would amuse me to no end to see Robert chasing his own tail. Going round and round while I crushed his business. I wondered if he would ever figure out that I had been on to him from day one, but even that satisfaction no longer mattered.

All that was important was that his fate was sealed. And with him, Savannah's was too.

The thought was strangely painful and depressing. I turned to look out of the window and the world seemed barren and gray. Without joy. I dug among the papers on my desk until I found the one I wanted. If Savannah was a rat, I might as well start leaving some cheese for her. I photocopied and folded it. Before I left home this evening, I would place it where it could not be missed when she slept over. A minute part of me held out hope that Savannah was not an accessory to Robert, but if she took this test bait, I would have my final answer about her.

I asked Sheila to make reservations at what used to be one of our favorite restaurants when we were dating. When I got home, I placed the sheet of paper in plain sight on the counter where I worked when I was home. I stared at the piece of paper for a few seconds. Part of me wanted to snatch it away and just trust her. She was my Savannah, the woman I was going to marry. I was wrong about her.

Then I picked up my keys and headed out.

It was going to be an eventful night.

16

SAVANNAH

https://www.youtube.com/watch?v=MOlzxfBSvp4
-The time of my life-

I examined my reflection once more and frowned. Was my lipstick too red? No, I was just not used to it. In fact, it contrasted well with my plain, but figure-hugging, black dress. The hem modestly stopped just below my knees. But my hand was already reaching for a tissue to blot it so it didn't look so bright.

There, much better or did my lips just look dull now?

I twirled and looked into my eyes. Was that panic I saw there? Deception was not in my nature and this whole charade did not sit well with me. So why did I agree to it? Not because I wanted to help Robert, that was for sure. I was doing it for myself. Somehow I had to get Max out of my system, and the best way I knew was to get close to him again and see him as he really was. A man who would betray anyone for money. Maybe that way I can start to truly reject him. All this while I had been pretending to reject him. Now, I was going to do it for real.

The memory of him howling when he heard I'd lost our baby flashed into my head.

"There you go again," I scolded my reflection. "Always grasping at straws. He was crying for his baby, not you. He doesn't love you. He just wants your body. Get that through your thick head."

I saw tears begin to pool in my eyes.

"No self-pity now. You can do this, Savannah. Max is not the nice guy you've made him out to be so get your sexual kicks out of the way and start to put things into their proper perspective."

I leaned my forehead on the cold mirror and closed my eyes and tried to believe the words I was saying, but no matter how hard I tried to convince myself Max was the bad guy, there was something niggling at the back of my consciousness. A tiny seed of doubt that had me wondering if maybe, just maybe, I was wrong about Max. Perhaps apart from manipulating me with the donation, he was in fact, the good guy. One thing I knew for sure, every instance when I spent any time at all with Robert my instincts were screaming at me not to trust him. That and the tiny seed of doubt made me remember the Max I knew before that fateful night: the playful Max, the kind Max, the hard-working Max, the loving Max, the Max I adored with all my heart and soul.

I pushed the contradicting thoughts aside and focused on my assignment. No matter what I thought about Robert, the fierce desire for revenge I had seen in Max's eyes was bordering on the obsessive and very unhealthy. If I could somehow make him see how destructive it was to him, perhaps as Robert said, we could all heal and go our separate ways.

I applied another coat of red lipstick, took one last look at myself before picking up my purse and heading downstairs.

THE RESTAURANT MAX had chosen surprised me. Admittedly, I had not given a thought as to where we would dine, but when we pulled into the parking lot of *Monticello*, I could not help the genuine smile that creased my face. This had been our favorite Italian restaurant when we were dating. I wondered if the menu was still the same.

"Still hankering for their caprese salad?" he asked.

I looked at him, his profile illuminated by the lights from the dashboard. That was the thing about Max. He was so beautiful I wanted to touch the skin stretched over his cheekbones. "Haven't had it in years," I murmured.

He threw me a glance. "Why not?"

I shrugged. "A teacher's salary doesn't stretch to the delights of *Monticello*."

He said nothing else until we were seated at the table. Unexpectedly, the evening was far more relaxing than I could have ever imagined. Conversation flowed freely and easily between us. It was like the four years apart had never happened. The caprese salad was exactly as I remembered it. Delicious. He forked some of his carpaccio into my mouth, and his eyes glittered when my tongue came out to lick at some oil that would have otherwise run down my chin. It was like a dream. Sometimes I even caught myself laughing. All too soon we were having coffee.

Some trepidation returned as I remembered what was next.

"Relax, Savannah," he drawled. "It's been a good evening. Don't spoil it. I'm not going to force you to do anything you don't want to."

I ran my finger on the rim of my coffee cup. "That's easy for you to say. You're not the one being led to the sacrifice."

He tilted his head to the side and considered me. "Is that how it feels, Savannah? Like you're a sacrifice?"

I dropped my eyes, unwilling to answer.

"What if I tell you, you don't have to come home with me? What if you get to decide when we have sex again."

My eyes flew to his. His gaze was steady and inscrutable. "What do you mean?"

"Exactly what I said. You don't have to spend tonight with me. I'll take you home and we'll call it a night."

I stared at him confused. "What if I never want to sleep with you again?"

He shrugged and leaned back in his chair, totally relaxed and supremely confident. "I've never had a reluctant woman before, and I don't intend to start now."

I knew Robert had already agreed to pay the unforeseen costs, but I was curious as to how he would react. "What about the money for any extra costs?"

His mouth twisted. "My word is good. Send a bill to my account's office and they'll take care of it."

My mind was a confused mess. He was giving me an escape route. He was giving me a way out of this agreement. I was thrown for a loop.

What was I going to do? I had given my word to Robert that I would help him and at the very least, I owed it to him to help him after he had been a rock in those dark days. I cleared my throat and spoke softly.

"I'm a woman of my word. I agreed to your terms. Your terms stand."

I saw something like a shutter come down over his eyes and a nerve in his jaw ticked. He dropped his gaze to the tablecloth. "Good. I hope the price you pay is not too high." Then he lifted his hand and made a writing gesture to a waiter standing nearby.

My heart was pounding as he paid the bill and came around to lightly place his hand on the small of my back. The heat from his palm seared me. I could not help but shiver slightly in the night air as we waited for the valet to get out of the car. I turned to look at Max. Gone was the easy-going man I had been with for dinner. This Max had anger rolling off him in waves, but he was getting what he wanted.

Why would he be angry?

The drive to his apartment was made in silence. I refused to break it. We walked through the lobby and were soon in the elevator. I looked at his profile as he watched the numbers climb. I wanted to reach out and ask him what was the matter, but we were no longer in that place. He was a stranger now. A stranger who had paid for the use of my body. The doors swished open and he made a gesture to indicate I should step out first. I walked out and felt him fall in step next to me. He stopped at a door and I waited for him to fish out his keys.

The instant we were inside, he kicked the door closed, and spun me around forcefully, his hands clamped at my waist.

"Let's get this over with, shall we?"

Before I could respond, his mouth crushed mine violently. I was stunned at first as I tried to figure out what was wrong. I allowed my mouth to open beneath his, barely stifling a moan, as his tongue surged in forcefully.

The arousal I had wondered if I would ever feel inside this sordid business arrangement came roaring to the surface as something feral in me took over. I was in Max's arms. Of course I was going to be aroused no matter what the circumstances were. He was my first and, as much I hated to admit, my only.

The only man for me.

I raised my arms and wrapped them around his neck as his hands yanked on the zipper of my dress. The dress slid into a dark shadow on the highly polished dark green granite floor. Wasting no time, he hoisted me into his arms and deposited me on the kitchen counter. It felt cold. I looked at him, puzzled. He held my gaze as he flicked my bra open and let my breasts spill out. Then he flicked my nipples with his thumbs almost insultingly, the way I imagined a man who bought a whore would, but there was a heat, real heat that he could not hide in his eyes.

It set my blood on fire.

He slid his hands down my side and into my panties. Automatically, I braced myself and lifted my hips for him to slip them off my legs. I realized his intention when he pulled up one of the bar stools and sat between my legs. He opened them wide. It was like old times. So illicit. Me completely naked and him fully dressed. I bit my lips as he reached out and stroked my clit with his forefinger, still holding my gaze. Then he closed his eyes and leaned forward and...

I was a goner.

Max knew my one great weakness. Eating me out was that one thing. As his tongue licked and sucked me, I struggled to stay on the counter. He chuckled and I felt the vibration of it ripple along my clit. I squirmed feverishly in his grasp as I felt that familiar tingle low in my groin.

"Oh fuck!"

He lifted his head. "Soon."

His fingers were pumping in and out of me and I could hear the sucking wetness of my pussy with each thrust. I lifted one leg and draped it over his shoulder, giving him better access. I lay back on the cold hard counter helplessly as I thrust my pussy up to meet his fingers and mouth.

"Ahhhhhh!!!" my hands balled into fists as my climax washed over me. My chest rose and fell with the deep breaths I was taking as I tried to regain my breath.

I felt him move away. Then he took my hands in his and pulled me into a seated position. Slowly he pulled me off the counter and I stood on legs that were still a little wobbly. He turned me around and I found myself facing the counter. I heard the rasp of his zipper then felt him nudge my legs apart.

I arched my back as he entered me from behind. I braced my arms on the counter as he thrust into me, hard and fast. I could hear the slapping of our bodies as each thrust brought our flesh together. I felt my juices running down the inside of my thighs as I felt as though I was creaming like never before.

His hand came around to find my clit. He rubbed it hard and that was the beginning of the end for me. My eyes rolled up as I pushed back against him urgently. There was no discussion of protection. I pretended to myself that it was fine, because I had just had my period, but the truth that I refused to face was I wanted his seed. I had always wanted his seed. In my mouth, in my pussy, in my ass. I always wanted it.

"Max! Oh fuck. Right there. Oh, yes."

I shuddered as yet another climax rushed upon me. I felt him thrust hard and deep and then he went still. His cock swelled inside me and I felt the heat of his explosion as he poured his seed into me.

I rested my head on the counter, my mouth open and my eyes staring vacantly. All that could now be heard in the room was the sound of both of us breathing raggedly. I put out my hand to try to stabilize myself and felt my fingers slide along the counter as they encountered a stack of papers. They fluttered to the floor.

"Sorry."

"I'll get them later." His voice was husky.

Slowly, he withdrew and I felt our combined juices sliding down the insides of my thighs. Turning me around, he hoisted me into his arms once more, and walked into the bedroom where he threw me into the center of the bed. For a couple of seconds, he did nothing, just watched me bounce on the bed through heavy-lidded eyes, his expression slightly cruel. Feeling naked and vulnerable I pulled the sheet over my body, but he reached out and ripped the sheet away. Then he undressed quickly. His cock was hard and pulsating angrily.

I knew it took a good two ejaculations before he was satisfied.

Wordlessly, I took the enormous shaft into my mouth. God, it had been so long. I could taste myself on him. I sucked him deep into my throat and a deep growl came from his throat as his hand came to fist my hair. A long, long time ago he taught me how to deep-throat him, but today I wanted something different.

"Fuck my mouth," I whispered.

And he did. For some reason it was exactly what I wanted. Maybe I wanted to be punished for my deception. For not telling him what I had agreed with Robert. He came deep in my throat and I continued to suck him until he finally pulled out of me.

Gently, like a cat, I licked his semi-hard shaft. I did it assiduously until he was as hard as rock once more.

Then I fell back on the bed and opened my legs wide. He captured my hands between one of his and held them above my head. I pressed my body up to meet his as he slipped his cock inside me. Our bodies picked up the rhythm of our tongues and we were soon moving in synchronization. I could not stifle the moans which rose up from within me as he twisted and turned his hips, knowing exactly which angle would bring me the greatest pleasure.

He brought me to a shaking climax before I felt his thrusts become harder and faster. I held him tightly as I felt him swell within me for the second time that night.

Sweat poured off our bodies as we lay entwined in each other's arms. I felt him shift his weight off me. Against my will, I felt my eyes begin to close. That was how it had always been with Max. I knew, though, that even if I slept, it could not be for long.

I allowed my eyes to close.

Hours later I woke up. The room was dark and I could feel the heat of Max's body beside me. I lay still for a few moments, making sure that he was fast asleep. Then slowly I moved out of his embrace, checking to make sure he was not disturbed.

When I was finally free, I moved quietly to the living room. As if drawn to a magnet I walked towards the paper that had fallen to the floor earlier. I picked it up. I was not wrong. Robert's name was on it. It was dated Monday. I felt so incredibly sad, I wanted to curl up into a ball and cry as I read through the document.

Robert was right! My instinct about Robert was wrong. He was not the bad guy. It was Max who was the bad guy. It was always him. Here was the written proof that Max was trying to destroy Robert. Here was the next client of Robert's that Max was targeting.

I put the paper back on the floor and when the hallway light came on, my heart almost flew out of my mouth when I looked up and saw Max standing at the doorway of the kitchen.

"What are you doing?" he asked softly.

"I... I." I had to think fast. I picked up the paper and put it on the counter. "I was thirsty. I came for a drink of water."

"Okay."

I turned to walk back to the bedroom.

Just as I brushed past him, he reached out and buried a hand in my hair. He turned me to face him, looking into my eyes.

"I thought you were thirsty."

My whole face burned with embarrassment. "Yeah, that's right. You... distracted me."

His face was expressionless. "Here, let me get a glass for you."

I waited while he got a drink of cool water from the refrigerator and returned with the glass.

"Thanks," I murmured.

He watched as I drank half of it.

"That'll do now," I said awkwardly.

"Sure?" he asked softly.

"Yeah."

He took the glass from my unresisting hand and placed

it on the counter. Then he scooped me into his arms and carried me back to the bedroom.

"Want another blowjob?" I asked softly.

"That would be nice," he replied.

That was the only way I knew to explain away the tears that were already burning the backs of my eyes. I could pretend he had made me gag.

I pulled out of her mouth and watched her wipe the tears off her cheeks.

"Are you okay?"

She smiled tremulously. "Yeah, just out of practice. Need to get my overactive gagging reflex to calm down."

I nodded and turned away so she wouldn't see the way I really felt.

When we had first started this 'game' I had been too blasé. I thought I could handle it. Her betrayal. Perhaps I had not really believed it, but I had been wrong. God, so fucking wrong. Now, even while I was fucking her mouth all I felt was pain. How could she not see what a scumbag he was? After everything we had been through, she still chose him.

Fuck her!

That was the whole problem. I couldn't say fuck you and walk away. Not from her. Not yet. Maybe if I kept on fucking her I would get over her eventually. Eventually it would get through my thick head that she was no good.

She lay on the bed with closed eyes. I looked at her

profile, wondering how an act that was almost divine when it was done with her could leave such a bitter taste in my mouth. I guess I didn't want to believe it, and I had done everything in my power not to acknowledge she was not the Madonna of my dreams, but a whore.

A fallen woman.

I had felt her crawl out of bed, and it had killed me to feel the warmth of her skin leave me. It was as if she was killing all my dreams. I had given her enough time to read the 'fallen' document before 'catching' her.

It gutted me she was such a traitor, but there was not a fucking thing I could do about it. All I could do was focus on my anger and try my best to turn it into hatred.

I resisted the urge to stroke her cheek as she slept, the same way in which I resisted the urge to engage my emotions while we had sex.

I closed my eyes. I was not quite sleeping, hovering on the periphery of consciousness. I was not sure how long afterwards it was when I felt her slip out of bed. I opened my eyes just in time to see her shadow slip out of the room.

I lay still, my mind whirling until I saw her trying to slip back into bed. Deliberately, I moaned and rolled over and she froze in her tracks. I kept up the act by stretching out to 'find' her side of the bed empty. I made a big show of fluttering my eyes open and starting to sit up in bed.

"Sorry if I woke you," she said. "I went to get a drink of water."

"Another drink?" I asked innocently.

She slipped back into bed beside me.

I lay back down, taking her with me. She turned her back and spooned into the curve of my body. I placed a thigh between hers and a hand on her hip as usual. I listened to her breathing. She was awake. But neither of us spoke. I trailed my finger down her hip and over her mound, slipping them between her labia. I found her clit, soft and hidden between the folds. With a light touch I began to stroke her. I moved my hand to my mouth to moisten my fingers then resumed stroking. I heard her sigh and felt her legs relax against mine as her clit grew hard.

Her hand came around to find my erect cock. She held me and began stroking.

I rolled her over to face me, keeping my hand between her legs. While my thumb continued to circle her clit, my middle finger dipped into her traitorous sweet pussy.

Silently, I rolled between her spread legs and entered her body. As I felt the tension heighten in my knees, I knew this would be a quick trip. I pressed and twisted, bringing her to the peak of pleasure before following her over the edge.

I rolled off and pulled her into my arms and, just like that, she was out like a light. I lay looking up at the ceiling, falling into fitful sleep only when the first fingers of dawn shone in the distance.

I DROPPED Savannah home before proceeding to the office.

Work was good, because it stopped me thinking of her. I got down to business and it was way past lunch time when Sheila brought me a very thick ham and beef sandwich.

"Eat," she ordered.

"Thanks," I said, as she slipped out of my office.

The afternoon ran off, and before I knew it Gerald was sitting in my office, shedding his coat and jacket.

"I'm not cut out for this cloak and dagger stuff. Sure, I

can build it into an app, but man, the drive over here was nerve-wracking!"

Gerald and I used to work together as the top programmers at Robert's. He knew I was innocent. Through him, I had direct access to Robert's operations. We very rarely met in person.

"So, what's so urgent you had to see me, Gerry?"

"I have some information that I think will be useful to you." He took a folder out of his shirt and slid it across to me. "I stayed back last night and took pictures of the originals and printed them at home. I haven't been to work today: I called in sick. I get the feeling I'm being watched."

I opened the folder and scanned the information. My eyebrows rose at intervals.

"Well, well, well. Robert is getting a little smart isn't he." Before me lay bits and pieces of the fake software I'd been planting. Somehow, Robert had found someone to work out the errors I had built into them and was in the process of using the remnants to build legitimate software. I was duly impressed.

"I think we need to step up the heat a bit. This cannot go on indefinitely. Right now, he's hanging by a thread. But if the jackass figures out this software it could put him back into a fighting position. If you're going to ruin him, you have to strike soon, like within the next few weeks. I'm trying to delay the test runs as much as possible, but there's going to come a time when it's completed and I won't be able to delay it any longer."

I nodded. "Got it." I tapped the folder. "It's vital information. Good job, Gerry."

He smiled and nodded. "Anything I can do to help. He did you wrong, Max. If only there was some way to prove it."

"Or someone who would confess. He had to have had

help. Still it's okay if I never get to the bottom of that. Everything crashing down around his ears will be revenge enough for me."

"And I, for one, will be glad when it happens. Things were so much better when you were around. I can't wait to see the back of him."

He stood and began to put his jacket on, then nodded towards the folder. "That's yours to keep by the way. If anything else pops up I'll pass it on."

"Sure thing. Thanks again."

"No problem."

I walked him to the lift through the empty offices, and waited until the doors swished shut. Then I got back to my seat, picked up the folder and carefully went through it. So the bastard had wised up and hired experts to figure it out for him. Whether this was the work of one person or a group, they were good. Very good, but little did Robert know that I'd been waiting for this moment when his people would crack the code built into the bait. Now I had to change my strategy, and, as Gerald had advised, fast. My brain was already beginning to turn at a mile a minute and I soon had my notepad filled with a new code of glitches and errors to keep them busy for weeks. I smiled. Nothing I enjoyed more than a stimulating challenge from professionals on my level. Perhaps when this was over I would hunt them down and hire them.

I put my pen down and picked up my phone. This would be the next bait I set for Savannah. Maybe this time I'll give her enough time to take a photo.

"Hello, Max?"

"Do you have plans for this evening?"

She paused. "Well, I was supposed to hang out with Tracey, but it's not set in stone or anything."

"Take a rain check?"

"Okay."

"I'm still in the office. Meet me at *Friction*?"

"Sure. What time?"

"Eight-thirty?"

"Okay."

"See you then." I disconnected the call, a ball of anger in my gut. She was willing to give up a night with Tracey for Robert. How fucking wrong I'd been about her.

My eyes went to the papers I was working on. I would have to find a creative way to leave this whole folder lying around and make sure to give it an incriminating title.

I sat in my usual spot at the counter and ordered another drink. I checked my watch again. Savannah was a stickler for keeping time, but it was now past eight-thirty. A sudden fear pierced through me. What if something bad had happened to her? I calmed myself down. I shouldn't care this much about her.

She was just someone I was fucking and using. A means to get my revenge on Robert.

Nevertheless, I felt restless and uneasy. My stomach churned and my mind filled with images of her caught up in a traffic accident somewhere. I had just picked up my phone to call her when I saw him approaching. The raw rage that welled up inside me made me tighten my fists until my knuckles whitened.

"I'll have what he's drinking," he called to the bartender as he took the stool next to me. I smelled the liquor on his breath and could tell he'd already had a few.

I kept my gaze on the row of bottles. Was this the reason

Savannah was late? To give him a chance to gloat? He always did count his chickens before they were laid, and he must be feeling he'd won ever since his people figured out the code. He had no idea the last part was the cracker.

"Isn't this like old times, Maxxie boy?"

"Go to hell, Robert," I said without looking at him.

"Max! Is that any way to greet your old friend and partner?" he said in a fake jolly voice.

I turned to look at him, and there he was puffed up with hairspray and confidence. He could barely contain his narcissism and swagger. "You were neither a friend or partner if you could even think of doing what you did to me."

His eyes widened dramatically. He was really enjoying this. "What I did to you? All I was trying to do was protect my company."

"Cut the bullshit, Robert. You have no audience here. You're talking to the guy you framed."

"Are you still harping on about that? You've got no proof I did anything of the sort. Money was going missing and the trail led to you."

"You know, I've always been curious. How did you do it?"

He laughed strangely, victoriously, knowing that he was beyond the law. I turned to find him staring at me evilly. He leaned in closer. "Signatures, my boy. You were too involved in your numbers and codes to notice all the checks going out with your name on it."

I could not believe what I was hearing. Robert was finally admitting that he had indeed framed me. At that moment, in my peripheral vision, I saw Savannah approaching. She had a small smile on her lips which slipped the instant she saw Robert. I saw something akin to panic as her steps faltered. She took a brief moment to school her features before coming to stop behind Robert. He turned to look at her, then he laughed, and looked back at me.

He shook his head. "Poor Max. You always were a sucker for a pretty face and so damn easy to manipulate too. Why do you think our little gold digger here has rekindled her relationship with you even though she saw you spread out on the bed with a whore? Because I paid her to. It was so easy was too!"

Trust Robert to use people and discard them. What a way to compromise Savannah and expose her as his ally. Two things occurred to me in that split-second I watched as the color drained from Savannah's face before she turned and ran out of the bar. One: she was not working for him. Two: she might be a gold digger, but she was *my* gold digger.

A part of me wanted to punch Robert's lights out, but he was not my most important consideration. He would keep for later. I wanted to go after Savannah.

Wordlessly, I threw a bunch of bills on the counter and moved past Robert as he continued to laugh drunkenly.

"That's it, run after her, Maxxie. Gosh! One of these days I hope she gives me a taste of that body. It must be one hell of a pussy to—"

Whatever else he was going to say was silenced when my clenched fist slammed into his face. He slid into an unconscious pile between the stools as I raced out into the night and looked around. Savannah's car was nowhere to be seen. I jumped into my car and sped into the night. I could only hope that she had gone back home.

I got to her complex just as she was parking. She looked up at me as she hastened across the parking lot.

"Savannah!"

"Leave me alone," she jerked out.

I raced after her, catching her on the landing. She

turned to face me and I could see the tears coursing down her cheeks. I pried her keys from between her fingers and went ahead to her apartment. She followed.

As soon as the door closed behind us, I pulled her into my arms. Her hands curled into fists which she pressed into my chest, fighting my embrace. I crushed my lips against hers as I pressed her against the door. My hand found hers and I forced her fist open and intertwined our fingers. I took advantage of her gasp to slip my tongue into her mouth. I felt her go soft against me. Without hesitation, I pulled up the hem of her skirt and cupped her pussy. Then I moved the crotch of her panties to the side. I found her clit and worked my magic even as I maneuvered my zipper down to free myself.

I pushed her up against the wall and plunged into her eager pussy. My mouth continued to plunder hers as she wrapped her legs around my waist. We moved with an urgency as our bodies thrust and strained against each other. When I felt the first flutters deep within, a surge of blood rushed to my cock. I ripped my mouth away from hers and threw my head back.

"Oh fuck!"

Belatedly, I realized I had broken my vow of nonchalance. I pressed my forehead to hers, kissing her softly as I held her waist tightly. Holding her tightly in my arms, I took her to the bedroom and undressed her.

I did not know how many times we made love that night. All I knew was I wanted to erase the pain Robert had caused her. Despite the fact Savannah had allowed herself to be bought by him, she still did not deserve to be humiliated by anyone, let alone a useless lowlife like him.

I lay looking at the ceiling as she slept and I wished I could tell her not to worry and this was all a part of my plan.

I wished I could tell her it was all going to be alright soon. But I could not. Not yet. All in due time though, all in due time.

I closed my eyes and allowed sleep to come, knowing that I did not have to think about watching her snoop around for information tonight.

18

SAVANNAH

When I woke up the next morning, my apartment was empty.

All that remained of Max was the scent of our coupling. I felt as though there was a gaping hole in my heart and tears pricked my eyes. True I had deceived Max in one way, but my motives were pure. I wanted us all to heal. Robert had betrayed me and made it seem like I did it purely for money, but it was not drunken Robert's betrayal that hurt me, it was having him remind me of the other woman.

It tore open the old wound of his infidelity and made it bleed all over again. Somehow while Max was in prison, I'd managed to push those ugly photos into the far recesses of my mind and numb the pain, but now the memory of him spread on the bed with her hurt like hell.

In shock, I realized I'd done what I'd vowed I would not do.

I'd gone and fallen back in love with Max.

I got out of bed and headed to the shower. Sometimes, I wished I had never chosen to go to that bar after class all those years ago. Then I would not have met Robert, or been introduced to Max, and had to contend with all the pain that unfolded in the last four years of my life. While they played their games it was me that was getting hurt in the middle. I could not take any more of this. I literally felt as though I was going crazy.

"Fuck you both and damn you to hell!"

I was too confused and hurt to think clearly. I needed some alone time to think. A seed of an idea popped into my head. Yes, that was what I must do.

I showered quickly, then dressed and pulled a small suitcase out of my wardrobe. As I packed, I made some calls. Half an hour later, I headed out of my apartment. I stopped by the building manager's office briefly to let him know I would be away for a few days and to give him an envelope addressed to Max to post for me. Outside the sun was shining brightly, but my heart felt heavy and blue. My last task before I drove out of the parking lot was to send a text message to Max.

Going away for a few days.

I briefly thought of turning off my phone but remembered that they were not the only people who would need to contact me. Instead, I set Max and Robert's numbers to mute for all calls and messages. There. Now even if either called or texted, I would not know.

I stopped and filled up at a gas station for the two-hour drive ahead of me. Closer to my destination, I could stop for groceries.

I must have been really stressed and needed the time out, because just leaving the city limits sign behind me made me feel as though a giant weight had rolled off my shoulders. I did not know how anyone could live a life of dishonesty. I was definitely not cut out for it.

I found a radio station playing oldies and let the familiar sounds wash over me until I was half an hour from my destination. I pulled off the highway and followed the signs to the shopping mall a few minutes away. I knew exactly what I needed so I was in and out in less than fifteen minutes.

Being back on the highway turned my thoughts back to what I had left behind. I felt anger at them both come flooding back.

"Forget about them. This week is not about them. Relax and enjoy yourself. Okay?"

I took a few deep breaths and let the anger melt away.

A few minutes later, I turned off the highway. Almost immediately, the road narrowed and I found myself going slower as the road grew bumpy. A few miles later I passed through a set of double gates which stood open. In the distance, I saw the tops of several buildings with vehicles in front. Now I knew why the agent had said I was lucky as I had gotten the last available single. A few miles more and I went around a corner and came to a stop in front of a small cabin. I hooted my horn and a short woman appeared on the porch, her round face wreathed in a massive smile. I couldn't help responding to her infectious grin.

"Savannah Maitland?" she queried.

I stepped out of the car. "Present."

"Awesome! I'm Jo-Anne. I've just got everything done for you. All cleaned, towels and sheets changed, refrigerator plugged in, hot water running. All that was left was your beautiful self and here you are."

I laughed. For the first time since I saw Max across the field, I was filled with the feeling I had done the right thing, made the right decision. I reached into the back for my travel bag.

"Let me give you a hand with that."

"Thanks."

I handed her the bag and went back for the groceries. She placed the bag just inside the front door and I placed the grocery bags on the kitchen table.

She held up a bunch of keys. "This opens the back door, and this is for the front. We operate on solar here so keep your eye on the battery. If you need to get in touch with the main house or any other emergency services, there is a list of numbers on the wall beside the refrigerator. I know it's summer so it's pretty warm, but just in case a chill passes through these hills, there's firewood. I think that's it."

"Thanks, Jo-Anne."

"No problem, sweetie."

I escorted her to the porch and watched as she headed back to the main house. She turned after a few steps.

"Oh. There's one more thing. If you plan to go hiking or anything like that, check in with us so we can know. The trails are clearly marked and are very safe. But still, you can't be too careful. We provide GPS and maps at the main house as well."

"Thanks."

"Enjoy, hon."

After she had disappeared in the distance there was a peaceful quiet. Some leaves shivering in the wind, some birds singing in the branches. Other than that. Beautiful silence. I stood for a moment, enjoying the absence of city sounds and taking in the scenery around me. Jo-Anne's mention of the hiking trails made me glad I had picked up my hiking boots at the last minute, even though I had not hiked in years. The last time had been on a weekend camping trip with—

I swallowed the lump that suddenly formed in my throat. Memories of that first time I went away with Max rose up before me. I pushed them aside hastily.

"Get it together, Savannah. Don't let them intrude. They are the reason you had to run away in the first place. Don't let them mess up your little peace right now."

I headed inside and put away the groceries in the refrigerator. I left a frozen pizza out for dinner and changed out of my travel clothing.

The next morning when I woke up to silence, it hit me that I was free, if even for a few days. I had taken a few books with me and for the first time in years, I was able to indulge in one of my favorite pastimes of reading. I became so engaged I found that I spent most of the first two days in the hammock on the porch, voraciously devouring pages of novels, taking a break only to eat or answer the call of nature. By day three, I felt the stress begin to leave my body. I decided to take Jo-Anne up on her recommendation of a hike and so, shortly after breakfast, I presented myself for accountability at the main house. With my backpack filled with water and snacks, and armed with a map and GPS, I set out on one of the trails. I was sorry I had not taken my camera. The scenery was beautiful.

When I returned that afternoon, my body ached in a good way. I discovered muscles I had not used in years and they were not averse to making their presence felt. I committed to finding more time to do more of this. I stopped at the main house to return the GPS and map before trudging back to my cabin. My mind started to spin out ideas for a committee retreat. I could see us camping out here one weekend in the fall in one of the bigger cabins. It was an idea I would pitch when we had our next meeting.

I showered, grateful for the hot water as it eased the ache in my sore muscles. Tonight, I felt like having soup and in a few minutes, the aromatic liquid was simmering on the fire. I heard thunder rolling in the distance as a summer storm brewed. By the time the lightning began flashing and the first fat drops of rain plopped to earth, I was snuggled up with my laptop which I had tethered to my phone for the internet.

I finished my soup and retreated to the bed with the laptop, falling asleep to the sound of the rain and the drone of the mechanical laughter from the comedy in the background.

The next morning, the air felt crisp and there was a cleanliness to it that could only be achieved after a storm. The ringing of my phone interrupted my thoughts. I frowned at the strange number.

"Hello?"

A few moments later, I turned as white as a sheet. Without hesitation, I raced inside to pack. Within the hour, I was heading back to the city, my heart in my mouth.

19

MAX

I wasn't exactly delighted to receive Savannah's message, and did actually entertain the thought of rushing to her apartment and cutting her off at the pass, but rationality prevailed. Obviously, she needed time to figure things out, and I would give it to her.

I needed time to sort my head out too.

I was quickly becoming utterly and completely obsessed with her. She thought I was using her for sex. Little did she know I was crazy, actually insanely crazy, about her. More than I had ever been. She was all I thought about day and night. I was even having trouble concentrating on work, and work had always been my oasis of peace. No matter what was going on in my life I could slip into the immutable, unchangeable world of numbers and codes and forget my troubles even existed. I was just trying really hard to do that when, any hope I could return into my safe world and forget her even momentarily, flew out of the window.

Sheila brought in my mail.

She had placed an A4 envelope marked PERSONAL in Savannah's handwriting on the top of the pile. For a second,

I was too stunned to react. Then, I snatched it up, tore it open... and froze.

What the fuck?

I couldn't believe what I was seeing.

I put the photograph on the desk and stared at it incredulously. So *this* was the proof of infidelity Savannah kept referring to. Clearly, I had not paid enough attention to her claims. Not only had I been too consumed with my own plans of revenge for Robert, but I had also made the mistake of dismissing her accusations as another facet of her jealous nature. In my defense I had good reason. When we first met, more than once, she had harbored feelings of insecurity and expressed unfounded suspicions about women I barely even realized were in my vicinity.

I stared at the photo curiously.

Was it a fake? CGI? If it was photoshop it was excellently done. I picked it up and peered closer. No, it was not a fake. The photo was of such high resolution I could even see the pores on my skin. I stared at the naked woman entwined with my naked body. Nope, no recollection of her at all. Nothing.

Carefully, I studied my surroundings in the photo. It looked like a hotel room, but not one I would have frequented. Still, I had obviously been there. I focused on the painting above the bed. Something familiar about it. I closed my eyes, frowned, and tried to cast my mind into the past. Where did I see that painting? Suddenly, my eyelids snapped open. Of course, the hotel room in Dallas when I went to the developer's convention held a few months before Robert framed me.

But I didn't go to bed with anyone!

I scowled as I tried to recollect the totally unremarkable occasion. Now when I think of it I had a very vague recollection of one of the nights when I had one glass of whisky at the bar downstairs, felt strangely dizzy and went straight to my room. The last thing I remember was falling into bed. I woke up the next morning with a terrible hangover and I had put it down to jetlag and too little sleep.

Bending my head, I restudied the photo more closely.

To anybody looking at this image, especially if they were in shock, it would indeed have seemed as if the woman and I were in the throes of mad passionate love, but I noticed something crazy. I was under the woman and she appeared to be kissing me deeply, but my body actually looked sort of passive, my hands were hanging around her loosely, as if they had been positioned around her. The more I concentrated on that fact, the more certain I became that I was not even asleep, but passed out so dead to the world I didn't even know there was a woman on top of me. Still, someone had gone to a lot of trouble. I noticed other details, what appeared to be sweat glistening on our bodies. I supposed that was easily achieved with an Evian spray can.

I sat back and steepled my fingers under my chin.

It came to me like a bolt of lightning. Robert was involved in this. This was part of the set up. And then, as if the universe itself was helping me out of the mess of my life, Robert suddenly burst into my office, with a flustered Sheila rushing in after him.

"I'm sorry, Max. He just burst through. Shall I call security?" she asked, glancing nervously at him.

"That's okay, Sheila. I'll call if I need anything else," I said softly, turning the photo face down while not taking my eyes off him.

"Told you it'd be okay, Sheila." Robert grinned, then winked at her. "Don't forget to put that business card away carefully now. I'm looking forward to a call."

As he considered her retreating ass with wolfish interest, I watched him. He was wearing make-up, probably to cover the bruises around his eye. When the door closed he turned his attention back to me.

"She's a dead ringer for Savannah that one. It must be easy to make up for the real thing. I'm sure you're tapping that, huh."

I remained calm. "What do you want, Robert?"

He took a seat, propped an ankle across a knee, then leaned back and looked around. "Nice setup. Cool office, and a spectacular view, too."

"What do you want, Robert?" I repeated, this time I could barely conceal my disgust.

"Nothing really. I just came by to say hello. This 'war' between us is juvenile and bad for both of us. Don't you think it's time for us to let bygones be bygones and call a truce like adults... like men?"

I observed his smug, carefully made-up face with narrowed eyes. To think I once thought he was my friend. Jesus, I must have needed my head examined.

He stood suddenly, and walked towards the large painting on my wall. "I'm not your sworn enemy, Max. I promise you."

I had always tried to give Robert the benefit of the doubt, even when others told me to be careful, I had trusted him as my friend. But now as I looked at him, I saw him for what he truly was: a creep. "Aren't you?"

He turned away from the painting and faced me. "No, I'm not, Maxie boy."

The Maxie boy grated, but I kept my cool. "Four years of my life spent behind bars says different."

"You keep harping on about those damn four years.

What about the more than ten years before that we were friends?"

"Friends?" I murmured.

"Yes, fucking friends," he shouted suddenly red with anger. "That was exactly what I was. A friend. A good friend who took a chance on your hail Mary scheme and helped you to build your dream with *my* money, and you repaid me by stealing my girl?"

"Your girl?" I drawled insultingly. I needed him to be angry and out of control. "Surely you're not still living in that world where you thought Savannah was ever yours to begin with?"

"I met her first!" he yelled as he pointed a furious finger at me. "I introduced you to her and you stole her from me."

"Savannah chose who she wanted to be with and that man was me. You were just a sore loser. But what's new? You've always been living in my shadow and dining on my leftovers." I leaned forward. "It ate you up that she wasn't impressed by your name or money, didn't it? The only way you could get her was framing me for embezzlement and catching her while she was in shock."

A strange look came over Robert's face, it was a mixture of loathing and frustration. "You think I've got Savannah? Then you're an even bigger sucker than I thought." He shook his head, and his voice was bitter. "I've *never* had Savannah and it's not from lack of trying. She's all yours. Now that we got it all cleared up, can we stop this war?"

I stared at him with narrowed eyes. "You're not in a war... but at the fair..."

He shook his head. "I've been bluffing all this time. That was just pure luck. I believe the surprise she experienced from seeing you after all these years gave me an advantage. It was easy to make you believe she and I were an item because you were so ready to believe the worst of both of us."

I felt anger rise within me. "Why? Did you not feel you had destroyed me enough?"

He shrugged. "I was mad with you, but I have been trying to make it up. I gave a check to not cut you off."

I laughed suddenly. "You paid her to fuck me?"

Robert's jaw dropped with horrified surprise. He looked like someone who thought he paid well below market price for a priceless painting and just realized he was the target of a scam. "You're sleeping with her?"

"Do you think we were going to sit around drinking tea? Of course we're fucking."

"She is a gold digger," he ranted vindictively. "She took money from me and you. She's played us both for fools."

I laughed at him. He just never gave up. "Are you trying to sell me the same old gold digger myth *again*?"

"Don't fool yourself into believing that, that bitch is with you because she wants—"

I was out of my seat in a flash and I'd thrown the first punch before he knew what had hit him... and boy, did it feel good!

I stared him down while flexing my fingers. *Go on, give me another reason to give you another reason to wear make-up.* He didn't disappoint. He retaliated with a punch to my gut, but I'd spent four years keeping myself fit and I jerked back so fast it landed as a weak jab. In fact, I was so hyped on adrenaline I did not even feel it. I grabbed him by the collar and delivered another blow to his precious face.

His hands flailed wildly in the air as he crashed to the floor. He didn't even try to get up. He just sat there looking up at me with a slightly dazed expression. Blood trickled from his cut lip. His hair was crushed down on one side and

I suddenly realized why he took such care to present it so perfectly coiffured. The perfection of his buoyant hair distracted you from his dead eyes. He had the emotionless eyes of a cold-blooded snake.

Standing over him, I felt a sense of triumph, not for having laid him on the floor, but for knowing that there'd never been anything between him and Savannah. I strode to my desk, picked up the photo, walked back to within three feet away from him, and flung it at him. He caught it, glanced at it, then looked up at me, a furtive look in his eyes.

"Go on. Explain that," I invited silkily.

"I'm not taking the blame for this. This is just as much your fault as mine."

I took a threatening step towards him. "I swear I'm going to turn you into a bloody pulp if you don't stop acting like an asshole."

"You made it super easy because you always had your nose buried so far into your stupid computer codes, you couldn't smell bullshit if you were drowning in the damn thing."

I took another step and he instantly shifted backwards on his ass.

"Okay, okay, calm down. You want to know what happened that night? Well, your whiskey was spiked. The bartender made you a little concoction. The way he reported it, you would be out cold by the time you got to your room. A little surprise was waiting for you there. While you were dead to the world the prostitute did her thing. You have to admit this is a particularly good photo. She deserved every penny of what I paid her too."

The hatred I felt for him boiled over and I wanted to throttle him once more, but I kept my mouth shut. I needed him to finish playing his hand.

"After that it was easy to have Lillian park the photos in your desk drawer after you stormed out of our meeting. You had let it slip earlier that it was Savannah's birthday and you were going to celebrate where you had your first date so I gave her time to know you were not going to show up. I actually sat and watched her through the window for almost an hour. When I saw her make a move to leave, I went to her. She was going out of her head with worry so I offered to take her to the office and help her locate you.

Savannah found the photos in your desk. She was devastated. Selling the idea of you embezzling to pay off a whore who was blackmailing you was as easy as taking candy from a baby."

"Get the fuck out."

"Look for what's it worth, I'm sorry, I—"

"Get out, before I decide ending you might be worth another bout of prison time," I said between gritted teeth. I watched as he stood shakily and walked to the door. Later, I would deal with him properly. First, I had to find Savannah and tell her the truth, but in a way to ensure that there was no chance of her doubting my sincerity. I had a fair idea of where I would start on the journey towards building my case.

20

SAVANNAH

"Priscilla Maitland, please."

My heart was pounding as I watched the nurse move in seeming slow motion as she checked the list. She looked at me over her glasses, her lips pursed. "And you are?"

"I'm Savannah Maitland. Her daughter. I got a call—"

"Oh yes! She's been asking for you since she came out of surgery."

"I got here as fast as I could. Is she okay? Is she in any danger?"

"Mrs. Maitland is fine. Let me show you to her room."

Impatiently, I stepped into the corridor and followed her as she walked slowly down the corridor. Only the fact that I did not know where I was going forced me to follow her. Finally, she stopped at a door and turned to face me.

"She has been out of surgery for a few hours, but sometimes the local takes a little longer to wear off so she might still be a bit groggy."

She opened the door and I stepped in. My face broke

into a relieved smile as my mother's face lit up at my appearance.

"Savannah."

"Mom."

"I'll leave you now. Please remember visiting hours end in twenty minutes," the nurse said, as she closed the door behind her.

I hastily pulled up a chair and sat, reaching for my mother's hand. "What happened? You gave me such a scare! The last thing I expected today was to come to the hospital because you've been in an accident!"

"It's not anything to raise a commotion over."

"It is when they say you've just come out of surgery."

"I told them not to call you unless I said so," my mother said stubbornly.

I smoothed a lock of her hair back from her face, allowing my fingers to caress her soft cheek. "What happened, Mom?"

"It's not a big deal. I was doing some yard work and slipped. They said I popped my Achilles' tendon. I guess I'll be in a leg cast for a few weeks."

"Slipped? On what? What were you doing?"

She went red and her eyes slid away from mine.

I narrowed my eyes suspiciously. "Mom? What were you doing?"

"I was trying to clean the gutters. A bit of a storm passed through and I had a few leaves that were stuck in it."

"Mom! Where was Benny? He's supposed to be doing all the labor yard work. You had no business being up on a ladder at your age."

Her lips compressed with annoyance. "Excuse me. I'm barely fifty. Not some old granny, Sav." Her eyes suddenly twinkled "At least not yet."

I was not going to be put off. "Where was Benny?"

"He was stuck in traffic. He got there when the ambulance did. Don't blame him."

"Where were you anyway?" she asked, skillfully turning the conversation spotlight on me.

"In the hills. I needed a bit of a break from the city."

"Oh no! I'm so sorry to spoil your little vacation." She reached out and caressed my cheek affectionately.

"You didn't," I said instantly.

"Did you get any rest? You look as if you've been out in the sun."

"I've been hiking along some fantastic trails."

"I'm really sorry you had to cut your retreat short because of my foolhardiness."

"Oh, Mom, I would have been back in a day or two, anyway. You haven't spoiled anything. I'm just glad you're okay."

I wanted to stay and talk some more with her, but visiting hours were over and I had to leave. When they discharged her in a couple of days, I planned to pick her up and take her home. I also intended to stick around for a few days to make sure she was truly able to take care of herself.

When I got back to Mom's, I reluctantly re-activated Max's number. That evening as I prepared dinner, the phone rang. I took a quick second to take a deep breath before answering.

"Hello?"

"Are you back?"

"I'm... back in the city."

He must have picked up on the pause. "Good trip?"

"Yeah, I could have stayed longer but something came up and I had to get back."

"Oh?"

The change in his tone was obvious and I could have kicked myself. I had been doing so well with my short, non-committal responses. I tried to sound as casual as possible.

"Yeah. Mom had a little accident so I'm at hers to sort things out for her."

"Is she okay?"

"She's being discharged in a day or two."

"Is she in the hospital?" he shot back, sounding genuinely concerned.

I gritted my teeth. *Way to go, Savannah. You're such a chatterbox!* My plan was to relay in as few words as possible about my mother's incident, and make it sound as casual as possible.

"She fell and hurt herself bad enough for her to land in the hospital. Fortunately, she's not too bad. At her age, it could have been worse. Much worse. She could have broken her hip and that kind of injury lasts a lifetime. She's not getting any younger and her bones have stopped growing. They're not sold in the stores either. You can't just place an order and a waiter comes out and delivers. She has to be more careful at her age."

I could hear myself babbling, but I couldn't stop.

"That's what I told her, but she did not take kindly to being reminded of her age. Pretty damn near snapped my head off when I said it!"

He laughed. It was a musical sound I'd always loved to hear. For a split second, it felt like old times, but I forced myself back to the present, breaking whatever spell was being cast on me. "Anyway, I've got to go," I said and ended the call.

After that I sat looking at the silent phone. The beeping of the oven timer broke me out of my reverie. I pushed all thoughts of Max out of my head. It was only a few more weeks till the end of summer and the end of our arrangement. I could only hope that the news of my mother would give me a reprieve from holding up my end of the bargain.

21

SAVANNAH

Finally, my mother was discharged and I went to pick her up. She was waiting in a wheelchair in the foyer, a pair of crutches across her lap and her overnight case at her feet. With some maneuvering, the porter and I managed to get her into the car.

When we got to the house, Benny, who rented the cottage at the bottom of her garden, was waiting to help her into the house. He easily swung her into his arms and I watched as her cheeks turned pink. I watched as he fussed over her, chastising her for not waiting for him to come from work to clean the gutters as he had promised. She took his fussing with much more grace than she had taken mine. I eyed them curiously, noticing how familiar he was in her kitchen and knew where everything was to be found.

When at last he left with a promise to check on the gutters as he did not want her finishing the job with a cast on her leg, I turned to her with raised eyebrows. I got straight to the point.

"Is there something going on here that I should know?"

She looked at me, a too-innocent smile on her face. "What do you mean, darling?"

I pointed my thumb in the direction in which Benny had gone. "Are you two into something? Am I going to be hearing wedding bells any day now? Am I getting a new dad?"

"Savannah, you always were so dramatic. He's just my tenant."

I chuckled. "A very good-looking hunk of a masculine tenant who lifted you into his arms like he was posing for the cover of a torrid romance novel. And the way he was fussing over you—"

"Don't be so silly, child. He's just a kind and caring man."

"I can see he cares for you." I raised my eyebrows. "Mom, you don't have to hide your romance from me. I like Benny. He has always been a gentleman and you're still young and good-looking. There's no reason he wouldn't be attracted to you. Dad would be happy with your choice too. Benny is the kind of man that would have been Dad's friend."

"So, I'm no longer a geriatric old woman who has no business being on ladders?" Mom asked sarcastically. "Now I'm a sprucy young bird who could be out strutting her stuff?"

We dissolved into laughter at the comparison. She quirked an eyebrow at me. "How come I'm getting a lot more action in my love life than you? You've been so down in the mouth lately."

"Me?"

"I don't see another Savannah Maitland here, do you? Of course, you. I've been meaning to mention it, but I don't want you to think I'm prying."

"Mom, first of all, I don't have secrets from you, and secondly, there's nothing to pry about, though."

"Oh, isn't there? I think when your only child suddenly seems down in the dumps after the man she was madly in love with is released from prison, it is reason enough to worry." She pinned me with a searching gaze. "Especially when she doesn't say a word about him contacting her."

"How did you know——"

"I've got my ways, dear. And it doesn't hurt when a friend casually asks if Max and Savannah are back together as she's seen you out with him. And for the record, it's not Susan. This is someone I trust and she has seen you together more than once."

I looked at my mother incredulously. "The FBI and CIA have nothing on you."

"Actually, it's called a mother's love. And no matter how old our children become, they will always be children in our eyes, and we will always be concerned. So?"

I look at her. "So what?"

"Have you been seeing Max since his release?"

The thought of lying to my mother did not even remotely exist. Nor could I put up a front where she was concerned. And for the first time in months, I felt as if the burden I had been carrying about this whole situation needed to be done away with. I sighed and curled up next to her on the couch she was sitting on.

"Yes, I have, but it's not what you think."

"How do you know what I'm thinking? Are you a mind-reader now?"

"Mom... I know that you loved Max to pieces and wished with all your heart that things had worked out between us."

"I've never hidden my affection for the man. If I'd had a son——"

"It would have been Max, I know, I know."

"So what's going on with him?"

"Seeing him was a mistake. I mixed business and pleasure and it's not worked out. When school starts, our connection will be over. So please don't get your hopes up about our relationship being rekindled."

"Savannah, I never raised you to hold someone's past against them. So, I hope you're not snubbing him because he's been to prison."

"Mom, you raised me better than that. That is not the reason why things are not working out with him."

"Well, from where I sit, that could be the only reason standing in the way."

I shook my head. "It's not that simple."

"What's the complication?"

"There are things I can't ignore."

"Like what?"

"I can't tell you right now, Mom. But I will. One day. I promise."

My mother looked at me for a few long moments, her eyes boring into mine. I did not doubt that she could see my unhappiness, but I could not tell her why. No matter how disappointed I was with Max, I could not reveal that part of his character to her. She would be devastated to know he cheated on me.

Finally, she nodded. "I trust that if you cannot tell me now, it must be for a very good reason."

"Thanks, Mom."

"But one day I will hear that reason. And even more so, I will hear Max's side of the story."

"No!"

"Something's not right and I think he deserves a fair chance to clear his name."

We both looked up as the back door opened and Benny came in with his arms filled with freshly cut flowers. My mother's cheeks turned pink as he spread them across her lap. I could see the twinkle in her eyes and the affection in his. Though she said there was nothing between them, I had no doubt that all the ingredients for wedding bells to ring were there.

"Sweet flowers to brighten up your room while you recover."

"These are beautiful, Benny! Thank you!"

"And they are a bit of an apology too. I should have gotten to the gutter sooner."

"Oh, Benny! Don't blame yourself. I should have kept myself on the ground and let you get to it when you could."

I pointed to the flowers. "I'll go get a vase before they wilt."

"That's okay, Savannah. I'll get it."

We watched Benny as he went to the kitchen. I saw my mother's lips twitch as she smirked.

I nudged her. "He does have a nice ass, doesn't he? For a man his age, he isn't half bad."

"Savannah!" She covered her hot cheeks and laughed. I joined her. My spirits lifted slightly at the thought that after all these years alone, my mother might finally be ready to take a chance on love again.

That night, the three of us ate dinner together. After Benny left, I helped her in the bathroom and we figured out how to do a semi-shower without getting the cast wet. It was not as difficult as I had thought it would be. And I felt a little more at ease at the thought of leaving her to cope on her own in a day or two.

I helped her to the guest room which I had set up on the ground floor since navigating any kind of stairs was out of the question.

That night, I slept on the pullout couch to be near her in

case she needed help with anything. As I lay staring up at the ceiling, thoughts of the past two weeks raced around in my head. Talking about Max with my mother had been a bit cathartic. I had been as transparent as I could be given the circumstances. But the conversation still left me feeling that things were not completely resolved. My time in the mountains to think things through and get things straight felt as if it had been for nothing. And it did not help to know my mother was actually on Max's side without even hearing his side.

By the third day, I felt comfortable leaving my mother and heading back to my apartment.

22

MAX

https://www.youtube.com/watch?v=aJOTlEiK9ok
-girls like you-

I kept in touch with Savannah on her mother's progress. I gave her the time and space she needed to be with her mother, but the more updates I got about her mother, the more I wanted to visit her.

I'd always liked Priscilla. She was a good, honest woman. In her I saw what Savannah would look like in the future and I liked what I saw. It was almost inevitable I would turn up on her doorstep one evening. I rang the doorbell, a bouquet of flowers in hand. An attractive older man answered the door. Savannah had not said anything about her mother being remarried, but perhaps she had found someone after all.

"Hi! I'm Maximus Blackstone. I heard Priscilla had a fall. May I see her?"

"Of course. Come in. Priscilla is in the living room."

I followed him into the house and found Priscilla by the window overlooking the side garden. She turned at our approach, and her face broke into a huge smile of pure happiness. "Oh, Max! It's so good to see you again." She turned to the man who let me into the house. "Benny, this is the Max I was telling you about. Savannah's Max."

Benny nodded. "Oh! That Max. In that case, I'm going to make myself scarce for a bit and give you two a chance to catch up with each other. I'll be in the kitchen making dinner if you need me."

Benny nodded to me once more and disappeared. I watched him go before turning to look at Savannah's mother. I put the flowers down on the table and quirked an eyebrow as I took a seat on the couch beside her. I leaned in and brushed my lips against the cheek she offered.

"Is a wedding on the horizon? Should I be looking into tuxedo rentals?" I murmured.

"Oh, Max! You and Savannah are incorrigible. Are you sure you haven't been exchanging notes with Savannah? She said pretty much the same thing when she met Benny. He's my tenant."

I pointed to her cast. "So, you've been climbing on ladders."

"It needed to be done." She pursed her lips and looked at me keenly. "So you've been talking to Savannah."

I plucked a card out of my wallet and handed it to her. "Now you can call me and we can talk without going through Savannah."

"I would rather you went through Savannah, though. At least it would keep the two of you talking." She patted my arm gently. "Sometimes Savannah does not know what she wants or needs, and as a mother, I need to nudge her in the right direction. Now that we're on the topic of Savannah, let's talk about what happened between you. She never told me. Why does she want to have nothing to do with you?"

"She thinks I cheated on her."

Priscilla's eyes widened. "Did you?"

I looked her right in the eye as I'd always done. "Never."

"So why would she think that you cheated on her?"

"Let me start from the beginning."

"That would be best."

"As you know, I got out of prison a few months ago."

"I had heard about that and I have to say I was shocked. I wanted to come see you or even attend the trial but then ummm I had to see to an issue with Savannah around the same time."

"She told me about the miscarriage."

"Good. You know I don't like to mince my words. I hope you forgive me for not reaching out when I'm sure you needed someone in your corner, but I'm sure you understand now why I could not."

I nodded. "There's nothing to forgive. Robert set me up."

"Robert? Robert Steinberg?"

"The same. We had a business together."

"Somehow I never connected the dots. Anyway, go on with the story."

"Since my release I've been working on getting evidence. I have some documents which show duplicates of checks that Robert signed, but on the copy my signature has been forged. The books also show that the money did in fact go missing, but the payout was authorized by me. My inside link is still working on getting me the other documents I need so that I can make a report and have him arrested. Based on what I hear, in the last four years, these trumped-up embezzlement charges are child's play in comparison to what he's been up to."

"But what does this have to do with why Savannah wants to have nothing to do with you?"

"On top of the embezzlement, he also set me up with a prostitute and had pictures taken. By his own admission, he had me drugged and a photoshoot was staged. Again, by his own admission, he planted the pictures of me and the other woman in my desk. Then he orchestrated a chain of events which led to Savannah finding the pictures. Because I was already arrested for embezzlement I could not defend myself."

"And a few days later she miscarried," she muttered almost to herself. "Oh! You poor dears! And all these years she's blamed you."

"I'm not blameless either. I've resented her for abandoning me in my time of need."

"You have to tell her that Robert set you up with that woman, Max."

"I didn't know about the photos until recently. Robert's plan was to ensure that if he couldn't have Savannah, neither could I."

"Really now."

I nodded bitterly. "He's ruined my reputation and he's almost ruined my relationship. I will get Savannah back and once I've done that, God help him because I will sink him if it's the last thing I do. And you best believe that I'm working damn hard on it as well."

"I believe every word you have said, Max."

"I do take some consolation in the fact that after everything Robert did he still was not able to get Savannah."

"I didn't raise a stupid daughter. Stubborn and willing to cut off her damn nose to spite her face, but her heart is in the right place."

"I know that now."

"Good. Now let's figure out how to get Savannah to see the truth."

"Robert didn't pull this all off himself, though. He had help. He mentioned my previous secretary. She was fired shortly after my arrest, but I have hired a private investigator to track her down."

"I'm rooting for you, Max."

"Thank you, Priscilla. You have no idea how much good this conversation has done for me."

"You're welcome, Max. Now give me a hug and kiss."

I took my leave shortly afterwards.

MONDAY MORNING FOUND me in a quaint little café downtown.

As I waited for Byron, my private investigator, I nursed a cup of coffee. I felt the hairs on the back of my neck stand up as he slid into the booth behind me. It turned out that Lillian lived just an hour away.

I left work early on Friday to beat the rush hour traffic and arrived at the address Byron gave me in good enough time. I parked across the street and waited.

It was getting close to dusk by the time I saw any movement from the house. A car pulled into the driveway and I craned my neck to see who it was. I made out Lilian's wild curls immediately.

Just as I was about to approach the house, the door opened and Lillian emerged with a dog on a leash. Bruno. She still had Bruno. I gave him to her as a puppy. But look at him now

I watched them as they walked down the driveway.

Suddenly Bruno's ears perked up and he turned and looked across the street. He sniffed the air.

"Woof! Woof! Woof!"

"Come on, Bruno. Leave the squirrels alone."

I rolled down my window.

"I think he smells me, Lillian."

I watched as she tightened her grip on the leash with one hand while she reached into her pocket with the other.

I spoke quickly. "It's me, Max. I just want to talk to you."

I saw her defensive stance relax and I got out of the car. Bruno was now overcome with excitement and straining at the leash to get to me. I crossed the street and subjected myself to his excitement as he jumped all over me, just like old times. I laughed as he licked my face.

"Hey, Bruno old boy. It's good to see you fella." I patted his head and rubbed his neck a few times.

I turned to Lillian. "Let's take this chap for a walk and have a little chat."

There was silence for a few minutes as we simply walked. Bruno stopped a few times to mark his territory.

"How did you find me?"

"I hired a private investigator. We need to talk about what happened, Lillian."

She nodded. "I know. It should never have happened. But I thought I didn't have a choice but to do what he wanted. He said it was his company and you were stealing, but I think I always knew he set you up. I wanted to help, but then you confessed and I was confused."

"I confessed because it was the only way I knew to free myself from him. I trusted him and signed all my intellectual output away to him. Now that I'm free, I'm hunting concrete evidence to take him to court."

"Max, I cannot begin to tell you how sorry I am for what

I did. I really did feel like I didn't have a choice. Terry in accounts was in on it as well, but I hear that he's passed away. I hope he made his peace before he did."

"Terry?" I repeated amazed. I remembered him as a sweet old man.

"Robert's pockets are very deep. And he just had the knack of finding the right accomplices at the right time. You know my aunt Ruth?"

"Of course, how is she?"

"She's alive, but I paid a high price for her life. I'm sorry it had taken so many years out of yours to have her with me still."

I sighed. The lack of money was the root of all evil. "I understand, Lillian. It's a pity you didn't come to me first. I could have helped and kept you out of feeling obligated to Robert."

She pressed her left hand into her cheek and when she spoke her voice was full of regret.

"Your heart was always in the right place, Max. I don't even know why I let him manipulate me like that. There isn't a day that goes by when I don't feel guilty about what I did. Robert fired me shortly after, you know. The bastard did not even want to give me a recommendation. It was hard, but I managed somehow. I wish I had never met him and I don't want to have anything to do with him ever again."

By now we were back at her house.

"I'd like you to come inside. I have some things that might interest you. You need to know about the photos."

"I know about them. I need something that will convince Savannah I'm innocent."

Lillian smiled suddenly. "You've come to the right place. I have exactly what you need. Come inside."

We entered the house resplendent with the smell of a

great meal. Lillian grinned at me as she took Bruno off the leash.

"You came on a good night. Aunt Ruth made lasagna."

"Ah, the way to a man's heart, but perhaps not today. I am too stressed to do justice to your Aunt's fine culinary skills"

She nodded. "I understand. Come with me."

I followed her deeper into the house. Lillian preceded me to the back porch where she invited me to sit and did not beat around the bush.

"Once when Robert had a few glasses of wine he admitted to me he hated the fact that Savannah chose you over him. I also kind of guessed that he had always been a little envious of your software skills. He knew it was your skills that made the company what it was. At some point the feelings he had must have turned into hatred so he set up the accounts to look like you were authorizing checks. What he didn't know was that Terry kept a secret record. When I left the company he sent me a copy of everything with a note that simply read:

Just in case...

It looks as if 'just in case' is finally here. So you can have that. Also, I'm sorry to say, it was me who arranged everything with the prostitute, the photographer, the bartender to spike your drinks. Luckily, I too, kept records. Just in case."

I could feel my chest fill with a sense of victory. "So, Lillian, you owe it to me to help prove to Savannah I was set up with that woman."

"I'll do you one better. I kept her number. Her name is Rachel and she actually doesn't live too far from here. I happened to know she's no longer employed in that field.

She found Jesus, became clean, and studied to become a hairdresser."

My eyebrows rose. "You kept in touch?"

"Actually, no. I just happened to run into her one day at Target. She remembered me immediately. I have her number if you'd like it."

"I would."

Lillian read her phone number out to me and I keyed it into my cellphone.

"Call her. I'm pretty certain she would be more than willing to tell her side of the story to Savannah. And if you need me to go meet Savannah myself, I will too. Tell you what. Let me talk to Rachel later tonight and see if I can get her to agree to come along with me to see her. It's the least we can do to right the wrongs we did to you."

"I would really appreciate that, Lillian."

I said my goodbyes and headed back to the city. That night, I could barely sleep as I thought about all the information I had uncovered.

THE NEXT MORNING, even before I'd had breakfast, Lillian called.

"Rachel agreed to come with us. I told her we would pick her up if that's okay with you."

"That's fine by me. When would be a good time?" I'd have driven to the ends of the earth to pick Rachel up if it would help Savannah to see the truth.

"Anytime this morning would be fine."

A couple of hours later, we pulled into the parking lot of an apartment complex. I waited while Lillian went upstairs to find Rachel's apartment. A few minutes later she came back, accompanied by the woman I presumed was in the photo. Hard to tell as I'd only seen her profile and she had changed her hair color and style, and she had all her clothes on. She smiled gently and gave me her outstretched hand.

"You're even more handsome awake."

I didn't feel very handsome. "Thanks for agreeing to help me clear up this confusion, Rachel."

She shrugged. "I helped to cause it. It's wonderful whenever I am given the opportunity to set my terrible past right."

The conversation was casual as we made the ninety-minute drive back to the city, but I felt as if my guts were tied up in knots. I didn't call ahead to tell Savannah I was coming, as I didn't want to spook her, but I knew she was always in on Saturday mornings. I saw her car was in its usual parking spot, as I turned off the ignition.

"It's showtime, ladies."

They nodded and we entered the building. We walked up the short flight of stairs and knocked on Savannah's door. I heard the latch being drawn back. Then the door swung open and there she was, the love of my life. That soccer ball to the gut feeling was back. I felt as though I was drowning in her beautiful eyes. Fucking hell! Swallowing hard, I stepped to the side.

"These ladies have something they'd like to tell you, Savannah."

23

SAVANNAH

Though years had passed, I recognized 'the woman' instantly. There was no mistaking her. Her image had been burned into my brain that fateful evening. My heart began to race and I felt fury rise in me. How dare he bring *her* to my apartment?

"I've been telling you the truth all along, and these ladies are here to prove it. I think you're going to want to take a seat," Max said.

Blankly, I stared at the three pairs of eyes looking at me. The truth? Was there truly another truth than those terrible photos?

"Please, Savannah," Max urged softly.

I tuned in on his face. His jaw was tight with tension. He didn't look like a liar. Then again, he never did look like one. Yes, I wanted to hear *his truth*. He deserved that much. Wordlessly, I stepped aside and they entered.

I walked to the nearest armchair and sank into it. The women sat on the couch, while Max stood behind them. He looked like he wanted to pace, but was deliberately holding himself still. The older woman spoke first.

"We've never met in person, Savannah. I'm Lillian."

Immediately, I recognized her voice. "Lillian? Max's old secretary?"

"Yes, that's right. We've spoken a few times when Max got bogged down with work and was going to be late. I may have sent you a big bouquet of flowers or two as well." She smiled sadly. "It's nice to meet you even under these circumstances."

I felt no kindness towards her. She never once called me to ask how I was. I crossed my arms and said nothing.

"Let me get straight to the point," she continued. "Robert set Max up, Savannah."

My eyebrows rose skeptically. Not beating that old drum again.

"I have the documents from the accountant to prove it. Robert forged Max's signature on check authorizations over a period of months. My task was to find a woman and set it up to make it look as though Max had cheated on you and was being blackmailed, hence his need to steal money."

I gasped, my gaze flying over to Max. He was standing as still as a statue and his eyes were without guilt.

"I'm sorry, Savannah. I'm so ashamed of what I did and have regretted my part in Robert's scheme ever since. In my defense it was a very bad time in my life. My aunt was dying and I couldn't afford the surgery she needed. I was so desperate to help her I wasn't thinking straight anymore. Robert told me he would pay for her operation if I would help him. All he wanted to do was get rid of Max from the firm. He promised me you would never see the photos. He would just use them to ask Max to leave the company. The way I saw it, my aunt would have died without her surgery and it wouldn't really matter to Max if he got kicked off the company. I already knew Max's big dream was to start up his own company... and from a couple of documents I'd seen on his desk it was clear he was already in the process of moving away. I swear, I truly never dreamed Robert's intention was to send Max to prison. Not only were they childhood friends, but not once had I seen any kind of animosity between them. My circumstances made it easy for me to fool myself into believing that Robert was a greedy, ungrateful bastard and Max would actually be better off without him. Once Max was taken away, I was immediately fired and told in no uncertain terms that if I was ever to breathe a word about Robert's plot, I would be the next one going to prison for my part in it."

My jaw dropped, and I stared at Lillian in shock.

"That's my part in this sad, sordid story. I'll let Rachel take it from here."

Rachel leaned forward. There was an earnest look on her face. "At that time I was a working girl and a drug addict. I exchanged sex for money, so I was super pleased to get a job that paid me for pretending to have sex with a John. All I had to do was pose for some incriminating photos with him. As Lillian said, it was all staged. The bartender had spiked his drinks and he was out cold the whole time. I was there for twenty minutes tops, then I was gone with my money."

"We do a lot of things for the people we love, but believe us when we tell you Max is innocent," Lillian said softly.

"Robert's still insanely jealous that you chose me and not him, Savannah. He always has been."

I looked at the three of them and felt emotions overwhelm me. This was the missing piece all along. It sounded like the stuff of which movie scripts were made. I shook my head in disbelief, tears pricking at my eyes. Tears blurred my vision and I wiped them away angrily. I looked at the two women. "Thank you for sharing this information with me."

I stood and looked at Max. "I'm sorry, but this is all just too much for me to process and comprehend at once. I-I need a little time to think through all of this. I really need to clear my head. You need to go. Please."

I walked to the door, yanked it open, and stood gripping the door handle. The women cast worried glances at me as they slid past me in the doorway. Max stopped in front of me but I refused to look at him, keeping my gaze firmly on the second button of his shirt. Finally, with the barest of brushes of his lips, he touched my forehead. Then he stepped into the hallway, and I rushed to close the door before a hot tear slid helplessly down my cheek.

I dashed it away. Now was not the time to cry. I needed to think, and needed to think smart for a change. I gave Max and the two women a good ten minutes to leave before I headed downstairs. A good long drive would clear my mind.

The car automatically turned in the direction of the mountains as I drove. Could it really be the anger I had held against Max all these years was unfounded? He had proclaimed his innocence ever since his release, but to hear it from the mouth of someone who had helped to frame him felt surreal. Was it possible this was another big lie? Was Lillian being loyal to Max and corroborating his story of being set up to help him? That still left Rachel, a stranger in the whole saga. Unless she was an Oscar worthy actress, her explanation seemed authentic to me.

My thoughts went back to the night everything turned upside down. Suddenly, I had questions I'd not thought of asking before.

First of all, how had Robert known where to find me that night? Why had he been so helpful in helping me find Max? It was he who had suggested going back to the office. Why hadn't we gone to Max's apartment instead? Why had he allowed me to search Max's desk? Wasn't it risky to have a stranger do that, especially with the sort of sensitive information Max always had? I remembered how easy it had been to find the photos. They had stuck out like a freaking sore thumb in that well-organized drawer. They were *meant* to be found.

Obviously, Robert had played me for an idiot, but instead of feeling upset, I felt electrified and almost dizzy with excitement. My heart was pumping in my chest. I took a deep steadying breath. It didn't work so I pulled over to the side of the road, got out and started to pace on the dirt. I had been wrong about everything.

Max was innocent!

Robert was the guilty party.

I thought about how kind and considerate Robert had been over the years, and it made me feel foolish. True, he had duped me, but not completely. Even though my eyes saw the kindness and accepted his knight-in-shining-armor act as reality, some hidden part of me always knew it wasn't real. No matter how kind he seemed to be, there was always that secret revulsion inside me whenever he touched me. When his fingers brushed against my skin it was the same feeling I had whenever a blue bottle fly landed on my skin. The sensation of wanting to wash my skin clean again.

I had just got confused with all the mixed signals. I was too hurt to see clearly.

Max spoke the truth.

Robert was a liar.

My chest felt tight as I thought about how Robert had offered to donate to the school if only I would help patch things up between them. Why did he do it? Surely, if he was jealous of Max and me being together then why pay to make us get closer? Unless he had a hidden motive. Was he planning to make me betray Max, the way he had manipulated Lillian with money to do his bidding?

A dark blue sedan had slowed down next to me, and a man with gray sideburns put his head out of the window and asked, "Hey Lady, everything okay?"

I was so deep in my own thoughts his appearance made me jump. "I'm good, er... thanks."

"Okay, you stay good, little lady," he said with a nod before speeding away.

I got back into my car, turned it around and headed back home, when Stacey called me.

"I've just taken delivery of twenty desktop computers already loaded with software packages, all courtesy of BB Tech."

I blinked. "What?"

"Yes, that was my reaction too."

My fingers were shaking and gripping the steering wheel hard. "Look, let me get back to you."

I could not breathe. I had been so wrong. If I had still harbored any grudges against Max, they were all erased now. Every last one. He was a good guy. He was always a good guy.

Instead of driving back to my apartment I headed towards Mom's place. I'd promised her I'd drop by sometime later, but since I was so close I might as well go now.

I found her on the couch, reading as usual. Benny was already home and in the kitchen. I'd learned that he was an excellent cook. In fact, he claimed to be better than my mom. Mom looked at me for help, but no way was I getting involved. Not after eating his cornbread. I stuffed another spoonful of the delicious chocolate mousse he had made into my mouth and pretended I couldn't talk with a full mouth.

I sat next to my mother.

"What is it?" she asked.

I looked at her. "What is what?"

"You've got something on your mind. Talk."

I flopped back against the sofa. To be honest I was dying to talk to her about Max and Robert. I started from the beginning, ensuring that I left nothing out.

"... and they both said Robert put them up to it. So, all along, Robert has been playing me for a fool. Max was innocent all along."

"I could have told you that from the beginning. Max is a good guy and a hard worker. I mean, look at him now. How many people do you know who would start a successful business while in prison? Ill-gotten gains are not his thing. For what it's worth, I am glad that you've finally realized what I have been saying all this time."

"What bothers me, though, is how quickly I believed him to be a liar, cheat, and thief. If I loved him so much, how could I have believed the worst of him like that?"

"You were young, pregnant, emotional and probably hormonal. It happens to the best of us. But more importantly, you've come out on the other side stronger."

"I think I owe Max a huge apology. Mom, I have been so nasty to him. I actually took the side of Robert against Max."

She looked at me kindly. "That's life. You did what you thought was right."

"Mom, I fell for one of Robert's schemes."

"Savannah!"

I covered my face with my hands. "I know! I know! I'm so ashamed of myself. All this time I thought Max had betrayed me, turns out I'm the one who has betrayed him. I am surprised he doesn't hate me."

Mom smiled tenderly. "Max could never hate you,

Savannah. He loves you too much. Go to him. Sort things out. I want that boy as my son-in-law. Get him back before some other smart woman decides to snag him for herself."

I gave a weak laugh.

"Off you go," she urged.

I gathered my things and leaned across to kiss her cheek.

"I'll do my best to snag him. I promise."

As I sped through the streets, I tried not to think. If I allowed rational thought to intrude, I might abort my mission, I was so nervous. He must still want me. If not why go to all the trouble of getting Lillian and Rachel to come to my apartment... and that kiss on my forehead. It was tender. Maybe there were still some feelings there for me.

It was not until I was in front of his door that it occurred to me I should have called first to check if he was at home.

I rung the bell a second time and was about to turn away when I heard a sound behind the door. Instantly, the blood rushed to my head. He was home. Then the door opened.

24

MAX

She looked as though she had been about to leave. She looked up at me, her beautiful eyes huge and swimming with some deep emotion. "Ummm. Hi. I hope I'm not disturbing you."

"I was working," I said softly. She was a sight for sore eyes.

"Oh. Okay. I'll come back another time then," she replied quickly, taking a step backwards.

I reached out, grabbed her arm and pulled her inside.

"No you won't. I need a break," I murmured as I kicked the door shut behind us.

I took her bag from her arm and slung it on the hook by the door and guided her through the open plan space towards the large couch. She perched on one end of it.

"Would you like something to eat? Drink?"

"I'm not hungry. Perhaps some water, please."

I walked over to the refrigerator for a bottle. "How is your mother?"

"The leg cast is off now. She's wearing an ankle brace and moving around a bit more."

"That's good to hear. And Benny?"

"He's taking care of her like a mother hen with her baby chick."

"Good. She's in good hands then."

I handed her the bottle of water and sat next to her, deliberately letting my thigh touch hers... and she didn't move away. Good! I slipped my hand along the back of the couch and waited for her to speak. She twisted open the lid of the bottle, took a quick sip, and nervously licked her lips. Against my will, I felt warmth flow over me. It was an effort to restrain myself from pulling her close to me and kissing that plump mouth senseless.

She leaned forward and placed the bottle on the coffee table before turning to me. "One rainy night not too long ago you turned up on my doorstep because things did not add up for you, and you wanted an explanation. Now it's my turn."

I raised my eyebrows. "Oh?"

She nodded slowly. "First of all, I want you to know that I believe you now. You were right about everything. And I'm sorry, truly sorry for not trusting you. Can you forgive me?"

I drew closer to her on the couch and brushed a lock of hair behind her ear. "Forgiven."

She caught me off guard when she threw her arms around me. My arms went around her and I hugged her tight. For some seconds there were no need for words. I just thanked my lucky stars and soaked up the smell and feel of my baby in my arms.

Eventually, she pulled away slightly and looked up at me. "I'm so sorry for all you've been through, Max. I can't even begin to imagine how you must have felt. Being locked away for four years for a crime you did not commit and being abandoned by me too. Must have been so hard."

"Hard? Your absence gutted me, Savannah."

"Yes, I know exactly how you felt. What I took to be your betrayal ripped me to pieces, but now that we know the truth, we can mend things, again? Can't we?" she asked hopefully. Her eyes searched mine. For the first time since my return, I saw them shining with all those old emotions.

I smiled down at her, using my thumb to trace her lips. "Are you saying what I think you're saying, Savannah?"

She nodded. "I just want you to know that there has never been anything between Robert and me. Never. He did try to.. well, replace you, but he never could. I never took him up on any of his offers of something more than friends "

I placed my head against her forehead. "I know."

"It's always been you. Even when I was angry with you, it was only ever you for me."

I brushed my lips against hers. "The same for me. There is only you. No one else. I pretended I was furious with you, but fuck, was that ever a lie."

The first kiss was a soft one, reminiscent of old times. She leaned her head against my shoulder as her fingers buried themselves in my hair. I was already undoing her braid and pulling her onto my lap. My cock was rock-hard beneath her thigh, but I was not going to rush this moment.

No. This was a sacred reconnection.

I kissed her slow and sweet, exploring every sweet nook of her mouth with my tongue. Her hands slipped beneath my t-shirt and I growled at the sensation of her silky soft, warm fingers on my chest. Tightening my grip on her, I sucked her tongue hard. I was pleased to hear her groan low in her throat.

My hand went to the front of her slacks. I soon had the zipper down. Slowly I trailed my fingers along the elastic waist of her panties before slipping them beneath it. I brushed her pussy, it was soaking wet. Her legs parted open in invitation. Quickly, I tore my mouth away from hers, slid her off my lap, and stood. When I extended my hand to hers, she placed her hand in mine and I pulled her up. She pushed her body against mine and wrapped her arms loosely around me, looking up at me.

God, she was so fucking beautiful.

Kissing her softly I reached down to the backs of her thighs and hoisted her up. She curled her legs around my body and I carried her to the bedroom. I put her down next to the bed. She was trembling with need, but I took my time with the buttons on her blouse, leaning down to kiss every inch of shivering skin as it was exposed. Finally, it fluttered to the floor. I found the back snap on her brassiere and undid it. Her gorgeous breasts popped out. I leaned forward and took one then the other hard peak into my mouth. She fell backwards, causing us both to fall in a tangle of limbs. I turned my attention back to her breasts, enjoying the way she squirmed against me, her fingers raking through my hair.

When I was satisfied the nipples were quite swollen, I completely undressed her.

"Play with yourself," I commanded.

Then I stood and looked down at her as I removed my shorts. Her lips were parted, her legs were open wide, and her fingers were circling her wet, pink pussy. I wanted nothing more than to bury myself inside her, but first things first.

I slid down and placed my face between her legs. Oh, the musk-sweet fragrance of her. It filled my nostrils and turned my brain to mush. I swiped my tongue along her slit to gather all that delicious cream and her hips thrust up to meet me. I caught her clit between my lips and sucked softly. A groan of pure pleasure rose from her throat. I licked and sucked at the little nub until I felt her trembling uncontrollably. I knew what I wanted. I wanted her to come in my mouth. It'd been so long since she gushed into my mouth.

I shuffled and lay beside her. "Come on, ride my face, baby."

She swung her legs over my head and lowered her pulsating slit onto my mouth. I lapped at her like a man dying of thirst. It was heaven, then I felt her grip my cock. Oh God! Her thumb slid easily over the head of my wet cock. Precum flowed out and her hair brushed my thigh as she licked it delicately like a cat. As her lips stretched over my cock, I had to fight the need to thrust and bury myself in her throat. Instead, my fingers bit into her ass as I continued to ferociously eat her out. I could tell when I hit particularly sensitive spots by the ripples her convulsing throat made along my cock.

Suddenly, her mouth released my cock while her legs tightened and trembled as her juices gushed into my mouth. Once she had climaxed she went limp on my body.

Gently, I rolled her over, then covered her body with mine once more. I leaned in to kiss her, intoxicated by the headiness of our mixed flavors. I used a thigh to part her legs. She was trembling.

"Max?" she whispered huskily.

I placed the head of my dick at her entrance, and immediately she gripped my buttocks and pulled me forward. Locking her ankles around my waist, she waited, her eyes shining. I felt a rush of possessiveness. This was my woman, and mine only.

"Oh fuck! Savannah," I growled.

"I love you so much, Max. I don't want to be without you

ever again," she rasped breathlessly one second before I thrust hard and deep into her.

Yes, Savannah. I love you too and you will never be without me again.

Our bodies twisted and writhed as our pleasure mounted. This was what it was like before I went to prison. I could feel the difference between us again. That unnatural bitter barrier was gone. There was no holding back. I pressed on, urging her desire to once more meet mine. She did not disappoint. Our mouths fused, swallowing each other's cries of ecstasy as we reached our peaks simultaneously.

Our bodies were drenched in sweat as we lay panting, still joined as one. She took great gulps of air while I buried my face in her hot shoulder.

I waited patiently, waited for her to be ready, then I raised my head and my lips found hers and our bodies were pressing against each other once more. It had always been like this, and I wanted it to be like this always. I would never let Savannah go again. Ever again.

Over and over, we made love that night, making up for those four sad, lost years. We slept on and off then reached for each other throughout the night.

By mid-afternoon on Sunday, we finally made it into the shower. After that I made us eggs, then we curled up on the couch like old times and flipped through the channels on the tv. I wanted her to stay nude, but had to compromise with her wearing one of my t-shirts. Underneath though, she was buck naked. I caressed her cheek when she seemed to gaze off into space.

"A penny for your thoughts?"

"There's something I need to tell you, Max."

"Yeah?"

She sighed and played with the hem of the t-shirt. "Since we're starting with a clean slate, there's something you need to know. Robert was not lying when he said he gave me money. He... well, he said he wanted me to patch things up between the both of you. I... uh... I'm sorry, but I believed him at that time and I thought it was quite a good idea."

"Since we're doing the clean slate thing. I have a confession too."

Her eyes flew up to meet and search mine. "You do?"

I nodded. "Yup."

"What is it?"

"I've had Robert under surveillance since I got out so I knew you had a lunch date with him. Right after receiving those pictures of you and Robert together, out of the blue you changed your mind and accepted my offer... so I thought he had recruited you to be his spy."

"Wow. So why did you let me in?"

"I was going to use you to give him corrupted information."

"Ah... and I walked right into your trap. Now I know why information about Robert's company was lying around and accessible on the first night we spent together. You planted it."

I nodded. "Damn right. The man was trying to destroy me. Of course, I was going to fight back."

"I'm so sorry, Max."

"We've both been angry and hurt for a long time, but the good thing is we've got everything out in the open now. Unless..." I raised my eyebrow. "You have any other confessions to make."

She shook her head. "None that I can think of right now."

"Good."

"Mmm... now that we're on the same page and the air is cleared between us, I don't want Robert to get away with what he has done to us. He's stolen so much from us, and it's time we get it back with interest."

I smiled with amusement. Revengeful Savannah was so cute. "How do you propose we do that, my lovely Savannah?"

She leaned forward, her beautiful eyes flashing. "Well, as far as Robert knows, I hate your guts. Why don't we keep him believing that? I'll put on the act of a lifetime. And, while we're at it, I'll accidentally feed him the corrupted information you left around for me."

I shook my head. "You are sweet, Savannah, and I know you want to help, but I don't want you involved. Robert's my problem not yours."

"No, your problems are mine," she insisted stubbornly. "Do you think I haven't suffered? I lost my baby because of him. I want to be a part of his punishment."

I nodded slowly, the anger I felt returning when I thought of the child we lost, but I forced the anger away. Robert had already taken up too much of my time. This was my time with Savannah and he wasn't going to have one second of it.

"Okay, you can help, but enough about Robert now, let's talk about what we're going to do tonight to make up for all those lost years, hmmm. Any ideas?" I slipped my hand up her thigh.

She dissolved into giggles and I leaned forward and kissed the inside of her thigh. The giggles became sighs. Then all that could be heard were groans of pleasure as our bodies yearned for each other once more.

25

SAVANNAH

I checked my watch again before I returned my gaze to the restaurant door. He was already ten minutes late for our lunch 'date'. This was not how I had envisioned spending my Sunday afternoon, but I was a great believer in moving swiftly. Time was of the essence. The sooner we got Robert dealt with, the sooner Max and I would be able to forget him.

I hid a small smile as I remembered how Max played with my clit while I was on the phone with Robert making plans to meet him. By the time I got off the phone, Max was like a demon. He made me climax twice and even then he was not satisfied. This was the first time I had gone out since I had gone to Max's apartment a few nights ago. I'd had just enough time to stop at my apartment to change clothes before coming to meet Robert.

Impatiently, I checked my watch once more. The bastard was fifteen minutes late.

I looked up at the door and breathed with relief to see his ridiculous blond head. He was flirting with the hostess.

My stomach rolled at his audacity. Now that I was seeing Robert for who he truly was, I knew I had dodged a bullet all those years ago when I had felt no chemistry with him. Thank God, there had been no crackling of electricity the way it was with Max.

Taking a sip from my glass of water, I watched the hostess blush and giggle at whatever Robert, the womanizer, whispered to her. I saw his hand meet hers – probably passing her his card. He threw a parting grin over his shoulder as he made his way towards me. If she knew what was good for her, she would rip that card to pieces and head for the hills. I had never felt so happy to deceive someone in my life. I plastered a big, happy smile on my face as he approached.

"Savannah! It feels as though it has been ages, but I guess we've both been busy."

I offered my cheek for the kiss he bestowed, and resisted the urge to wipe my face when he was done even though the revulsion was even stronger now that I knew the truth.

"I have to say, I was ridiculously elated to get your call." His eyes never left me as he slid into the seat opposite me and picked up the menu. "For a minute there, I thought you'd gone over to the dark side."

A waiter came by. "We'll have two dry Martinis," Robert ordered without looking at him.

The man went away and I pressed my lips together as if I was hiding great pain. "Yes, I allowed Max to seduce me all over again. It was a great mistake, but I'm finally, finally over him. I can't believe how deluded and blind I've been about him. I feel sad to think I've wasted all these years mourning for the loss of him."

Robert stared at me with a mixture of curiosity and glee,

then as if realizing that was not the appropriate reaction, he schooled his features and reached out his hand to gently pat mine. "The important thing is you've finally realized what a snake he is."

I sniffed and nodded. "I truly have. You know, I truly believed he was one of the good guys. Hell, I was going to marry him, but now I know he's just a narcissistic, self-absorbed prick who doesn't give a shit about anyone else but himself. Once he knew I didn't want to be with him he refused to honor his word and fund our lab project. Because of his selfish actions the whole project is now in the lurch. I feel as if I hate him. How could I have thought even for a second he still cared for me? Clearly, all he cares about now is taking revenge on you."

Robert's eyebrows almost disappeared into his hairline. "Taking revenge on me?"

"Yes, taking revenge on you," I repeated, injecting what I thought was the right amount of vindictive anger. "It's all he can talk about. I mean, he's obsessed with you. It's actually ugly to watch. To be honest I think he's planning something, some trap either for you or your business."

"Really?" His voice was soft, but there was now a hard glint in his eyes.

I nodded. "Yes, I believe so."

He leaned back in his chair. There was a strange expression on his face, the first sign of suspicion and doubt. His fingers played with the knife as he spoke. "This is a dramatic change of heart for you. What happened to cause this 180 degree turn?"

Let the real acting begin. I looked down as if I was ashamed, then up again so I could see his expression.

"It's a bit humiliating, but you're an old friend so I'll tell you. He's been secretly having sex with strangers he meets online. More fool me to expect a leopard to change its spots, huh?"

"Mmm... yes," he muttered distractedly.

"I'm so furious. He's really let the school down bad. I wish there was something I could do, but there isn't."

"Hmmm..."

The waiter came back with the martinis. He wanted to know if we were ready to order, but Robert waved him away.

"Anyway," I said, "I'm glad I got all that off my chest. It's time for me to finally move on."

"Yes, yes, good." He raised his glass to his lips and took a sip. "So... uh... did he ever reveal anything about his plans for revenge?"

I frowned, as if I was trying to recollect a memory. "Well, I once saw a file with your company's name on it on his desk. I didn't open it, of course, but I kinda wish now I had. It's wrong what he did to you and what he is still planning to do. I'm sorry, Robert, I didn't look. You've been good to me and I've never done anything to repay you."

"Hmm... I suppose now that Max has let you down, you need another benefactor, don't you?"

I nodded. "Yes, we do."

"I could help..." He let his voice trail away.

I widened my eyes. "Really?"

"Yes, and... perhaps in return, only if you wanted to, you could help me find out how Max is planning to ruin my business."

"Oh, that would mean me seeing him again," I murmured doubtfully.

"Don't worry." Watching me keenly, he smiled bravely. "It's okay. I never want to force you to do anything that would make you feel uncomfortable. No, of course not. I'll find another way to save my business and myself."

I pretended to think for a few seconds, before I spoke again. "You know what, I'll do it for you. You've always been good to me and you deserve the same loyalty from me. I won't sleep with him again, but I'll try to get close to him and this time when he talks about you I won't shut the conversation down, but encourage him to tell me more. It'll be easy enough for me as he still wants to see me, it's just he wants those other women too."

"My God, Savannah. That would be great." There was a big smirk on his face.

"Feels like I'm spying on him though," I ventured tentatively. My capitulation shouldn't seem too easy.

He leaned forward eagerly. "Of course, you are not *spying* on him. Think about it, Savvie. The man wants to destroy me. You're doing the right thing to stop him. Not only are you helping me, you're helping the school, and those poor kids that don't have anyone else but you."

I nodded slowly, consideringly. "You're right. What he is planning to do to you is wrong."

He leaned back and considered me gravely. "Thank you, Savannah. I will never forget what you're doing for me."

Our conversation was interrupted by our server coming to take our orders. I stayed silent and Robert ordered for both of us. As soon as the waiter left, he turned his attention back to me.

"I want you to be very careful. I don't think you are in any danger from him, but it's better to be safe than sorry."

"I'll be careful. In fact, I might even be able to take some photos of his files for you."

His eyes shone with excitement. "My God, Savvie, that

would be amazing. If you can get your hands on some of those files I'm sure I'll be able to turn the tables on him. With your help I'll defeat him. I feel that in my bones."

"All right. I'll do that for you."

"Well, let me start showing you my appreciation right now."

I raised an eyebrow. "What did you have in mind?"

"Every girl likes a spa day. You choose where. You choose when. I'll foot the bill. You know money is no object to me, so choose the best. I'll throw in a few extra thousand for a shopping trip as well. What do you say?"

I looked into his cunning eyes and felt a sense of exhilaration at the freedom I now had from his lies and schemes. Was this how easily he had manipulated all the parties four years ago? As Max had predicted, he had simply reached for the wallet he had inherited from his father.

He stroked my hand gently. This was worse than a fly landing on my hand. I felt as though I was being touched by a reptile.

"Well? Will you follow through on the plan? Stick it out with him for a few more weeks, figure out what he's working on and get it to me, so we stop him once and for all. Hopefully this time he stays down. I get my revenge for him trying to put me out of business, you get your revenge for him breaking your heart again. Do we have a deal?"

I looked at him, amazed. How had I not seen Robert's true colors all this time? I was grateful that there had always been something that kept me from going beyond friendship with him. He was wicked and devious to the core.

"Savvie?"

"Yes?"

"Do we have a deal?"

"Yes. We have a deal."

He patted my hand. "Good girl."

The meal went by in a blur. Finally, we said our good-byes and I was in my car heading home. As I thought about everything that had transpired, I was grateful for the fact that I had come to my senses in time. My phone jarred me out of my thoughts as it rang. I tapped the screen of the dashboard to activate the Bluetooth call feature.

"Hey, Mom!"

"Are you busy right now?"

"I'm actually heading home. Is everything all right?"

"How far away are you from me?"

"Ah... maybe fifteen minutes."

"Good. Could you be a dear and swing by here, please?"

My heart skipped a beat. "Is everything okay?"

"Yes. Just come. Please."

Without another word she hung up. My heart began to race. She had not sounded as if she was in pain or anything, but to be summoned so suddenly was not normal.

I switched lanes and headed in the direction of her house with my foot heavy on the gas pedal. Exactly ten minutes later, I parked in her driveway. At least I was not being met with ambulances. I raced inside.

"Mom! Where are you?"

"On the back porch, darling."

I raced through the house and came to a grinding halt at the scene before me.

There was a trail of red rose petals leading from the doorway to the table that was set up on the porch. A huge heart had been formed by the petals around the table and on top of it sat a sign with the words, *Will you marry me?*

Benny stood behind my mother, his arms draped loosely around her waist. She was beaming and had her left hand outstretched. There was no mistaking the engagement ring on her finger.

I looked from him to her, then back at him. He took my mother's hand and walked towards me. Tears suddenly filled my eyes and I clapped my hand over my mouth. My mother hugged me tightly, matching tears glittering in her eyes.

I hugged her back. "I'm so happy for you, Mom. You deserve this. You really do."

She laughed and sobbed at the same time as she looked over at Benny.

"I told you she would approve."

I pulled back laughing and wiping at my damp cheeks. I looked from one to the other.

"I knew there was something going on between you two. I just knew it."

"Honestly, Savannah, there wasn't anything. This fella plays his cards close to his chest, you know."

"And your mother played clueless too. I'm a shy guy but heck I must have dropped enough sweet crumbs to lead Hansel and Gretel back home. And still she pretended not to notice. I do thank you for your approval, Savannah. It means the world to us. I know I can never replace your father..."

"And I would never ask you to do that. I am genuinely happy for you both Benny. I couldn't have asked for a better man for my mother, after my father, of course."

"Will you be my maid of honor, darling?" Mom asked, her cheeks tinged with red.

"Of course. I would be offended if you asked anyone else and I would have had to disown you."

Mom just laughed.

"And I'd like to ask Max to be my best man, if that's okay with you." Benny looked at me with a hesitant smile.

"Max?" My eyebrows went up. "That's an unexpected choice."

"He and Benny have built quite a rapport and bond, you know. He's been to see me a couple of times and they've hit it off quite well."

"But if that would make you uncomfortable in any way..." Benny started. I could see the disappointment in his eyes and hear it in his voice.

"I don't have a problem with Max being your best man. Not at all. Ask him." I smiled at both of them.

"Sure?" Mom asked.

"I guess if we're sharing good news, now is as good a time to share mine. Max and I worked things out and we've decided to give our relationship a new start."

My mother grabbed my hands and squealed. "That's wonderful news. Perhaps we could have a double wedding."

I laughed. "No, Mom. Max and I are going to take it one day at a time. We have a lot of stuff to get over. We are nowhere near wedding bells. Besides, your day is your day. I won't take away any of your shine. Do you have a date yet?"

"Priscilla wants it to be tomorrow."

"Mother! Can't wait to get into his pants, can you?"

"Look at him. Would you want to wait?" Mom quipped.

It was my turn to blush as I turned to look at Benny. His face was scarlet.

"I think that's my cue to exit and leave you ladies for a bit," he mumbled.

He leaned down to kiss my mother's cheek then mine. I suspected that had I not been there they would have kissed on the lips instead. We both watched as he went inside. I took my mother's hand.

"So, tell me how this proposal went. I want every little detail. Did you suspect anything? Did he go down on one knee? I want details!"

"Well, there I was doing the Sunday gardening as usual, when he pops up and says there's something on the back porch he wanted me to look at if I had the time."

We spent an hour catching up and recounting her surprise proposal before I left for home. As I walked towards my door I saw Max leaning against it holding a couple of familiar bags from one of our favorite take-out places.

"I should give you a key," I said softly.

"Yes, you should," he replied, a slow grin spreading on his face.

While he reheated the food I had a quick shower, and by the time I came out a tantalizing aroma filled the apartment. I dressed hastily and went to the kitchen to find he had put out two plates and the table was resplendent with fried rice, sweet and sour prawns, cashew-nut chicken, barbequed pork in honey sauce, and chili noodles.

I sat down and dug in, not realizing how long ago lunch had been until I heard my stomach growl. We ate in relative silence, speaking only to ask for condiments and extra servings. When at last we were both satisfied, we retreated to the couch with the remote control. I curled up against Max's side like old times while he lounged on the couch. He flipped aimlessly through the channels.

I reveled in the feeling of his arms around me. There was a newness and freshness about us. I wondered if he felt it too.

I looked up at him, reaching my hand up to caress his cheek. He looked down at me and smiled.

"Love you."

"Love you more." He leaned down to brush his lips against mine. As the kiss deepened I thought about all the things I wanted to tell him about my day, but they could all wait. Right now, I just wanted to be where I was, doing what I was doing.

Everything else could definitely wait.

26

MAX

I fell back laughing as Savannah hit me hard with the pillow.

"I was sworn to secrecy," I said in my defense.

"But you could have told me!" She swung at me again and I ducked.

"Then it wouldn't have been a secret, would it? Besides, I'm sure it was as wonderful a surprise for you as it was for Priscilla. I wish I could have seen the look on her face when she walked out onto the back porch and saw the effort the guy had gone to."

"You don't keep secrets from people you go balls deep in!"

I grinned at her and wiggled my eyebrows. "I'm always going to be balls deep in you, babe, but the plan is to keep a reasonable amount of secrets from you. Don't you want Christmas and birthday surprises?"

"You still could have told me," she grumbled, before giving me a push. I grabbed her and let myself fall onto the bed. As she lay sprawled on top of me, I intertwined my fingers with hers and we looked at each other.

"I hope she liked the ring we picked out."

"She loved it, but I still don't get how you found the time to help Benny go ring shopping."

"Where there's a will, there's a way. The ring was selected and bought on the same day."

"It was very kind of you to help."

I looked into Savannah's eyes and smiled gently. "Actually, it was practice for me, for when I go ring hunting for you."

Her beautiful eyes were like a green galaxy. Gold and honey colored stars swirled in them. I smoothed a lock of hair away from her forehead and kissed her. Her lips parted beneath mine as my tongue traced their fullness. I pulled her more fully on top of me and held her close as she straddled me, grinding against my cock slowly. I was already hard for her, but I resisted the urge to meet her and instead gently rolled her off me. She protested by gripping my shirt and trying to remain on top. I laughed softly.

"If we're not careful, all we will do is stay in bed all day every day."

"What's wrong with that?" She pouted.

"Because I have an office to run."

She leaned up on her elbow and trailed a hand along the front of my shirt. "I haven't told you about Robert. I met him at lunch."

My eyes narrowed. I was not totally okay with the idea of her helping me bring Robert down, but she seemed determined to get involved. "You did?"

"Yup."

"Why didn't you tell me?"

"Because I knew exactly what I wanted to do and I didn't want you to worry about it."

I frowned. "I will always be worried when you are around him. I know what he is capable of. You don't."

"I believe I now know him quite as well as you. I met him in a public place. Anyway, long story short he took my bait, hook, line and sinker. I've convinced him that I hate your guts and will spy on you for him. The funny thing is I got the feeling I wasn't the first spy he's recruited. He seemed too comfortable with the idea. There was a smoothness to the whole discussion. As if he's done it all before."

"You aren't the first, and I know who they are as well."

She looked taken aback. "Wow! Really?"

I laughed. "There is very little about my business I don't know, Savannah. I have spies of my own in his organization too. Robert has no idea how much rubbish I've fed him through them. By now he should have got the codes that Paul stole from my safe."

"Paul?"

"The assistant Rick hired for me while I was in prison. The minute I met him, I knew he was on Robert's payroll. There are three others scattered between research and development as well."

"So, really you don't need me at all." She ran a forefinger along my eyebrow.

I looked into the green galaxy. "I need you to complete my life, Savannah. Without you everything is colorless, tasteless, and without meaning."

"I know and I feel that too, but I really, really, really want to be part of everything that's going on. I actually had fun today, knowing I was helping you bring him down. I liked the idea of being a double agent."

I smiled at her simple, child-like delight. "Oh, Savannah. You will be the best mole he has ever had. He knows he's been getting crap so far and although he has managed to salvage something, it is nowhere close to where he needs to be just to keep up with my firm. I suspect he's near his breaking point and you're going to give him the little push he needs to tip him over the edge."

"Are things that bad for him?

"He's been doing his digging and snooping, but so have I. I can't give you the details right now, but trust me when I say Robert is in so much financial shit, sinking me should be the least of his worries. It'll be a fucking miracle if the check he gives you clears. The noose is closing in on him. I'm just ensuring that I cross every 't' and dot every 'i' before I drop my final bomb. But in the meantime, we are going to give him what he thinks he wants – my new software."

"So the info I take to him will cause him to blow a fuse?"

"He's going to do more than blow a fuse. He's going to explode. And when he does, he will make the wrong move. And we'll have him where we want him. And it will be all thanks to you."

She smiled at me. "I'll do my best. It's payback for what he did to us."

"Let's give it a few days though. It would seem a tad suspicious if you got your hot little hands on my prized software in less than twenty-four hours after he ropes you in. Let it appear to happen naturally."

"How about we delay until he has to call me. That way we know he's getting desperate."

"Good idea. I'm going to drop a few hints at work about the new software as well. When the information gets back to him, he'll become anxious. I predict he will be calling you before the week is out."

"And when he does?"

"Make him sweat. Let him call a couple of times first.

Then when we're ready, you'll answer. We will let the chips fall from there."

"Can you imagine me being a Mata Hari type creature?" She smiled sultrily as her hand reached down to trace the front of my pants. Though her touch was light, it made me hard in just a few seconds. She smiled as she continued to stroke me.

"If you keep that up, neither one of us is going to make it out of here for a whole week," I warned huskily as I rubbed my hand across the outline of her nipples beneath her t-shirt. She leaned over to kiss me and I could feel my resolve slipping away.

"Would that be such a bad thing?" she whispered against my lips, her tongue coming out to trace my lips lightly.

I grinned wolfishly. "Sure, I can put off my meetings, but don't you have a grand assembly planned for the official opening of the renovated lab tomorrow? Think of those disappointed children and parents and donors."

She groaned and sighed as she flopped onto her back. I laughed.

"Duty calls." She rolled her eyes.

I laughed at her expression. "How about a quickie?"

Her hand slid into my pants and I stifled a soft groan.

"You're a stubborn little wench. Did you know that?"

"I've found that it pays to be stubborn. You usually end up getting what you want."

With a quick move, she slid down my body. I raised my hips and she slid my pants and boxers half way down my thigh. As her warm mouth covered my cock, I felt fire lick through my veins.

My hands tangled in her hair as she worked my cock.

When I felt as though I was going to explode, I pulled her up to me and stripped us both.

I pulled her atop me as I lay back and held her tightly with her pussy hovering over my cock. With one thrust upward, I buried myself into her, loving the feel of her heat and wetness closing tightly around me. She arched her back and ground her pussy down on me as I fucked her hard. I watched desire dance across her face as she rode me. I felt her legs tremble and her pussy grow even hotter as her juices came gushing from her climax.

Taking advantage of her lapse in activity, I rolled her down to her back.

I pulled her legs around my waist as I thrust hard and deep. From the tingles in my groin, I knew I was close to my climax. As the first rush went through my cock, I buried my face in her neck, my eyes closed so tightly I saw sparks. And as I poured my seed into her, a strange thought full of clarity flashed into my mind: was this the moment we created a son or a daughter?

It was hard to leave Savannah's bed, but my plans for the future now that I had Savannah's dreams to care for were bigger than ever.

As I drove home, my brain was already clear about the changes I would make to the program that Savannah passed on to Robert. But we would stick to the plan. If my guess was correct, Robert's time was short and, if the reports I was receiving were true about his accounts, the powers that be would soon be breathing down his neck.

We would wait until he got even more impatient and desperate. Then he would get what he had been after. Then all hell would break loose.

27

SAVANNAH

I checked my watch anxiously as I sat in Max's car in the restaurant parking lot. I fidgeted with the bracelet on my wrist as I looked around. Max's hand covered mine and I felt his fingers close over mine.

"Relax, babe."

"But what if he leaves before I get there?"

"He won't. We're watching him. He's waiting for you." His phone pinged and he looked down at it and gave a low whistle, before returning his attention to me. "And it looks like he's upped the ante this time too. Has he ever had anyone else at any of your meetings?"

"No. It's always been him alone."

"Well, he's got company tonight. I guess he is very desperate to expose them like this."

"Expose what? Expose who?"

"You will see," Max said mysteriously.

I could not get anything else out of him so I peered through the windshield into the gathering dusk and recalled every phone call from Robert that I had deliberately missed as per Max's instructions. The voice messages reeked of panic. When I responded it was only to tell him I'd been busy with school, but I'd be seeing Max on Friday night, and I'd let him know when I had something. I then called him around one on Saturday morning and whispered that I'd found a flash drive which I thought contained the program he wanted and managed to copy it. We made arrangements to meet.

And here I was, waiting in the wings like an actress awaiting my cue to enter the stage.

My phone rang, breaking into my thoughts. Robert. I looked at Max.

"What do I tell him?"

"You're five minutes away."

I nodded and answered the phone.

"Savannah? Where on earth are you?" Robert's tone was almost shrill.

"Five minutes away. Got caught up in traffic. Sorry."

I hung up before he could say anything else.

Max ran his fingers along my cheek, his voice grave. "Are you sure you want to do this, Savannah? As I said before, Robert is a dead man walking with or without this flash drive."

"He killed my baby and stole four years of my life so I absolutely want and need to be part of his downfall."

"Okay. He has company and I don't know if that's a good thing or bad thing, but I'm here and I'll be watching like a hawk."

"Stop worrying about me. I'll be fine."

I sat for a minute longer, taking deep breaths, then I turned to Max and smiled. "It's showtime."

Max nodded, but did not smile. I knew he wasn't totally happy with my involvement in his revenge plans, but as I told him this decision was not his to take. Clutching the flash drive in my hand I got out of the car. I closed the door and suddenly I felt flustered and nervous. Maybe it was Max's anxiety that got to me or maybe I wasn't cut out to be a double spy, but I felt like a nervous wreck. Ignoring the voice screaming for me to get back into the safety of Max's car I literally ran into the restaurant.

I almost screamed when I barreled into Robert in the foyer. His eyes flashed at me. All I could think of was that it was a good thing I had entered when I did. Otherwise, he would have seen me getting out of Max's car. And that would have been a dead giveaway.

He scowled at me. "I was beginning to get worried. You're never late. If anything, you're always the one waiting for me."

"Sorry," I mumbled, surprised by how impatient he seemed to be.

He took me by the elbow and unceremoniously steered me towards a booth in the corner. I felt his fingers bite into my flesh as we walked quickly. I could feel tension emanating from him in waves. Gone was the suave, sophisticated man of our previous meetings. And in his place was a tightly wound and tense man. As Max had warned there were others at the table – four men to be exact. Something about the men bothered me. They seemed cold and watchful. My heart began to pound. I did not like the look of them or my situation. My head swung around to look at Robert.

"I wasn't expecting company."

He smiled tightly. "Call it a staff meeting. As you're now a member of my staff, do take a seat."

Without ceremony, he pushed me into the booth ahead of him, effectively sandwiching me between himself and another man.

"Do you have what these dimwits have failed to find?"

I looked around at the table at the surly expressions which followed Robert's insult. I opened my hand to reveal the flash drive. He smiled coldly and looked around.

"It seems I should have hired pussy from the get-go instead of you dicks and the job would have been done long ago. Maybe I wouldn't be losing clients to that asshole faster than a whore opens her legs."

Something was very wrong. I shot to my feet. "I'd like to go please."

Robert grabbed my hand and tugged me back down. "Not so fast, sweet cheeks. We're going to check the information on your drive and make sure it's legit. Let's see if it's the real thing or more of the rubbish he's been feeding me until now. If I wasn't sure I have my tracks covered I'd be tempted to think you're all double-crossing me and working for him behind my back."

Cold sweat beaded on my forehead. "I want to leave. I don't like the vibe here."

"Let her go, Robert." The man to my right spoke.

"No fucking way. I want to make sure this is legit. Because if it isn't," he fixed me with a glare, "she's going to have to explain herself, just like you'll all have to explain yourselves. For the money I've spent on the sorry lot of you, at the very least, I should get something of use."

I sank back in silence, not daring to look at the others directly. A furtive glance here and there showed they were just as nervous as I was. We all held a collective breath as one of the men, obviously an expert in the matter, inserted the flash drive into his laptop. I felt as though my heart was going to beat right out of my chest. Everything seemed to move in slow motion. Was Max nearby as he had promised he would be? I was about to look around when the man suddenly slammed his laptop shut and shouted. "Fuck, it's malware. That will corrupt your whole system."

Robert moved so fast I didn't see it coming, let alone have time to react. His hand shot out and grabbed my wrist in a vice-like grip. "You fucking worthless, lying bitch! You've set me up, haven't you?"

I looked at him in a shocked panic. I'd never seen Robert like this before. He was like a stark raving madman. His eyes bulged and a big angry vein throbbed wildly in his temple.

"You're hurting me," I gasped.

"After everything I've done for you, you spread your legs for that piece of shit, spin me a bullshit story, and betray me."

He raised his hand and, reflexively, my free hand came up to block my face. Fortunately, the man next to me caught and held Robert's hand before it could connect with my face.

"What the hell do you think you're doing? Do you think we're going to sit here and let you hit a woman?"

"Thank you, Steven. I'll take it from here," said a cold hard voice.

Six pairs of eyes swiveled towards Max as he stood a few feet away from the table. He held my gaze for a few moments and I felt calm sweep over me. Then he looked at each of the men, except Steven who had stood up for me, and was obviously in Max's employ.

"Was it worth it, gentlemen? I could have told you it wasn't, but why take my word, I'm just an ex-convict." The men had the grace to hang their heads shamefully.

Max turned his derisive gaze on Robert. "Hello, Robert."

"Well, well, well. Come to rescue your girl?" Robert asked. He was trying to appear cool and sarcastic, but his voice came out shill and desperate.

"Of course," Max drawled.

I cried out when Robert's fingers bit suddenly into my forearm.

Max held up a flash drive similar to the one he had given me. "Let her go, Robert, unless … you no longer want this, of course." His voice vibrated with anger.

You could have cut the silence with a knife. It seemed to me as though the strange hush had fallen over the restaurant too. Beyond Max's shoulder, I could see a tall man speaking quietly to what seemed to be the restaurant manager. The manager looked worried but the tall man patted his shoulder and kept speaking softly. I assumed it was another of Max's men. I looked back at Max who was staring at Robert. He moved the little device in his hand as if it was a fan.

"Do you want it or… nah?"

Without a word, Robert released my hand and stood. I wasted no time in dashing out of the booth away from him. Max pulled me to his side and instantly, his warmth flowed into me.

"Perhaps you'd like to ask your monkeys to leave so we can get down to business."

Robert made a dismissive move and his men scrambled out of the booth in record time and made their getaway, not one looking back at us.

"Want me to stay, boss?" Steven asked.

Max shook his head. "No, but good work. See you at the office tomorrow morning."

As Steven left Max spoke again. "Have a seat, Robert."

Robert sat and Max slid into the seat opposite and left enough space for me so I slipped in beside him. He dangled the flash drive in front of Robert, but as Robert reached for it, he pulled it back and laughed softly.

"Not so fast. There are a few things that I want as well."

"I knew it. Money."

"I don't want your dirty money, Robert. All I want in exchange for the damn software is for you to stay out of our lives for good."

Robert's laugh was brittle and humorless. "That's it? You could have at least asked me to throw in a vacation for two." He turned his gaze on me. "Maybe one day you'll tell me what he's got in his pants that's so damn addictive, huh?"

"Fuck you, Robert. What part of stay out of our lives for good do you not get?" Max snarled.

"Jeez. Calm down. I was just messing with her."

"And if you ever cross our paths again, there will be hell to pay. This I promise."

"Yeah, yeah." Robert put his hand out, his voice was deliberately bored and dismissive.

Without another word, Max handed him the flash drive. We watched as he inserted it into his own laptop and tapped the keys. He frowned at the screen for a few moments. Then I saw his face light up. He grinned maniacally and tapped the keys a few more times. I heard a few chimes and he laughed, before looking up at Max.

"You always were the whiz kid with code, but I was the moneybags with the real plan, and you forgot that. We made a great team until you got in my way. No hard feelings, bro, it's a pity you didn't stay out of the way when you got out of prison. No. You had to try and get revenge. Now, I have you where I want. This," he gestured to the laptop screen, "together with my secret Gennie software is going to put my business back where it belongs. So, say goodbye to all those clients you've been stealing. They'll come running back to me with their tails between their legs, begging me to take them back. It's going to be sweet!"

"Gennie software?" Max asked, and I heard the surprise in his voice.

Robert threw his head back and laughed. "Yes, you didn't know about my little Gennie, did you? Well, no doubt you'll hear about it from your clients. Before the year ends, BB Tech will be mine. I know I shouldn't gloat, but it's not every day you get to destroy someone twice in their lifetime."

We watched as he closed his laptop and placed it into his crocodile skin briefcase. Then he stood and looked down on us. His gaze moved to me and he smiled coldly.

"We could have had it all, Savannah, but you had to choose him. I could have given you the moon, but you settled for his worthless rocks. You're not very smart."

"Not everyone can be bought, Robert." I lashed out angrily.

He caressed his briefcase. "I won't send you to prison this time. I think you will find the healing is not rewarding; the hurting... is rewarding."

He turned on his heels and walked out. I watched him go with my jaw dropped. I turned to Max as he disappeared through the door.

"You've got someone to mug him and take it back, right?"

"Nope." He picked up the menu calmly.

"But you heard what he said. He's going to use your Gennie and your own software to bankrupt you."

"Yup" He raised his finger and a waiter was by his side almost instantly. "We're in a celebratory mood. What's your special tonight?"

The waiter rattled off the options and Max placed his order and I just said, "same for me," as I didn't hear a word the waiter said. When we were alone once more, I turned to him.

"You're not worried at all?"

"Nope."

"But I don't understand. You gave him your software. You worked hard on that. And he's going to use it to destroy your company."

He placed his hand over mine and smiled.

"And it's okay, Savannah. I have everything I want right here. And he is out of our lives for good."

"How can you trust him? He's lied so many times. What makes you think he won't break his promise to leave us alone and the next thing you know is the police will be on your doorstep again?"

"Because he will have other things to deal with. Relax babe and trust me when I say Robert is officially in our past."

I frowned. "And what on earth did he mean by that healing and hurting line?"

"Ze healing is not rewarding; ze hurting... is rewarding. Robert's only call to exquisite taste is a line from *Koyaanisqatsi*, one of the most hypnotic films of all time."

"*Koyaanisqatsi*? I've never even heard of it."

"Then we must watch it together. It is more prescient now than when it was made almost forty years ago."

Another waiter arrived with a bottle of champagne which he proceeded to pour into two flutes.

Max raised his glass to me. "To new beginnings, my Love."

I clinked my glass against his. "To new beginnings."

I took a sip of the bubbly liquid, loving how the cool bubbles slid down my throat. I had no idea what the future would bring, but I felt a sense of calm and hope.

Now and forever, I would trust Max completely.

28

MAX

https://www.youtube.com/watch?v=dsCl2kXJca4

-What a feeling-

I swung Savannah into my arms and kicked the bedroom door shut behind us. There had been so many stages in our rekindled romance, but tonight truly felt like a new beginning.

I laid her on the bed and covered her body with mine. I kissed her and she began to pull at my clothing. I pulled back to gaze down at her face.

"God, you're so beautiful I sometimes can't believe you're mine."

She smiled dreamily up at me. "You're beautiful too... and sexy, very freaking sexy." She reached up to bury her hand in my hair and pulled my mouth back to hers.

In the tangle of arms and legs we undressed, as our hot bodies pressed against each other urgently. At last, even the smallest scrap of silk was discarded and with a long, low growl, I entered her. She arched back as her lower body pushed up to meet mine. It was hard and fast as we devoured each other hungrily. Soon our cries of ecstasy echoed throughout the room. It seemed as if we could not get enough of each other, but that had always been us.

Never could get enough of each other.

Later as I lay with Savannah sleeping in my arms, my brain was on fire for the series of events I needed to instigate. Gently, so as not to wake her, I slipped out of bed and padded to the living room, taking my cell phone with me. The clock on the microwave read half past four. I picked up the phone and dialed. It rang a few times before a sleepy voice came over the line.

"Hello."

"Sorry to pull you from your bed, dude. But it's time."

"He bought it?"

"Hook, line and sinker. He even checked it on the spot to make sure it was the real thing."

Jasper Jackson chuckled on the other end of the line. "You sure read him right."

"Yes, it's the one thing he forgot. His enemy knows him too well. You ready?"

"Just say when."

I smiled in the dark. "When."

I listened to Jasper tap a few keys on his end. "Done."

"How long?"

"Thirty-six to forty-eight hours. That should give him enough time to make his move."

"If I know him, he's already loading it onto his company's platform. This is the system he jerks off to. He thinks it's going to solve all his problems."

"Good. He won't know what hit him."

"Thanks, Jasper. The balance will be in your account first thing Monday morning."

"No problem."

I disconnected the call and sat looking out of the window for a few moments. The world was asleep. I thought I would feel something different, but there was a vague feeling of relief. He was gone from our lives.

"Who were you talking to just now?"

I turned to see Savannah standing in the doorway. I smiled and went to stand in front of her, pulling her into my arms.

"Just a friend about a software issue I'm having."

"At this time of the morning?"

"No time like the present, babe." I kissed her softly as my body brushed hers.

She chuckled as she raised her arms to wrap around my neck. "You're insatiable."

"Can you blame me? I sat in a prison cell and longed for you for four long years, Savannah."

"I know. We have so much to make up for, but I don't want to be the death of you."

"Bury me at your feet."

"You've become morbid in your old age, but you'll do."

She stroked my already hard cock and led me back to bed.

WE DID NOT STIR until almost the next morning and only rolled out of bed because we were having lunch with Priscilla and Benny.

Lunch was a light-hearted affair. I only half-listened as they discussed their wedding plans. It seemed they were looking at a Christmas wedding. After lunch Priscilla and Savannah went off to the bedroom and Benny and I headed to the garage, where he kept a good bottle of cognac.

He poured us a glass each. The aroma of it filled my nostrils. I raised my glass. "Here's to married life."

"To married life," he echoed, taking a sip. "After fifty-two years, I'm going to have to turn in my bachelor card, but it's worth it. Priscilla is all I've ever wanted in a woman."

"It's clear that she feels the same way about you."

He sat on a battered armchair and looked sideways at me. "Savannah looks at you the way my Pris looks at me, you know.

I smiled. "I know."

"You should do something about that. Something like what I did."

"Oh, I intend to do just that, Benny. I have a few more loose ends to tie up, but as soon as those are done, I'll be joining you by hanging up my bachelor ways."

"I gotta say, we snagged the two best women out there."

"I'll drink to that."

29

MAX

https://www.youtube.com/watch?v=ydwBQhpFRıQ
-unstoppable-

I went into the office the next morning. It was business as usual. But then about noon, there was a buzz. I could hear loud discussions taking place and shouts of disbelief. Not even five minutes later, there was a frantic knock on my door.

"Come in!" I invited.

"Max!" Nina, one of my software specialists burst into the office. "You're never going to believe what happened! Have you seen the midday news?"

"No."

Without hesitation, she put my laptop on my desk and tapped the keys a few times before turning the screen back to me. There was a rebroadcast.

Information coming into the newsroom is that Robert Steinberg's company is responsible for a breach of client confidentiality. The breach occurred when their latest software malfunctioned, compromising the private information of clients. This compromise has led to some of their clients' databases being hacked and exposed, resulting in losses which are already in the millions and still climbing. As we speak, the lawsuits are piling up and from all indications Steinberg is in a lot of hot water. More at seven as we continue to track this developing story.

"Hmmm. Interesting."

"But I don't understand. Isn't this the same software system we're supposed to be working on for release next week?"

"One and the same."

"But how did he get it?"

"I gave it to him."

Her eyes popped. "You *what!?*"

I smiled. "Don't worry about it, Nina. Worry about this instead: the influx of customers who are going to be beating down our doors to reverse this damage."

"It's already started. Sales have already been flooded with calls."

"Good. Christmas bonuses are looking good this year."

She smiled and shook her head. "I don't know what you did, but I'm glad you know how to fight dirty. I wouldn't want to cross you."

I laughed. "That's good to know."

She left the office and I leaned back in my chair. Then I summoned my secretary.

"What's going on?" she asked, her face showing nothing except a natural curiosity about the unusual activity going on around her.

I marveled at her coolness. "Nothing much, other than you're fired."

"Sorry?" I could tell by her expression she honestly thought she had heard me wrong.

"You're fired, Sheila."

"What? Why?" she asked, shocked.

"Because you've been spying for Robert."

She frowned. "No, I haven't. I swear I'm nobody's spy. I mean he gave me his number, but I never called him. I don't know what he told you, but there's nothing going on between us."

"Did you take me for a fool, Sheila?" I asked softly.

"No, of course not, but what you are accusing me of is simply not true. How could it possibly be true when he only gave me his number a few days ago? You saw it yourself. Here, in your office."

"Robert didn't slip his number to you a few days ago. He hired you to apply for this job before I got out of prison."

She shook her head vigorously, but something flashed in her eyes. Fear. "No, that's not true."

"What are the odds that a woman who applies for the post of my secretary would be the doppelganger of the woman I was head over heels in love with?"

"We're not exactly alike," she said defensively. "We just have the same coloring and build. Strange as it may seem, these kinds of coincidences do happen in life."

"You were supposed to seduce me, weren't you?"

"No. Of course not. Not at all. It was just a coincidence. I swear it, Max. I'm not Robert's spy. I don't even like him. He gives me the creeps. I swear——"

"Don't bother, Sheila. I happen to have proof. The program that Robert stole from me bears the hidden code that I made sure only you had access to."

She took a step backwards guiltily, but her head shook vehemently in denial. "No. You have to believe me. It's not me. Someone else, I don't know who, must have stolen the program from my desk. It wouldn't exactly be a difficult feat as my desk is pretty much unguarded whenever I'm off running errands or away at lunch."

"I also took the liberty of having you investigated. Some intriguing things that are none of my business came up, but what interested me were some odd payments into your bank account from a shell company in Belize."

Her face reddened suddenly when she knew I knew about her feme fatale dominatrix website.

"The only reason I kept you on was because it suited me for him to think you were still his inside person. Now, I no longer have use for you. You have thirty minutes to clean your stuff out of your desk and leave."

A cunning expression crossed her face. "You mean you're not going to take any other action against me."

"No. Never having to see your face again will be reward enough."

"Thank you, Max. Thank you. I'm really sorry. He forced me—"

"Don't push your luck, Sheila. Get out now before I change my mind."

She fled then.

NEWS KEPT COMING in throughout the rest of the afternoon. By the time I tuned in to the evening news, the writing was on the wall for Robert, and I knew it would not take long either.

Within three days, he filed for bankruptcy.

I had been avoiding all his calls and told Savannah to do the same. It was the only way to make him so furious he would incriminate himself.

And he did.

The voice notes full of screaming expletives and threats
he left were perfect. As if icing on the cake he even did me
the unexpected favor of further implicating himself by
reminding me what he had done to me years ago. I saved the
time dated messages, knowing I would need them for my
next step.

On Friday, I made a phone call to Rick to check on our
financial position. Revenues were up due to the influx of
clients and it would be a few weeks before I could initiate
the purchase of Steinberg, but I wanted to make sure we had
the funds in place to do it when the time came.

On Monday, it came as no surprise to hear that Robert
and all his Belize connections were also being scrutinized
for tax evasion by the IRS. I smiled as I listened to that piece
of news. It was amazing what one call to the right person in
a government agency pointing them in the right direction
could do.

I gave that one another few days to sink in before I
added the cherry on top of the shit fest sundae of Robert's
destruction. More files. More incriminating proof of Robert
secreting money into offshore accounts.

A few weeks later, I had my day in court.

I walked in calmly and took a seat. Savannah sat beside
me while we waited for Robert to enter. We saw him before
he saw us. His swagger was gone, his face was gaunt, his hair
seemed brittle and a harsh yellow; and his expensive suit
hung on him. We watched as he took his place in the defen-
dant's seat, his lawyer beside him.

The trial was a quick one.

I had done my homework. As Robert's company fell
apart, I had seen to it that certain key players had been
rounded up, specifically those Robert had used to help

frame me all those years ago. In exchange for suspended sentences of collusion, they agreed to testify against him.

It was an open and shut case.

Testimony after testimony spoke of the plot to frame me for embezzlement. Each confirmed their role in getting me to initiate contracts which could be used as proof of my writing bogus checks. It had been a plot that was a year in the making.

When I took the stand and faced him for the first time in weeks, I knew he was a done man. His hateful sneer made him ugly, and I wondered how I could have befriended someone like him even as a child. I realized he must have always hated my guts.

As I sat in that witness stand and testified against my childhood friend and former business partner, I was surprised to feel all the bitterness I'd stored up inside me for those four years seep away. He stood up, and his lawyer tried desperately to hold him back, but his narcissistic personality was unable to accept he had lost, and he gave in to one last outburst filled with obscenities at me. I saw him for what he was. A washed-up, pitiful loser who could have had everything, but allowed his envy and greed to destroy everything. I didn't hate him anymore.

Finally, I could close the chapter on Robert Steinberg. With time I would get my criminal record expunged. After that I would never again give him even a moment of my time.

I turned my head and looked at Savannah. She smiled softly at me. There. That there, was my future. All rosy and beautiful. I smiled back.

30

SAVANNAH

Six Months Later
https://www.youtube.com/watch?v=AJtDXIazrMo
-love me like you do-

I t was six in the morning. and the vampires were all gone, but to be safe I would wait another hour before I ventured out.

I closed my book and stretched, luxuriating in the warm sun that kissed my bare skin. The weather was wonderfully warm and I could not have asked for a better birthday present than a trip to the beach. I rubbed a dab of sunscreen on my legs as a waiter approached us.

"Your Pina Coladas," he said, with a big smile.

"Thank you." I smiled and tipped him.

As he sauntered away, beside me, Max stirred from his nap. He yawned and looked over at me. Even in the shade of the umbrella, his eyes shone brilliantly. "Hello, Sexy," he drawled, his eyes skimming slowly over my bikini clad body.

I leaned over and dropped a gentle kiss on his lips. "Thank you for this gift. I needed it. As a matter of fact, *we* needed it. The last few months have been nonstop and it feels like we're finally slowing down to take a breath. Heck, I couldn't sleep for days until I knew he was locked away."

"Put him out of your mind, Savannah. Justice has been served. He's behind bars serving time for his crimes. Karma's a bitch as they say."

I took both cocktails and handed one to him. I took a sip of my cold drink. "I'm glad it's over."

"Do you know how beautiful you look right now?" he asked softly.

I looked into his eyes and felt my mouth dry. There was so much emotion in his eyes. "No," I croaked.

"Then let me show you," he muttered, as he stood he scooped me into his arms, and carried me across the hot sand towards our hotel suite. For a long while Max made me feel like the most beautiful woman on earth. Afterwards, when Max had gone to the other room to make some calls, I lazily turned to my side and dialed my mother's number.

Benny and her had a spectacular wedding in December on a rare sunny day. It had been a beautiful winter wonderland. Max and I had sent them off to a warmer climate for their two-week honeymoon. Ever since then both of them gave the distinct impression that they were totally enjoying married life. I could not be happier for them.

After the call I took a nap, leaving Max still on the phone. I dreamed I was running through a meadow of flowers, and behind me, two children followed. A boy and a girl. They looked like small chubby versions of Max. I turned around and gathered them into my arms. They were as light as feathers. My beautiful feathers.

"Where's Daddy?" I asked them.

"He's collecting seashells," they chorused, in their sweet little voices.

I woke up to the warm sensation of soft lips on my skin and smiled sleepily. Only the wisps of my beautiful dream remained. With a sigh I rolled into Max's embrace. "Their mouths were very red. They must have been eating cherries," I mumbled.

"Who?" Max asked.

"Our children. I dreamed of them. Twins. A boy and a girl," I whispered.

He stilled, and his voice became serious. "Are you trying to tell me something?"

"No, but I might be soon."

He nodded slowly. "Good, because there's nothing I'd like more than a boy and a girl."

I grinned up at him. "Yeah?"

He grinned back, only his grin was very, very wolfish. I knew what happened to me when he smiled like that.

"I'm hungry. Is it time to go down for dinner?" I asked.

"Yes, but you smell like sex. We can't have all the cabana boys swarming over you."

"And whose fault is it I smell like that?"

"Mine," he agreed readily, his eyes speculative. I knew what he was thinking.

"If you feed me well, I'll love you long time tonight," I said in my fake Bangkok accent.

He laughed and unpinned me from under him. "Off you go to the shower before I change my mind."

I vaulted out of the bed and hurried to the gorgeous marble bathroom. I let the warm jet flow over me as I marveled at how lucky I was. Wrapping a large towel around me I went back to the bedroom. Max was nowhere in sight, but I could hear him on the phone in the living room.

I dressed carefully. The dress I had selected was a gorgeous silk wrap around with a halter neckline. It ebbed and flowed around my calves in a mixture of browns and blues. The bronze high-heeled slippers matched perfectly. Gold earrings and a delicate bracelet completed my ensemble. I kept my make-up minimal as usual and was just spritzing on perfume when Max called out to me.

"Ready, babe?"

"Ready."

I stepped out into the living room and Max was waiting for me. He whistled softly when he saw me. He held out his hand. "Come on, my little Thai Princess. Food awaits."

Downstairs, I was stunned into silence to find the entire outdoor seating had been reserved by Max. The whole area was awash with candles and hurricane lamps. I could see that one table had been set for two. Smiling waiters hovered.

"Heck, I didn't smell that bad, did I?" I mumbled.

He looked down at me with a smile. "I wanted you all to myself tonight. I hope you don't mind."

"Well, since I want you to myself all the time, I don't mind at all."

He laughed as I slipped my hand into the crook of his elbow.

It was a beautiful night full of stars and we feasted like royalty under them. Max had left no stone unturned in the sumptuous five-course meal we were served. The waiter left us with an array of desserts and an additional bottle of wine. When at last we were alone, I reached across the table and put my lips to his, but he pulled back and smiled.

"If I followed your lead, we'd be heading to bed right now. And we will get there. Just not yet. The night is far from over."

"No?"

"No. Do you remember five years ago when you sat in that restaurant waiting for me before all hell broke loose?"

"I can't forget it."

"Neither can I. You see, five years ago, the night before your birthday to be exact, just like tonight, I was on a mission. I had made so many plans for your birthday, Savannah. We were going to go to the restaurant where we had had our first date. Then after I had wined and dined you I was going to take you for a walk along the pier. We would gaze up at the stars, pretty much like we're doing now. And I was going to take you back to my apartment and make sweet love to you before giving you something else."

I gazed at him as he looked down at me. In the light of the hurricane lamps I could see the love shining in his eyes.

"These lamps are interfering with the stars, don't you think?"

I laughed softly as the waiters went around extinguishing each lamp and candle, plunging the outdoor restaurant into darkness. He was right, the stars seemed much brighter without the other lights competing. Suddenly, out of nowhere, I heard something like an explosion, and almost jumped out of my skin.

"What the hell was that?"

"Looks like fireworks. Look."

He pointed to the sky. Indeed, there were the unmistakable bursts of fireworks. I watched as the sky turned red with a giant heart. Then a series of fireworks were released. I watched in awe as letters appeared. Then my mouth dropped open as I realized what the letters meant.

Marry me Savannah

I clapped my hand over my mouth as I turned to find

Max kneeling at my feet. He was holding up a small box which housed a beautiful diamond ring on a velvet bed.

"Savannah, so much time has been stolen from us, so it's only fitting that I pick up where I left off all those years ago. Savannah Maitland, will you do me the honor of marrying me and making me the happiest man in the world?"

Without hesitation, I threw my arms around him, nodding and showering his face with kisses.

"Yes! Yes! Yes!"

He laughed and pushed the ring onto my finger. Then he went and cupped his hands around his mouth and bellowed, "She said yes!"

I heard cheers and applause erupt from the waiters, the diners inside the restaurant, and the people on the beach. He pulled me into his arms. Even more fireworks filled the night sky as we sealed our deal with a blazing kiss.

Later that night as our bodies met, and I showed him, even though my Thai pronunciation was lousy, I knew how to love for a long, long time.

EPILOGUE

Savannah
Nine Months Later

My eyes blinked wearily. Everything seemed to be surrounded by a haze. I could hear machines beeping. I tried to move my arm, but it felt heavy. A tube was in it. My body felt sore.

"It's good to have you awake, Mrs. Blackstone."

"Water," I croaked. My lips felt dry and cracked.

The nurse gave me a cup with a straw and I sipped from it, a figure moved from the corner. Quite suddenly, Max was standing over me. He smiled down at me as he smoothed a lock of hair away from my forehead.

"Hey Beautiful."

I groaned. "I don't feel very beautiful."

He kissed my cheek softly. "You'll always be beautiful to me."

"Am I going to fall into your MILF category now?" I asked cheekily.

"There's only one woman in that category," he replied loyally.

"Better be," I mock threatened.

As if on cue, came two other nurses wheeling two carts. They each picked up a bundle. Tears filled my eyes as I remembered the last moments before they had put me out.

Max and I were at Mom's for dinner when I felt what felt like a cramp, but by the time we got home, there was just enough time for Max to grab my hospital bag and rush me to the hospital. My labor was complicated. One of the twins was a breech baby and they had to perform a cesarean birth.

The nurse handed me the bundle with my son. I smiled down at him, my eyes filling with tears. His face was wrinkly and red, but I recognized him from my dream. He yawned widely as he blinked up at me. His eyes were bright blue. Just like Max's.

"Dreams do come true," I murmured.

Max sat in the chair beside my bed while the nurse handed him our daughter. She was fast asleep and Max appeared speechless. The nurses left, and Max and I looked at each other. We smiled through our tears as we held our children. After a few minutes, he took our son and gave me our daughter.

"Aren't they beautiful?" I smiled at him. I watched as he leaned down to kiss our son.

"Exquisite. Just like their mother."

I shook my head. "No. They get it from their father."

He leaned over to kiss me softly. "Let's call it even."

The End

COMING SOON- SAMPLE CHAPTERS
MINE TO POSSESS

Chapter One
Amelia

I can't help my heart from sinking when I see the sign loom up ahead of me.

WELCOME
to
Sunny Vale.

I'm sure when it was put up in the late eighties, the image of the sun was a bright, happy yellow. All of the letters were there. Now the sun is faded to a dirty off-white, the 'L' from 'WELCOME' is missing, and the whole board is filled with tiny holes where kids have played target practice with their BB guns on it.

Maybe, back then when the sign went up, Sunny Vale was the sort of place that felt welcoming. Now it's the exact opposite of that. It's dreary, depressing and wholly unwelcoming.

I sigh as I pass beneath the sign, and step into the trailer park. The trailers are all as old and dilapidated as the sign. The front windows of one of them is boarded up. Another has patches all over it; patches my mom likes to pretend aren't there.

"Good afternoon, Amelia," a voice calls from the step of one of the trailers.

"Hi, Mrs. Mason," I call back, giving the woman a half-hearted wave.

She stands in the doorway to her trailer, a mostly smoked cigarette dangling precariously from her lips. She's at least sixty, and from what I can gather she's lived here since the park opened its doors. I kinda feel bad for her. What sort of mistakes does a person need to make to end up living here all of their live?

Maybe she's like my mom...

You'd think by husband number four my mother would have understood alcoholics don't make good husband material, wouldn't you? But no. She chose Dan. Another mean spirited, aggressive, alcoholic tyrant and on the wrong side of two hundred pounds. His trailer is his pride and joy, which I really think says everything a person needs to know about him. He's not trying to better himself and get out of this shit hole. To him, living in the Sunny Vale trailer park is living the dream life.

I still remember the day my mom announced we'd be moving here.

At the time we were living in a tiny, one-bedroom apartment and she was working two jobs just to keep us in that. By then I'd already met the cleaned-up, sober version of Dan once or twice. He seemed like an ok guy, so when she said we'd be moving into his place, which had three bedrooms, one of which, I was informed, would be mine, I was ecstatic.

My very own room!

God, the dreams I built up in my head. And then she brought me here and all my dreams faded away like the sun on that damned sign.

In that one day, I went from being Amelia from the ghetto (the charming name the kids in my school came up with to differentiate me from the other kid called Amelia) to Amelia the trailer trash girl. School was not fun for me, but I longed for a chance at college. No college for me, of course. When I hit sixteen Mom asked me to quit education and contribute towards the household expenses.

I understood, Mom needed me out working because Dan couldn't work due to his disability. I managed to find a job in a small clothing store and kept my mouth shut, but once, when I was giving over almost all of my wages to Mom and Dan was passed out on the couch, I couldn't help remarking that his only disability was the one he found every night in the bottom of a whisky bottle. For my trouble, I got a sharp back handed slap from my mother and a reminder we were living in *his* home.

That kind of closed that discussion.

Life went on, but my job only lasted until two months ago when Dan came into the store in a drunken stupor and demanded the owner give me a pay raise. He caused that much of a scene Mr. Jones told me not to bother coming back.

I'm job hunting right now but it's hard when the only job I've ever had refuses to give a reference and I have no real educational qualifications. God, my mom and Dan sure have a lot to answer for.

I reach our trailer and for a moment stand at the bottom of the steps leading up to it. I just stare at steps, wondering how the hell my life came to this. The trailer is one of the slightly better ones in the park, but it's still a shack. One of the steps is missing and the window has a crack in it. Stained curtains that are never open sit pulled taut against the windows, an inch or two too small to close properly.

The outside is nothing compared to the inside though.

Mom and I do try to keep the place in some sort of order, but Dan doesn't make it easy for us. Every day the place gets littered with take-out cartons, empty beer cans, whisky and rum bottles, and overflowing ashtrays. Thank God, I have my own little room. My sanctuary.

I skip over the missing step and go inside.

"Violet? Is that you?" Dan shouts.

His voice is slurred. Great. I can tell he's not close to drunk enough to pass out, but he's nothing like sober either. He's in that horrible middle place where he thinks he's a charming comedian, but one wrong move on my part can send him into a blind rage.

"No. It's me, Amelia," I shout back, praying he doesn't bother coming out to talk to me.

I open the grubby fridge and put the milk into it. As close the door my eyes dart around and I sigh. The ashtray is already full and six beer cans are scattered around the living room. I cleaned the place only two hours ago before I went out. I should do it again; save my mom the trouble when she returns from work. Then a rebellious thought crosses my mind.

Fuck it, she chose this life.

I sure as hell didn't. I turn away from the mess and make my way down the narrow hall to my bedroom. I open and close the door as quietly as I can. My bedroom is by far the cleanest room in the trailer. There are no scattered cans, no half eaten take-away remains, or plates with gravy crusted onto them. It even smells like perfume which is really something considering the dense fog of stale alcohol fumes and cigarette smoke that hangs in the air in the rest of the trailer.

I hear Dan approaching, his footsteps shambling. The

trailer rocks slightly as he stumbles and bumps into the wall. I move away from the door just as he crashes it open.

Bastard!

He's wearing grey sweatpants that are covered in stains, stains I can only hope are beer rather than piss. He's shirtless – not a good look for him. His beer belly hangs out, the skin tight, shiny, and so white he almost glows in the gloomy hallway. He's also in desperate need of a shower. The smell of stale alcohol and sweat that clings to him reaches me immediately and I try hard not to react.

Chapter Two
Amelia

"Where's your mother?" he slurs.

"At work. It's Friday," I remind as politely as I can, even though it's freaking irritating that he cannot even keep *her* schedule in his head.

"And yet you're here. Why aren't you at work?"

I resist the strong urge to roll my eyes. I don't want to set him off on another rant about how ungrateful I am.

"You got me fired, remember?"

He snorts and I'm not sure if it's laughter or disgust. "You're too good for that place anyway."

Place comes out as "plashe", which tells me he's a bit more gone than I originally thought. I shrug my shoulders. I'm not sure what he wants from me and I'm very wary of saying the wrong thing and sparking his temper.

"Pretty girl like you, you should be a dancer or something," he says, a speculative, admiring look in his eyes.

I'm sure somewhere in his drink-addled brain, he imagines it's a compliment, but it sure doesn't feel like one to me. I feel disgust swirling in my stomach. He doesn't have to come right out and say it. I know exactly what he means by dancer. Stripper.

He smiles at me, and it's not a normal smile. It's... oh God, lecherous!

And just like that the disgust in my stomach turns to outright fear. For the first time I have to deal with Dan as a predator and me as his prey while I'm trapped in this small space.

When my mother is around, Dan is either mean to me or pretty much just ignores me. These things I can live with, especially where he ignores me. In fact, that's my perfect scenario with him. But recently, more and more whenever we're alone together, which I try to avoid whenever I can, this new side of him comes out. Where he looks me up and down like I'm a piece of meat he'd like to devour. I've not failed to notice either the way he brushes against me whenever we pass each other, even out in the living room where there's absolutely no need for it.

Right now, I keep my face totally impassive.

"I said you're pretty," he repeats.

"Yeah. Thanks," I say tightly.

Just go away, I think to myself, but he doesn't go away. He stands propped against the frame of my bedroom door. I don't move because moving would bring me closer to my bed and I don't want him thinking for even a second it's some sort of invitation.

He grins. "You know Amelia, we've always had this chemistry between us, haven't we?"

My eyes widen. Is he mad? I can't stand him. As a matter of fact, I detest him. I'm dying to tell him exactly what I really think, but I have to keep this little gem to myself. Sleazy Dan is bad, but angry Dan is wore, by far worse.

"I should call Mom and tell her to bring home some

orange juice. I forgot to get it at the grocery store," I say, mentioning Mom in the hope he'll remember to be loyal to her. Unfortunately, it's too subtle a hint for him.

He grins at me. "Aww... look at you. All shy and shit. But I get it, really I do. You don't want to hurt your mom. And neither do I. Violet is great. Fantastic. She takes good care of me."

"Yeah, she does," I say with a touch of desperation. I don't want to risk angering him or encouraging whatever the hell he thinks this is.

He pushes himself up off the wall and I flinch slightly. Dan notices and laughs cruelly. "Don't pee yourself. I just thought someone should tell you how attractive you are."

I feel myself flush, the searing heat rushing up my neck.

His eyes note my embarrassment and he laughs, the sound unfamiliar. There is something cruel and sexual about it. For a moment it seems as if he wants to say something else, then he checks himself, turns and stumbles away, heading for the living room. I hear his body crash into the sofa.

I step forward, close the door, and lean back against it, my heart beating like crazy. Jesus, what the hell was that all about?

Then I quickly move to my tiny bed, sit down and pull my laptop towards me. My heart is still fluttering as I start browsing the jobs' boards. I have to find something. Something that pays enough for me to get the hell out of here.

I check the time. My mom is due home in an hour. I'll just lie low and hope Dan forgets I'm home. It wouldn't be the first time he's done it. One time, I came out of my room and Dan ran from the bedroom he shares with my mom with a baseball bat raised over his head. I managed to duck as he swung it at me.

Instead of apologizing he lost his temper with me, scolding me for sneaking around like a thief, and telling me that I should have the manners to greet him when I get home. I bit my tongue and didn't remind him I'd been home for almost three hours and I'd spent the first fifteen minutes of it making him a bacon sandwich. I think that was the time I realized exactly just how drunk Dan could get.

The hole he made in the wall with the baseball bat is still not fixed. It is a constant reminder to me that Dan can be unpredictable and downright dangerous.

I freeze suddenly. I can hear him moving around. The fridge door opens, then slams closed. A beer bottle is opened and the opener thrown on the counter. For some reason him not bothering to put the bottle opener back into the drawer irritates me. Mom's out there working herself to the bone for this lazy jerk. I mean how hard can it be not to get shit faced through the afternoon and put the damn thing back into the drawer for fuck's sake?

Like, everyone else manages it.

I grit my teeth go back to my laptop. My rage is pointless. I find a few promising openings. A waitress at a diner. A shelf stacker in a grocery store. Shitty, low paid jobs, but if I can just get one of them, then maybe I can get out of this life. I fill out the applications to a couple of openings, hit send, and shut down my laptop.

I pick up my cell phone, ready to text Lucy to see what she's up to tonight. I might see if I can go over to her place. She lives in a clean and tidy little house and her parents are normal. They work for a living and the only time her dad drinks is a glass of wine or two with dinner and the occasional night cap. Like a normal man.

I hear Dan stumbling back along the hallway towards my room. I put my cell phone down. Great. What now?

"Do you need something, Dan?" I call, hoping he just wants a sandwich made.

I hate that I'm practically Dan's hired help (without any pay or benefits, of course) but if making him a sandwich gets him away from my bedroom, then right now, I'll happily do it.

My door has no lock and he opens it without knocking just as I stand up from the bed. He grins at me and blinks twice, fast. I frown and he does it again. Oh God, he thinks he's winking at me. It should be tragic, but it's not.

It's terrifying.

Chapter Three
Amelia

"I've been thinking," Dan says, then pauses.

I nod tightly for him to go on. feeling that's what he's waiting for.

"You want me to notice you."

My eyes widen and my mouth drops open. Jesus, I was expecting him to ask for a sandwich. What on earth is going on with him today?

"Don't give me that butter wouldn't melt in your mouth look. You strut around here in your little short shorts and your skimpy little tank tops, tempting me. What else can it be?"

Has he gone stark raving mad? The only thing I've ever worn that even vaguely matches what he's saying is a pair of baggy shorts that are about six inches away from my knees, and not once have I strutted in them.

I swallow the thousand different sarcastic thing that fly into my head and make the mature decision not to respond. If I try to reason with him, he'll just get mad and who know what could happen. I'm trapped here for the moment, but Mom should be home soon. I just have to keep him at bay until she gets here.

"I'm going to make a sandwich. Shall I make one for you?"

Dan doesn't seem to notice or care I'm not responding to what he's saying. He just keeps right on looking at me like he's undressing me with his eyes.

"I've tried to resist your coy advances, but I mean I'm only human, Amelia. I have to give it to you, you played it well. You knew I wouldn't be able to resist you for long. And I mean your mom is great and everything, but she's not what she used to be, is she?"

My mom hasn't changed one bit in the time he's known her. Dan takes a step into the room and I take a step backwards, the backs of my legs meet my bed. He grins, but it doesn't meet his eyes. His eyes are suddenly nasty, lecherous, moving up and down my body. I feel sick as I imagine what he sees when he looks at me.

"You win," he grins. "You've worn me down."

He steps closer again, and again. I have nowhere else to go. Dan reaches out and caresses my cheek. My stomach rolls with nausea. His fingers smell of stale cigarette smoke and beer,; and his palms are rough, although I have no idea why – it's not like he's ever done a hard day's work in his life.

"I'll be honest with you Amelia. I've wanted this for as long as you have, but it felt wrong you know? Still... now you're eighteen, you're a woman now."

"I'm only seventeen," I say in a panic. "I'm not eighteen for another five weeks."

He smiles and does the blink thing again. "I won't tell if you won't."

My whole body goes cold as Dan reaches out and pulls

me against him. I have to resist the urge to retch as his hard beer belly digs into my body. He tries to kiss me and I turn my head to the side. He slobbers on my cheek, leaving it wet. His breath stinks of stale beer and something dirtier than that, and I can't help but wonder when he last brushed his teeth. The thought isn't a good one. I can feel bile rising in my throat. I swallow it quickly as Dan lunges his lips at me again. I try to wriggle out of his arms, but for a drunk guy, he's shockingly strong and his vice-like grip is impossible to escape.

"Dan, stop it," I say as firmly as I can. If I can just get the upper-hand here, I might be able to talk my way out of this.

"Dan, stop it," Dan mimics. "You've pushed for this for months and now you're going to pretend like you don't want it to happen? Why? You think you're too good for me all of a sudden?"

I think literally every woman on the planet is too good for him. "You're very attractive and all that, but it's not right. You're married to my mom," I say, keeping my voice from becoming shrill.

"Since when has that bothered you?" Dan snaps.

He releases me from his hold and I breathe a sigh of relief. It's over. Except it isn't. Dan is only just getting started. He shoves me hard on my chest and I fall backwards onto the bed.

"Fucking slut. You really think you're something, don't ya? Well, let me tell you something about girls like you. You're only good for one thing."

I scoot backwards across my bed, but it's so small and there's nowhere for me to go. My back is already pressed up against the wall. I can feel angry tears filling my eyes as I try to think of something to say to calm my mother's husband down. Nothing comes to mind. Since there's nothing I can grab to smack him with I get ready to kick him in the nuts. He'll crumple into a heap and that will give me enough time to get the hell out of this room.

Then I'm never coming back.

He smiles down at me and his eyes shine wickedly. I don't know if he really believes I've somehow been leading him on, or if it's just something he's telling himself to justify what he's about to do to me. Either way, he's coming for me. As if he knew what I planned to do, he grabs both my ankles and clambers onto my bed. He pulls my ankles wide, and roughly pushes me onto my back. He clambers on top of me, breathing his disgusting breath all over me.

I try to throw him off, but it's like he's made of wet sand. His weight holds me in place and he grabs my flailing arms. He pushes my hands together over my head and holds them in place with one large fist.

I am screaming now, shouting for help at the top of my lungs. I don't know how much good it will do. Our neighbors all tend to keep to themselves, not getting into each other's business. And no one around here will call the police. Not if they don't want their windows smashed in as a paint can comes crashing through them.

Dan is slobbering over my neck. It's only a matter of time until he goes further. My screams are doing nothing to stop him. Mom's figure appears suddenly at the bedroom door and relief floods me. My scream freezes in my throat.

"Dan. Get off her right now," my mom commands.

Dan jumps up like I'm hot coals.

"Oh Mom," I whisper, pulling my legs together.

Tears run freely down my cheeks now. My mom is here. Everything is going to be okay. She can see what a creep Dan is. She'll get rid of him and it'll go back to just being the two of us. We'll find another little apartment. I'll get a job and we'll make it work.

"You just couldn't see me happy, could you, Amelia?" my mom asks, shaking her head.

For a second it doesn't compute. I shake my head?

"How could you?" she screams.

"What?" I blurt out, shocked.

"Don't you want me to be happy?" she asks, her voice suddenly breaking.

Happy? Am I stuck in a nightmare? "Mom, he's a fucking useless alcoholic who just tried to rape your daughter."

"You seduced me," Dan mutters, all the slur gone from his voice.

"Shut up," Mom throws at him viciously before she turns on me again. "You walk around here in your little outfits, begging for Dan's attention," my mom says, mirroring Dan's untrue observation about my skimpy attire. "But I let it go. I told myself you were just seeking attention. You wouldn't actually try to steal my man, but..."

"Steal your man? Can you hear yourself, Mom? You're delusional." I look Dan up and down and shake my head. "You think I want to steal *him*? I wouldn't have him if he was the last man on earth."

Mom steps forward and slaps me hard across the face, leaving behind a stinging, burning patch.

"Show a little respect," she snaps, her face white with anger and hurt.

Dan grins, triumphant. I have no idea how this has happened. My mom came home and literally caught Dan trying to force himself onto me, and somehow, it's my fault?

"Mom, you heard me screaming," I plead. "Why would I have been screaming if I wanted this?"

My mom pauses for a second and then the hard look on her face softens.

"You're a pretty girl Amelia, and you like to show yourself off. It would be a strange man that didn't find you attractive. Maybe you're just naïve and didn't know this would happen. This is my fault. I should have warned you what you were doing. You need to be more considerate of Dan's feelings."

"It's not your fault, Vi," Dan says quickly. "It's hers. She's been flirting with me ever since you two moved in here. I should have said something, but I didn't want to hurt you."

My mom shakes her head and sighs. "I know it's been hard for you."

"I love you, babe," he says pathetically.

Mom nods. "I love you too, hon. Let's just put this behind us, ok? Amelia, apologize to Dan, then you can go and start peeling the potatoes."

I just stare at her, my jaw hanging open. The betrayal is too much. I almost can't recognize my mom. Does she really want me to apologize to him knowing what he just tried to do to me? Well, maybe it's ok with her, but I know I'm sure as hell am NOT going to apologize to Dan.

"Amelia?" Mom prompts.

I stare at her defiantly.

"It's ok, Vi," Dan says sweetly. He puts his meaty hand on her shoulder and she looks at him. "Give her some time to think about this. She'll come around. Right Amelia?"

I'm too shocked and distressed to say anything. I can't bring myself to even look at Mom, but I shrug my shoulders. I want them out of my room and I think this might be the only way to do it.

"Fine, Mom says in a hard voice. "Stay in your room and take a moment to think about how you could have broken our family up. And don't come out until you're ready to take responsibility for your actions and apologize to Dan."

"And to your mom," Dan adds. "You've caused her a lot of stress over these last few months, but you really outdid yourself this time."

Mom leaves the room, and Dan follows her. On his best behavior now. He closes my door quietly behind him. I stare at the old wooden door

I want nothing more than to lay on my bed face down and sob my little heart out. How could my mom take his side like this? Turning a blind eye to his drinking and his temper is one thing, but this? He was going to rape me. Does she really think so little of me that she believes I tried to steal Dan from her? Even if I did flirt with him which I would never do. Not just because he disgusts me, but also out of principle, how could she accept him back after this. She obviously doesn't think much of Dan either. She obviously thinks he's too weak to say no to anyone who flashes him a come-on.

I take a deep breath. No, I won't give myself the luxury of wallowing in self-pity.

I have to get out of here. Right now. I don't know where I'll go or what I'll do, but nothing can be as bad as this. I stand up and go to my wardrobe. I pull out a duffle bag and throw in some clothes and my makeup bag. Then I put slid in my laptop and my cell phone charger. I move to the bedroom door and stand listening. I can hear Mom and Dan talking in the living room. If I'm quiet, I can get to the bathroom and back without them noticing.

I sneak to the bathroom and grab my toothbrush, half a tube of toothpaste, my deodorant, a razor and a bottle of shampoo. It'll have to do. I sneak back to my bedroom and pull a brush through my hair. I toss it into the bag. I put my coat in the bag and zip it up.

I open the tiny drawer in my nightstand and pull out the little amount of money I've managed to save. I count the money. I have a grand total of one hundred and twenty-two dollars and fifty-three cents. It's not going to do much for me, but I'm going to have to make this work. I put the money in my pocket and straighten up. I pick up the duffle bag, take a deep breath and leave my bedroom for the last time. I make my way down the hallway to the kitchen. My mom hears me and looks up. She nudges Dan and they both sit looking at me. Dan is now bleary eyed and holding a bottle of what I think might be rum. He takes a swig as he looks at me.

"Well?" my mom says. "Are you ready to apologize?"

"Yes," I say. "Dan, I'm sorry you're a fucking rapist who blames everyone around him for his actions. Mom, I'm genuinely sorry for whatever happened in your life to make you think this is the life you deserve."

Then I turn and leave the trailer, leaving Mom and Dan staring after me with open mouths. I've officially burnt my last bridge there, but that's alright. I'd sooner die on the streets than go back into that hell hole.

Chapter Four
Amelia

I have been desperately walking the streets since I left the trailer. I swear I've been into every business I've passed, practically begging them for work, but it's the same old story everywhere. They're either not hiring or they tell me to send in my resume. I feel like curling up in the gutter and crying my burning eyes out...

But I won't do that. Or go back to the trailer.

I'll make it or I'll die trying.

Sure, it's been three hours, I'm no closer to finding a job than I was at Dan's place, and I've discovered the tiny amount of money I have would pay for two nights in a cheap motel. I have no intention of using it up like that.

I try to think where I can go. Lucy's place is out of the question. Her parents are super strict about having people staying over. Maybe if I told her mom what happened, she would let me stay, but knowing her she'd probably want to call the cops and social services and God knows who else. I don't want that.

I don't want anybody thinking ill about my mother. No matter what she is *my* mother and I'll never betray her.

I don't really have any other close friends. Sure I have a few acquaintances, girls I hang out with now and again, but I can't just turn up at their doorstep and ask them to house me until I sort my shit out.

I scrunch my forehead and try to think of my options. Obviously, I had colleagues at work and did get quite close to some of them. If I had to guess Jason might put me up for the night, but the truth is I really don't know him well enough to lay my problems on him. He might even have a girlfriend by now. The more I think about it, the more I shake off the idea. I've been ghetto Amelia and trailer trash Amelia for too long. I'm not going to let myself become slutty Amelia or seductress Amelia.

No, I'm on my own with this one.

I'm pulled out of my thoughts as a door opens in front of me and a drunken man stumbles out. He gives me a lopsided grin and I shrink back, but he just stumbles along on his way. I have to stop thinking everyone is like Dan. I look at the door the man stumbled out of. The Pink

Flamingo. It's a bar and the biggest dives around here. Always full of people drinking too much too early. And fights like you wouldn't believe.

I can't help but look at the sign taped to the door. Help Wanted. I've seen it already since I've been past this place twice already.

I'm just going in circles now, figuratively and literally.

This is the one place I haven't been to. I mean do I really want to work in a place like this? The answer is no. I most definitely don't. But it's starting to seem like it might be my only option, and anyway it can't be much worse than what I just left.

Maybe this bar and I are a good fit.

Maybe we deserve each other. We're both at the bottom of the barrel. We're both the thing people come to when they're all out of other options. Maybe working here won't be as bad as I think.

I lean against the steamed up window for a moment and think about it. If I can get a job here I might make enough money to rent a little studio apartment, but even better if I stick it out for a few months and get some experience, I might be able to find a new job in a decent place. I think for another few minutes, pretending to myself like I have another option, but I don't.

This is my last shot.

I push myself off the window, take a deep breath and push the door open. A cloud of humid heat hits me. The place is heaving and everyone looks drunk. The tables and booths are all taken and several people mill around in groups, standing in the open spaces around the place.

The bar is crowded too and even from here I can hear people screaming, they're next. The jukebox is playing in the background; a country song I don't recognize. It's barely audible over the sound of drunken laughter, conversation, and shouts.

Well, they all sure look happy. Actually, very happy.

No one is fighting or arguing. No one looks like they don't want to be here. In fact, everyone seems to be having a great time except the harried looking waitress who pushes through the crowd with a tray loaded down with drinks. I could do that, I tell myself.

I push deeper into the room, squeezing through the throng. My rucksack hits the back of a seated man's head as I push through towards the bar and I cringe, waiting for him to go off on me as I stutter out an apology, but he just laughs and waves away my apology. Whoa. Maybe this place isn't as bad as I thought it was.

"What you got in there honey? Are you running away from home or something?"

"Something like that." I grin back at him.

"Cheers to that," he says cheerfully.

He picks up a shot glass filled with clear liquid and swallows it down to a round of cheers and whoops from his table. The grin on my face widens. This place is sure growing on me.

I make it to the crowded bar, and wait until the couple waving money in front of me are served, then push my way into the spot they've vacated.

"Hi," I chirp brightly, when the bartender gets to me.

"ID," he barks.

"I'm not here for a drink. I saw your help wanted sign in the window," I explain.

He turns away from me, leaving me standing there, unsure of what to say or do.

"Larry?" he yells. "Someone here for the job."

He comes back to the bar, and ignoring me, moves onto

the next customer. A voice yells something indistinguishable through an open door from the back of the bar. The bartender looks back to me.

"Go on through," he says, jerking his head towards the open door.

I have no idea how I would get to the door and I stand staring at him dumbly for a moment. He rolls his eyes which makes my cheeks sting with embarassment.

"Coming through," he shouts at two drunk looking men who are standing at the side of the bar.

They back up a little and the bartender lifts a section of the bar up and beckons to me. I push past the men and squeeze through the gap. It's so loud here that I can barely hear the bartender as he speaks to me and I wonder vaguely how they have any idea what drinks people are ordering. I don't catch a word the bartender says, but he points through the door behind him and I step through it.

It's cooler back here and a little quieter and I take a deep breath, square my shoulders, and start moving along a corridor carpeted in an ugly red and green carpet.

"Hello?" I call out timidly.

"For fucks sake, get in here," a voice shouts.

I follow the sound of the voice and find myself in what I take to be an office. It's a small room, carpeted in the same cheap stuff as the corridor outside. The furniture is shabby. There's an overweight man sitting with his booted feet up on a chipped desk. A lit cigarette smolders in an ashtray on the messy desk. The man is wearing a suit, but even that looks cheap and ill-fitting.

"You're looking for a job, huh?" he asks.

Chapter Five
Amelia

I'm kinda speechless by the situation I find myself in, so I just nod.

He gestures to the chair in front of his desk. I don't really want to sit on it. It looks grubby and sticky, but I park myself on it. I need a job. I can always wash my jeans.

"What's your name, kid?"

"Amelia Till," I reply.

"Till what?" the man says, and laughs heartily at his own joke.

I smile politely, and mumble, "Good one."

"I'm Larry Hall, the owner of this fine establishment."

I don't know if he's joking or not when he says that. He doesn't laugh and I'm glad I didn't.

"How old are you?" He looks me up and down as he asks me the question and I can see the look in his eye. It's the same look Dan used to give me when my mom wasn't home.

I don't think Larry is the sort of man who is worried about following the law, but this is my last hope and I'm not going to blow it with honesty. I swallow hard. "Eighteen," I lie.

Larry's smiling at me now, a smile that makes me want to shrink away from him. The look on his face takes away any guilt I might have felt about lying to him.

"Have you worked in a bar before, sweet cheeks?" he asks.

I can't lie about that. Two minutes behind that bar and he'll know I don't know the first thing about bar tending.

"No. But I'm a fast learner," I say.

"Nah, I ain't got time to be teaching you nothin'," he says. "Can you put on a pretty smile and carry a tray?"

I nod and do my best to smile at him.

He laughs and shakes his head. "You'll need to do a lot better than that kid. The regulars here like their waitresses smiling and happy as a pig in shit... and showing a little cleavage. You get me?"

I get him alright. I nod, forcing my smile to be wider, showing more teeth.

"That's better. If you work here, you'll be working late most nights. Definitely weekend nights. You ok with that?"

I nod again. It's not like I have any sort of social life, anyway.

"And there'll be none of this bleeding heart feminism bullshit. Our regulars like a joke and sometimes, those jokes could be seen as offensive. Your job is to laugh at them and not get your panties in a twist. Clear?"

It's clear. If I work here, I'll have to accept all of the pervy comments thrown my way and any groping without complaint and with a smile on my face. But at least here, I'll be able to leave when my shift is over.

I nod again. "Sure. It's all said in fun right?"

"That's the spirit. No snowflakes in this establishment." Larry grins. "One more question. Can you start right now? One of my waitresses called in sick today and I think you can see we're kind of short staffed tonight."

My eyes widen, trying to take his words in. Wow, I got a job.! I actually freaking did it. The smile on my face is genuine this time as I nod vigorously.

Larry laughs. "You'll be working around twenty hours a week, maybe more. The pay is rubbish, but smile like that honey, and you'll make a king's ransom in tips."

Crappy hours, bad pay, horrible customers, and a lecherous boss. It sounds like hell on earth, but it's a job. A life saver! I can do this for a few months. I am certain it won't be half as bad as living with Dan.

"Wait here," Larry says, pushing his heavy body upright.

He leaves the office and I take a moment to compose

myself a little bit. I can't let myself seem too thrilled about this. Larry will think something strange is up if I do.

"Greg. Greg. Get out here," I hear him yelling.

He comes back into the office a few minutes later with the bartender I spoke to when I first came in.

"Greg. Amelia. Amelia. Greg. Amelia's starting as a waitress tonight. Get her the right uniform and show her where everything is. Ten minutes," Larry says.

I get to my feet as Greg rushes me out of the office.

"Don't I need to fill out any paperwork or sign anything?" I ask.

Larry shakes his head and he and Greg laugh. It seems like lying about my age had really been totally unnecessary. Larry and employment laws seem to be living in different worlds. I shrug. I remind myself this is not a bad thing. *Just suck it up, Amelia. You need the money. Badly.*

I follow Greg down the grubby hallway into what I assume is the staff room. It's reasonably clean and there are lockers which must be a good sign.

"Grab locker two," Greg says.

There are only five lockers. I go to locker two, open it, shove my bag in, turn the lock, take the key out, and turn back to Greg. He's looking me up and down critically. Not again. My disgust must have shown on my face because Greg laughs.

"Don't flatter yourself," he says. "I'm working out what size uniform would fit you."

"You could just ask me," I point out.

He grins. "I could, but it wouldn't help much. The uniforms are pretty old. Most of the labels are washed clean."

"Ahhh."

Greg nods and disappears, leaving me standing there.

I'm still in shock so I appreciate the little alone time to gather my thoughts, but he comes back quickly, holding up a black short skirt, a frilly little apron, and a black top that looks smaller than what I'm used to wearing.

He looks at my sneakers and winces. "They'll have to do tonight, but for your next shift, you'll need black stilettos. At least three inch heels, but the higher the better," he says. He holds the clothes out to me. "I'll wait in the hallway while you put these on. Don't be long."

I change quickly, wanting to make sure I don't give Larry any reason to come looking for me while I'm undressed. The skirt is a decent enough fit, but the vest... wow, it feels as if my boobs are falling out of it. I stuff my clothes into the locker with my bag and push the key into the pocket of my skirt. Then I open the door go out.

Greg looks at me. "Not a bad guess, huh?" He smiles. "Hell, Larry always knew how to pick em."

I frown and he quickly makes his face expressionless.

"So basically, the left hand side of the bar is table service. You'll find some people on the right hand side want it too. You can serve them if you want to, but your priority is the tables on the left."

He pauses his explanation for a second and hands me a notepad and pen before going on.

"They go in the pocket of your apron. Write down the orders bring the tickets to the bar, and take the drinks to the tables. Think you can manage that?"

"I think so," I reply sarcastically.

Greg ignores my sarcasm, and nods to top.

"Open the top two buttons," he says.

It is already so tight and small. I frown.

He shrugs. "Totally up to you, but if you want to make decent tips, you'll do it."

I almost don't, but I need money fast and so reluctantly, I open the top two buttons and show off even more cleavage.

He grins. "Perfect. Let's go." He turns and heads back towards the bar. He points to a door on his left. "That's the staff toilet. Unless you have a weird fetish for bodily fluids, never ever use the customer toilets."

"Got it," I say, instantly deciding I would rather pee in my panties than go into the customer toilets.

Greg leads me out into the bar and opens the hatch for me to leave through.

Before I can even respond he turns away and starts serving customers.

I stand at that spot, unsure of what to do, but I don't have long to dilly around wondering. A man spots me and beckons me over to his table. It's on the left side of the room, so I quickly make my way over, a massive smile on my face.

Chapter Six
Amelia

"Good evening gentlemen. What can I get for you?" I ask, my notebook and pen out and ready.

The men at the table laugh.

My smile goes so wide my face is in danger of cracking.

"You're new here, aren't you?" one of them asks.

"First night," I admit.

"I can tell. You haven't gotten the standard Flamingo exasperated greeting of 'what'd want next' down yet."

"Ok, what'd want next?"

Another laughs. "She'll do."

"Yeah, she'll do all right. Here's a nice simple order to get you started, cream pie. "Five pints of pale ale; three rum and cokes, no ice, and eight shots of tequila."

I write the order down quickly and flash them another big grin. "Coming right up."

I go back towards the bar and stand waiting for one of the bartenders to spot me. Greg spots me and rolls his eyes, pointing to the end of the bar. The opposite end to where the entrance hatch is.

"You work here, Amelia, Greg explains dryly. "You don't have to wait in the line. When you have an order, come straight up here, ok?"

I nod and hand him my ticket. He turns away and another table yells, "Hello, sweet cheeks."

"That'll be you," Greg calls over his shoulder.

"Right." I plaster another smile on my face and head towards them. When I come back with their order, there's a large tray waiting for me with all of the drinks for my last order.

"I have to take all of these at once?" I ask the female bartender who holds her hand out for my new ticket.

She nods. "Yeah. And if you drop them, Larry takes the money out of your fucking wages, so watch your step."

Wonderful. I pick the tray up cautiously. It weighs an absolute ton and my hands are shaking with nerves. Beer starts to slop over the top of the pint glasses and I feel tears starting to form in my eyes. This is not fair. I've not even been given a chance to practice. Just thrown into the deep end without a float. I put the tray back down on the counter and blink hard.

The woman behind the bar comes back, obviously taking pity on me. "Like this," she says.

Then she crouches slightly and pulls the tray to the edge of the bar. She holds her palm out and slides the tray onto it. "Do it with both hands to start with it if you need to."

I nod. That does look easier than my way.

She quickly tops up the spilled beers and nods for me to go.

I take a deep breath and do it the way she showed me. The tray sits neatly on my palms. Yup, I can do this. I take my other palm off. My arm shakes from the weight, but the drinks hold steady and nothing spills. I take a deep breath and with my spine straight I make it to the table before I realize I have no idea how to get the tray back off my hand.

I look around frantically and watch another waitress. She takes the drinks from the tray one at a time, announcing them and handing them to the people who claims them.

I copy her actions, and I soon have all of the drinks off the tray and on to the table. Breathing a sigh of relief I thank the man as he pushes a ten dollar tip into my hand. I put the money in the tight little pocket in the ass of my skirt and go back for the next tray of drinks.

The next few hours go over reasonably smoothly. Granted I make a few mistakes I run left, right and center, but I don't drop any trays, and most important of all, I manage to resist the urge to tell any of the customers to fuck off, even when they make comments about my body that men their age really should know better than to say to a girl.

Larry keeps popping out of his door to see if everything is running smoothly. A couple of times he catches my eye and nods approvingly.

Finally, the place starts to quiet down as the night wears on. Eventually, I'm the only waitress still working. The other bartenders also having finished their shifts and Greg is the only one behind the bar.

I know it's too late to have any chance of finding somewhere to stay tonight now. With the money I've made from tips I could probably get a room in a half decent bed and breakfast place now, but I know I need to save the money for a down payment somewhere more permanent. I decide to hang around here as late as I can and then I'll either sleep in that small locked room or I'll spend the rest of the night walking the streets. Tomorrow, I'll try to find somewhere to stay.

My thoughts are interrupted when the entrance door opens and a group of three men enter. They're all wearing black suits. Two of them hang back slightly from the middle one, letting him lead the way. He is short, but broad with black hair and eyes that are strangely vacant and dead. There is something dangerous and cold about him. One of my tables is waving at me, but I am so transfixed by this trio I pretend not to notice. Even I can tell these men are not here for a drink.

They give off bad vibes and make me strangely nervous.

These men mean business.

At that moment Larry suddenly appears at the door behind the bar, his face is drained of color, and his eyes dart towards the three men making their way towards the bar. He must have seen them on the surveillance screens on his office wall and rushed out.

"Mr. Sorokin," I hear him say as he flashes the main guy a smile, but his smile looks sick and I can see the beads of sweat that have formed on his upper lip. "I wasn't expecting to see you tonight."

"Why not? Your payment is late," Mr. Sorokin explains in a thickly accented, but polite voice.

Greg passes me my drinks tray and although common sense tells me to move away from the bar area, I can't help being fascinated as to what's happening here.

Larry licks his lips. "Um... why don't you come around to the office. We can talk there."

"Or we can talk here," Mr. Sorokin says softly.

"Okay, sure," Larry says, his palms in a downward placating gesture. "We can talk here. I know the payment is late, and I'm really, really sorry, but you know, sales aren't what they used to be. Covid, you know? I've had to spend a lot to respect the new governmental regulations. I've even have to give up some of my tables to social distancing rules. But don't worry, it's just temporary. I'll get the money to you as soon as I can, I swear."

Mr. Sorokin doesn't say word. Just looks at Larry with those cold, dead eyes.

Larry tugs desperately at his collar... like it's choking him. "It's just temporary," he gasps nervously.

Then Mr. Sorokin curls his forefinger towards Larry in a beckoning gesture. Larry's head is shaking as he reluctantly steps forward. It's like a particularly bad B movie has become real. Lightning fast, Mr. Sorokin grabs the front of Larry's shirt and pulls him towards him, dragging him halfway over the bar and pressing his deadly calm face close to poor Larry's sweating, white one.

Jesus! That sure escalated quickly.

I look around me and it seems as if everyone else is too drunk to care or even notice. I try to catch Greg's eye, but he studiously ignores me. I know I should take my tray of drinks and move on, but I simply can't drag my attention away from the scene playing out next to me.

Chapter Seven
Amelia

"Did I just hear you say, as soon as I can?" Mr. Sorokin asks with exaggerated pseudo incredulity.

"No, no...I... I didn't mean it like that. You must know, I

didn't. You'll have the money. I promise," Larry says, his voice low and pleading.

"Listen you fuckin worm. Stop talking. The more you writhe and squirm, the more you piss me off."

"Sorry, I didn't mean to—,"

"I said, stop talking."

Larry nods vigorously, the sweat is pouring into his eyes, making him blink owlishly.

"I want last week's and this week's packet by Sunday. And by Sunday, I mean this Sunday. Two fuckin' days from today. And if I don't have it all, plus the interest, then you know what'll happen, don't you?" He pauses, letting the moment drip with menace.

Larry's eyes bulge like a squeezed frog's as he nods.

"Say it," Mr. Sorokin murmurs, his voice silky with enjoyment in his ability to make Larry totally submit to him.

"You will break every bone in my worthless body."

"Very good." Mr. Sorokin smiles coldly before he releases Larry.

Then the three men turn as if one autonomous body to head back for the entrance.

Panic seizes me. Oh God, I can't have Larry know I've seen him in such a humiliating position. He will be forced to fire me out of sheer embarrassment. Hastily, I pull my tray of orders from the bar counter and turn away, but I'm so totally shocked by what I've just witnessed, my fingers slip and tray jumps out of my hand as if it has a life of its own.

In helpless horror I watch as it flies into the air. In seemingly slow motion, I see the drinks launch into the air. Gold, amber, and white liquids splash upwards and spray everywhere. In a way it is all rather beautiful. Well, at least until the flying glasses meet the hard wooden floor. The crashing sound of the breaking glass echoes across the whole room making my heart stop in my chest.

In my wildest dream I could not have imagined myself in this scenario. Mr. Sorokin's suit jacket is so absolutely drenched with beer it is dripping from the edges. He turns in slow motion and trains his dead eyes on me.

He is the impersonation of evil.

My insides go cold. "Oh my God. I... I'm so very sorry," I stutter. "Let me get some napkins for you."

I turn on my heel to start back towards the bar, but Mr. Sorokin reaches out, grabs my arm, and spins me to face him.

He doesn't shout or scream as I expect him to do. Instead his voice is flat and emotionless. "You think you're so clever, so brave. Standing up for that fat, worthless worm."

My eyes widen with shock.

Oh shit! He thinks I did it deliberately. "No, no... I didn't spill the drinks on purpose. It was an accident. I swear it. Honestly. You have to believe me. It's my first day here. I'll pay for the dry cleaning bill, of course."

He doesn't say anything, just stares me intensely, with his tar black eyes. It is impossible for me to know what he is thinking, but he is so close I can smell him. He reeks of smoked mackerel. Strange, but his skin looks shiny and oily as a fish. It takes everything I've got not to step away.

"Oh, you'll pay all right, but not my dry cleaning bill." Something I've seen in Dan's eyes glitters in his eyes.

First my jaw drops, then I feel a flash of pure fury. The shock of having Dan almost rape me, the pain of my mother's betrayal, and the fear of not having a place to crash for the night rush into one boiling emotion that burns in the pit of my stomach. I straighten my spine and stare back at him.

"I've said it was an accident and I'm really sorry. I've also offered to pay for the cost of cleaning your suit even though it will probably mean I've worked all night for nothing. So... you can take up my offer or not, that's totally up to you, but don't imagine you can ask me to sleep with you just because I spilled some alcohol on your clothes. I swear, I'll call the police if you try to force me."

His mouth quirks with amusement, as if he is the devil himself playing with a helpless human. "Who said anything about sleep. After I'm done with you, little pigeon, you can call anyone you want, but think carefully first, it would be a such shame if I had ruin skin like yours. It is so smooth and... young."

Suddenly, I feel fear like I have never known before. Even with drunk Dan, I was just waiting for the moment I could knee him in the nuts and while he was reeling in pain make my escape. Sure, I was shocked, disgusted, and annoyed, and maybe even a little scared, but it was nothing, nothing like what I feel now, looking into this man's cold killer's eyes. Goosebumps scatter all over my body. My mouth opens, but I don't know what I can possibly say to save myself from a fate worse than death.

Then from the shadows a voice like whiplash, calls out, "Igor."

To my amazement the devil in front of me freezes. As I watch in disbelief his eyes narrow before he slowly turns to face a man who has stepped out of the shadows.

Chapter Eight
Viktor

"Let go of the girl," I command in Russian.

There is a flash of confusion in his eyes, then he recovers, and releases the girl as one would a piece of burning coal. "It's nothing, boss. She's just a dumb broad in a dive bar."

I frown, unexpectedly furious with him. She's no broad. She's just a kid. Hell, she looks like she just turned sixteen. Not that it is any of my business, but what the hell are her parents thinking letting her work in a shit-hole like this. I keep my tone pleasant so anyone listening would think we were just having a polite conversation in Russian. "Fuck off."

Igor's eyes show frustration and impotent rage, but wordlessly he nods, and moves towards the front door, the two goons who came with him follow closely behind. There is fear in their eyes but their faces are deliberately impassive.

I walk up to the girl.

Something about her caught my eyes as soon as I walked into the dive, but I couldn't see her properly before. Now that I'm closer I clearly see she is not only too young to be working in this place, with its stink of stale beer, where she's probably groped at every opportunity, but that she is also very, very, very beautiful. With a heart-shaped face and one of those swollen mouths that look like she has just given some lucky guy an unforgettable blowjob. Her hair runs down her back in a thick golden plait. It's so long, it goes all the way to her ass. And what an ass it is. Rounded and full. The perfect ass to grab onto while fucking.

I shake my head. Annoyed.

What the fuck is wrong with me? She's obviously way too young for me. As a rule I don't like them young. When they are this young they are too clingy and desperate for love. I like girls who've been around the block and understand the nature of the game.

Her sparkling baby-blue eyes jerk towards mine.

She is completely horrified, but as soon as she locks

onto my scrutiny, her eyes widen with confusion and some emotion I cannot pin point. For a few seconds she simply stares at me, her entire body frozen, as if the world around her has stopped revolving, and there is only me and her. Then, as if remembering herself, she suddenly tears her gaze away, dropping it down to the ground. Her long, luscious lashes make blue shadows on her silky cheeks. My gaze drifts lower.

Her top is open too low.

Showing off her pert, little breasts and I can't fucking help myself. The image of me sucking those breasts slams into my head. I shake the stray thought away, disgusted with myself. I hate predators like Epstein.

She's just a kid. A fragile thing that needs protecting, not hitting on.

How in heaven's name did I get here?

This is not me. Part of me silently fumes that through no fault of my own I'm now the owner of a loan shark outfit. In an ideal world, I'd never ever set foot in a place like this, but my cousin, Alexei, unable to meet all his financial obligations, ran away and left me with his mess.

So... I now own his business and I'm not sure I like being the owner of thugs like Igor bullying small-time business owner like Larry, or being in the position of saving under-aged damsels in distress that I am disgustingly attracted to. It all leaves a bad taste in my mouth.

"Are you ok?" I ask her.

She shakes her head slowly, not speaking, and the tears that were shining in her beautiful eyes spill over. I should push a few thousand dollars into her hand, apologize for Igor's brutishness and leave, but something about her holds me in place. I don't know what it is, but every instinct in me is telling me I need to protect her. Stupidly, I reach out to her.

She flinches back from me.

I raise both my hands, to show her I'm not going to touch her if she doesn't want me to.

"It's ok," I say in a reassuring voice. "I'm just going to take you outside for five minutes to get you some fresh air and let you calm down, ok?"

"I'll get fired," she whispers.

Larry is standing behind the bar, watching the scene with an open mouth.

"Are you in the habit of firing your staff if I ask them to step outside with me for a moment and they do it?" I ask.

"N-no, of course not," he stutters. Then he forces a smile to his white face. "Take all the time you want, Amelia."

Amelia. That's her name. It suits her somehow. I turn and begin to walk away. She follows me silently.

"Wait in the car," I tell Jerome, my driver, as I reach the entrance.

He nods without question.

I go outside and turn around to wait for her. She opens the door, but hangs back as if she is afraid of me.

"I'm sorry you got caught up in that," I say. "Igor had no right to put his hand on you like that."

"I should have been more careful," she answers, her voice breaking. She presses her lips together immediately and her eyes begin to swim with tears again.

"It was a bit of alcohol. No big deal," I say.

She swallows hard, as if she unsure of my motives. All the while tears are pouring down her face.

I smile at her, trying to think of a way to stop the rolling tears. "You probably shouldn't be quite so clumsy as a waitress though."

She gives a short laugh as sniffs. "I sure made a great impression on my first night, huh?"

I laugh, which is odd in itself. I hardly ever laugh out loud, but I can't help it. Through all of this, she has managed to keep a sense of humor. Which makes her quite the little heroine in my eyes.

"Can I ask you something without you thinking I'm coming on to you?" I ask.

She shrugs. "Sure."

"What's a girl like you doing working in a hole like this?"

Her bottom lip wobbles again and I find myself regretting the question. Another odd emotion for me.

"Hey, it's ok. I'm not judging you or anything, I'm just curious."

She exhales, a heart-felt sigh full of troubles. One girl of her age shouldn't have to express.

"You want the truth?" she asks.

"Nothing else will do."

"Are you sure? It's not a pretty story..."

I nod. "I'm sure I can handle it."

"Okay, today, my stepdad tried to rape me, but that's not the big deal. The real kicker is my mom took his side. So, I walked out of his house with a duffle bag of clothes and hardly any money. I took this job because it's the only one I could find. It was a choice between doing this or ending up on the streets. Which technically. I still am, but hopefully, if I can keep this job, not for much longer."

"You don't have anywhere to stay tonight?" I ask calmly, even though I'm furious on her behalf. I want to punch her step-dad and shake her brainless mother.

"Nope," she whispers. "But since the bar is open pretty late, I'm hoping to hang around here until the very moment it closes. And then it won't be that long to wait until daylight comes. I can hopefully find somewhere then."

I know I should walk away. This is the right moment to stuff some cash in her and walk away forever.

Amelia isn't my problem. I have enough of those. But there is something about her that I can't walk away from. I don't know what is it, but I tell myself it is because, her tough talking doesn't hide the vulnerability in her eyes. or the fact that I can see she's actually terrified of her situation.

"How old are you?"

"Eighteen," she lies.

I frown.

"Well, I'll be eighteen in a month."

I sigh. I'm probably going to regret this, but what the hell. "How are you at cleaning?"

She frowns. "Cleaning?"

"You know. Vacuuming. Polishing."

"That kind of shit, I can do with my eyes closed," she replies quickly, as if she has come into territory she recognizes and is comfortable with.

"Good. How would you like to join my team of maids? You'd be cleaning my private quarters and maybe one or two of my offices. Fifteen dollars an hour plus accommodation."

"Why would you do that?" she asks, raising an eyebrow suspiciously.

Why indeed? I shrug. "Because you look like you could use a break." I glance at my watch. "I have to be elsewhere soon, do you want the job, or do you want to go back in there and keep working for Larry?"

"I want the job," she says quickly, flashing a big smile at me.

"Right. Go on in and get your stuff. I'll be right here if Larry gives you any trouble."

She nods then turns and walks back into the bar, her head held high. I can't help but watch the way her ass sways in the tight little skirt Larry has her wearing.

As the door closes, I turn away, frowning.

Deliberately, I put her out of my head and turn to the very real problem I have to solve: Alexei's 'business' that I have unwillingly inherited is basically a loan shark enterprise enforced by brute criminals. I came to this bar to observe first-hand the operation he runs and I'm not impressed at all. At the very least, I should get rid of Igor and his goons. And I will, when Marcus, my operations manager comes back from vacation.

Right now, I'm a man down, but I'm not going to put up with this psychopathic bullshit for another week. I'll have to get Larry to go up to my offices to work out something reasonable with one of my guys, and put a very tight leash on Igor until Marcus's return.

Want to read more?
Pre-order the book here:
Mine to Possess

ABOUT THE AUTHOR

If you wish to leave a review for this book
please do so here:
The CEO's Revenge

Please click on this link to receive news of my latest releases
and great giveaways.
http://bit.ly/1oe9WdE

and remember
I **LOVE** hearing from readers so by all means come and say
hello here:

ALSO BY GEORGIA LE CARRE

Owned

42 Days

Besotted

Seduce Me

Love's Sacrifice

Masquerade

Pretty Wicked (novella)

Disfigured Love

Hypnotized

Crystal Jake 1,2&3

Sexy Beast

Wounded Beast

Beautiful Beast

Dirty Aristocrat

You Don't Own Me 1 & 2

You Don't Know Me

Blind Reader Wanted

Redemption

The Heir

Blackmailed By The Beast

Submitting To The Billionaire

The Bad Boy Wants Me

Nanny & The Beast

His Frozen Heart

The Man In The Mirror

A Kiss Stolen

Can't Let Her Go

Highest Bidder

Saving Della Ray

Nice Day For A White Wedding

With This Ring

With This Secret

Saint & Sinner

Bodyguard Beast

Beauty & The Beast

The Other Side of Midnight

The Russian Billionaire